Jane McLoughlin was educated [ ] went to university in Ireland. Sl[ ] Ulster for various national nev[ ] editor and women's editor of the Guardian and [ ] *The Demographic Revolution* and *Up and Running: Women in Business* (Virago)

coincidence

Jane McLoughlin

Published by VIRAGO PRESS Limited, April 1993
20–23 Mandela Street, Camden Town, London NW1 0HQ

First published in hardback by Virago Press Limited 1992

A CIP catalogue record for this title
is available from the British Library

Printed in Great Britain by
Cox & Wyman Ltd, Reading, Berks.

To Stanley Reynolds, who lent me his New England.

CONTENTS

PART ONE

A FOOL'S ERIN

page 3

PART TWO

A DROP OF THE HARD STUFF

page 73

PART THREE

THE HUNTER AND THE HUNTED

page 143

PART ONE

A FOOL'S ERIN

1

Expensively dressed young Mrs Brooks Acton Lawrence, with
American movie visions of Walt Disney's cute little Irish leprechauns
dancing in her head, came down the stairway of the plane and entered
Ireland, the land of her fathers.

Unlike the other passengers who, observed by visitors from
another planet or some such time-travellers, would appear to be
an amazing collection of refugees from some great natural disaster
that caught many of them unprepared on the golf links, baseball
diamond or tennis court (with here and there a sprinkling of deserting
soldiery, of either sex, who had not had time completely to cast off
their jungle kit), Mrs Brooks Acton Lawrence looked rigged out for
more sophisticated fun.

She was dressed for Paris. She had boarded the plane in Connecticut, bound for France, but she was disembarking now at Shannon,
making her own personal unscheduled stop.

Still, like the golfers, ballplayers, tennis champions, and jungle
insurgents all about her, there was something theatrical about young
Mrs Brooks Acton Lawrence's costume. She was dressed for an April
in Paris of another age, before the invention of the jumbo jet and
jogging clothes. Among all the tourists as Golfers and Guerrillas,
Mrs Brooks Acton Lawrence was the tourist as Traveller. And
Mrs Lawrence knew she was play-acting; but, she thought, she
was young, she had married young, she had just been divorced,
her young dreams of glamour had never been fulfilled. She wanted
some fun, she wanted life and liberty, she was eager in the pursuit of
happiness. She had been sad and now she wanted to be happy; it was
not, she thought, too much for an American of any age to ask.

Coming into the airport, Mrs Brooks Acton Lawrence became
aware that she was doing something unusual and not at all like

3

herself. Or, at least, she thought that this sudden varying from the normal or set plan of action (getting off the plane in Ireland) was not at all typical: her mother(widowed), her friends(many), her lovers (three), and her husband (ex), would not have agreed. They, and particularly her current lover, Dr Sidney Millstein, a psychiatrist (but not hers), a tall bearded figure, with a cunning brain full of as many twists and spins as his highly idiosyncratic tennis game, would have thought this sudden last-minute change of plan was all too like Kitty Lawrence. She was also aware that at her young age – not yet thirty, or at least not much above it – she was making 'history'. She was the first of her line to return to Ireland since 1848, the year of the Great Famine, when her family had come to America.

The married name Kitty Lawrence had carried for some eight or nine years was redolent of old New England (there were cities and towns that bore those names), but she possessed another and much more famous Irish name. She was Kitty O'Shea. This name of the beautiful adulteress, the passionate mistress of the legendary Charles Stewart Parnell, was the expensively dressed ex-Mrs Brooks Acton Lawrence's maiden name, and she had, since her divorce, reverted to it. She had booked the flight as Kitty O'Shea although her passport had her as Katherine Lawrence. At home some friends still called her Kitty Lawrence, and she herself sometimes hesitated before announcing that she was Kitty O'Shea, the same as when she was a girl.

Standing in the queue for Customs, Kitty tried to remember who played Kitty O'Shea in the old movie one still saw on TV, the one with all the clothes so complicated you could never imagine getting them off in a hurry. Strange, Kitty thought, how hard it was to think of those old-fashioned women, after all the trouble of putting on those clothes, taking them all off again to commit hasty adulteries in the afternoon. Kitty supposed literature was to blame for this inconsistency. They never seemed to fuck in any of the world's great masterpieces. She held a novel by Dostoyevsky in her hand, and wished now that she had brought James Joyce's *Ulysses* with her instead. She hadn't read Joyce since Mount Holyoke College. Then she remembered that years later, when she was committing adultery for the very first time, she re-read Molly Bloom's big closing number to see if it would sort out her own mind. All that Molly Bloom business about a great big red poker and lots of spunk. It didn't help. But Joyce's book would be just the thing for a trip to Dublin, but then she had not known she was coming to Ireland.

The Customs queue was moving ahead quite rapidly. She stopped, placed all her luggage down around her, banged her big hat down more solidly on her dark head, and put the bulky paperback she was carrying into her bag.

She passed breezily through Customs with nothing to declare; she was ignorant of the fact that certain medicinal rubber goods were contraband; she was a modern woman, and what she liked to call in humorous self-mockery, a 'college widow'.

There were no porters anywhere. Not like when Carole Lombard or Greta Garbo go places in the old movies on TV, she thought. There was this odd-looking dark man staring at her as though at any moment he might offer to help with the luggage. She was dithering about with coat and bags, and her hat was falling off.

The funny dark fellow came forward. Kitty hesitated, thinking he might steal her bags. Then nature called, and she thanked him hurriedly, and raced off, the wide brims of her Champs Elysées hat nodding, to the women's room.

Kitty, at the crowded mirror, looked around at the other women there. Would she, she thought, manage to find some O'Sheas who belonged to her? And one of those little white cottages, like President Kennedy and President Reagan managed to find? She had a sudden vision of some very nice cousins, women who were Irish versions of Mimi Vallard and Meg Putnam, the girls who had been at school with her, and the men like Tim and Frank, her brothers. One cousin might even be allowed to be something like Mr Brooks Lawrence, with hair, as Brooksie was when Kitty first met him, a Deerfield preppy and star halfback at Jeffrey College in leafy Dickinson, Mass. Sidney the Shrink, she thought, just could not possess an Irish counterpart.

For a nice Catholic country like Ireland, there were amazingly vulgar things written on the walls of the airport women's room. Must have been a foreign nympho passing through, she thought. A spunky gal indeed, I'll say, Kitty said to herself.

The dark unhealthy-looking man waited patiently by her luggage.

5

Should she tip him? He looked so poor. But then, he might take offence.

'Oh, thank you,' Kitty said, 'thank you, thank you so much, that's so kind.'

The man just stood there, staring at her, then retreated into the crowd. Kitty O'Shea gazed round her at the Ould Sod whence she and all the O'Sheas had come.

In spite of the wondrously rolling banks of grey mist outside, she was disappointed. She had expected something different: high hills, great lakes like inland seas, castles. Perhaps they were blotted out behind the mist. From the air the legendary River Shannon, glimpsed through a break in the clouds from a window of the tilting plane, had looked pathetic, like a fish on a green plate.

Still, this was another home, the Mother Country. Even though four generations of O'Sheas were American-born, they had always considered themselves Irish. Why, even the family dog, a cocker spaniel, was called Brian Boru. He was still alive, living with Kitty's Mom, the Judge's widow, in the big white-painted house with the black shutters in Holford Park, still running to greet her when she came to call.

Yet it had not occurred to her to visit Ireland at all on this trip to Europe, where she had planned to drown her sorrows in famous paintings and in classical music, and in all the empathy with the Art of Suffering that the great culture of Paris, Florence and Madrid had to offer. She had not thought she would walk off the aircraft in the Republic of Ireland quite overwhelmed with the need to seek her roots in a country which might as well be Camelot, for all the reality she knew of it.

Now the girl at the hire-car desk was asking 'How long will you want the car?' and Oh, Kitty O'Shea thought, the sound of that accent. It seemed to contain all that the exiled O'Sheas had lost in their long estrangement. How romantic it was. And how harsh and strange her own American voice sounded in contrast.

'I don't know for sure,' Kitty said, in this strange, harsh-sounding new voice of hers. 'I hadn't planned on stopping at all. Several days, I guess. I've come to look up family ties. I'm Irish, too, you see.'

The hire-car girl smiled. She saw Kitty before her from the waist up, all white silk and black cashmere, long black hair expensively cut under the wide brims of the Paris hat.

The hire-car girl was used to red-faced New York, Chicago and South Boston Irishmen. She did not think Kitty looked Irish at all.

Kitty filled out the form, handed the girl her credit card, signed, and was stooping for her luggage when that dark gaunt creature in well-worn black was there again. He picked up her bags and led her out to a line of toy cars, his coat flapping sadly as they came out of the building into the driving rain. Kitty O'Shea skipped across the puddles.

'Typical Irish weather,' she said, wiping wet hair from her mouth. 'Isn't it just wonderful?' God, she thought, how awful. Just listen to me gushing like a tourist.

Her smile met pale, blue-washed eyes as cold as the wind. His hair, the way it was plastered to his head, gave him the aspect of some large black, beaked bird.

'Oh, gosh!' she said. 'I need to change money.' She turned back to the building. She did not look to see if the unhealthy stranger followed her.

She was some time. The unfamiliar currency was difficult to check, and Kitty held up the queue counting it to the penny. By the time she returned with change to overtip her amateur porter, to placate those indifferent eyes, he was nowhere to be seen. But her luggage was all there. It was neatly stacked ready to put in the back-seat of the car.

Well, isn't that nice, Kitty thought, reaching up with her long arms, in a gesture now lost to the feminine arts, removing the wide-brimmed hat and skimming it into the back-seat, with the air of someone casting a hat into the ring.

Lurking dark against the rain-soaked concrete, Falk watched her. She looked as though she had happiness to throw away, as if people had always crowded round her, picking up any odd scraps she happened to drop. The sort who didn't see any reason to expect people wouldn't like her. Falk swallowed bitter saliva in his mouth. She didn't fool him. The vulgar thing she was, all shining. And the sound of her voice made the gums shiver in your mouth. Look at her now, with that great pearl necklace of a smile on her face as she watched Irishness on the rampage with the cousins, uncles, aunts, brothers and sisters coming through Customs to meet families waiting for them since some unholy hour of the morning. Look at that face on her as she sorted the coins they gave her at the bank as though she'd never seen money before, all full of delight at the leaping salmon and the metallic bull.

Falk pulled his collar closer, smelling his own sweat, cold and sour, watching her go. Nothing in her bags. Perhaps it was about her person. A woman might keep it up there. A certain sort of a woman. A key, perhaps. To a locker somewhere. Couldn't stuff a million bucks inside, no matter how large the denominations.

He began to move softly after her, sniffing the sweet pollution of her scent where she had passed. At least Tyler and the good clean-living Loyalists he worked for in the North didn't go in for such whore Papist hypocrisy. Whiskey patriots and women. Whore tricks, like that one before her, who bore the same name, although she started life as a decent Protestant woman, Parnell's whore.

Behind a display of bright alien greenery, another Irishman watched Kitty O'Shea. He was a short fat man, wearing a bright tan trilby hat. He put down the racing page he had been reading, and stood. He stretched and yawned with a great vulgar cracking of his jaw. Two bored kids from Cincinnati, Ohio, waiting with their mother for Irish aunts and uncles who had not arrived, beside a pile of brand-new plastic luggage, nudged each other and giggled, much to their travel-weary Mom's annoyance. 'Hey, look,' one of the children said, 'a leprechaun.' The mother turned and observed the truth of their description, and saw a little man, with slightly leprous, swollen, badly-shaven cheeks, and the gleam of drunken lechery in his inky eyes. The fat little man smiled at the Cincinnati kids, looked at his watch, sorted his change, and walked briskly towards the telephone. There was something comic in his walk. The small boys from Ohio relieved their boredom imitating it, to the further annoyance of their mother.

Some hours later, much to the relief of relatives and friends who had been waiting all morning long, the melancholy voice on the airport tannoy system announced the arrival of a delayed Aer Lingus flight from Chicago. The voice dispassionately apologised for inconvenience caused by the late arrival of the aircraft, which was due to technical difficulties at the point of departure.

Inspector Doyle smiled at Detective Sergeant Byrne. 'Well,' Doyle said, 'she's going to get quite a welcome.'

There had been some confusion earlier in the morning. Doyle's source in Chicago had said the American woman, who was carrying, or was carrying the access to, a million-dollar donation to the Provisional IRA from American supporters, would book the flight as Kitty O'Shea. But her passport bore the name Roberta Lobello, the young woman's married name. There had been some sort of slip-up in the passenger lists for another Kitty O'Shea appeared on the TWA flight from Hartford, Connecticut, via Boston, Massachusetts to Shannon and Paris. Doyle told Detective Sergeant Byrne that he blamed the computer for that. Byrne was a great believer in computers. The woman on the TWA flight turned out to be only a Mrs Katherine Lawrence. Chicago had given Doyle photographs of Mrs Lobello, who was short, just over five feet, and red-haired. Mrs Lawrence was tall with dark hair. The computers had messed up, Doyle said. Detective Sergeant Byrne was not so sure of that. Anyway, Mrs Roberta Lobello, aka Kitty O'Shea, came off the plane and was asked by a passport control official to please step into the office for a moment. There was, Doyle was told, a hell of a row. The woman started screaming and fighting. Doyle came into the office and witnessed this. The woman was wearing a wig and, later, it was found, she was wearing contact lenses rather than glasses, as in the Chicago photograph. 'But,' Doyle said, listening to her screaming, 'she's a redhead all right.'

Detective Sergeant Byrne smiled, but he was a contemporary policeman. He believed in computers and post-postfeminism – his chief, Doyle, had scarcely heard of feminism; he called it Women's Lib and thought it had to do with burning bras. The immigration officials had all been issued with the picture of the wanted woman (a curious little face, all eyes and teeth, Doyle thought) and physical details – height five foot one, eyes grey, hair red. They had all been told that she may have dyed her hair and be wearing thick spectacles or coloured contact lenses.

Or even lift shoes, though that lack of height would be hard to disguise.

Doyle and Byrne walked up and arrested her for terrorist offences.

'Fuck you, you Brit fuckers,' she screamed at them. An old Dublin Garda like Doyle thought this a great joke, but Byrne was young and very nationalistic. He took it wrong and kept talking about it all day. Doyle's information was from a very reliable Chicago source. They expected she would be carrying the money, either in her hand baggage, or in the luggage in the hold. They found it before it reached the carousel in the Customs hall.

Doyle had two Dublin policewomen with him. 'To handle the rough stuff,' Doyle told Detective Sergeant Byrne.

Mrs Lobello stopped fighting and swearing and began to weep. Then she got what Doyle described as sulky. He had hoped to collect her Irish contacts, but they had lost them or she was to meet them elsewhere. Detective Sergeant Byrne had been all for letting the woman go through the airport and 'snaring', he said, 'the lot.' 'Including Mr Big?' Doyle asked, but Byrne did not appreciate this sarcasm.

As they were taking Mrs Lobello away, Byrne said he wondered why she picked the name 'Kitty O'Shea'.

Doyle looked at the bitter little red-headed woman.

'I suppose she's a romantic,' he said. This time Detective Sergeant Byrne did laugh.

2

In Dublin it was only four o'clock; the rain had slackened, but the leaden sky had closed over the afternoon, and the cars hissing and spitting their way down the wet streets already had their headlamps on. In Merrion Square the lights were also on inside the National Gallery. Paddy Kiernan, a thin man in his late thirties whose spectral features gave the impression of something cut in a hurry from unseasoned wood, came out of the Gallery and across the forecourt to the street. He had viewed no pictures there, but had received the call from Shannon from Brendan on the Gallery pay-phone; and he had also made use, twice, of the visitors' lavatory – 'kidneys inflamed; seek a sunnier, drier clime,' the doctor (must be joking) said.

As he walked along the north side of the Square, Paddy Kiernan glanced through the lighted windows of the elegant Georgian houses, all converted to offices now, and saw the secretaries with their heads bent over typewriters and computers. He turned up his sodden coat collar, a pointless gesture against the rain (Paddy Kiernan possessed neither mackintosh nor umbrella), and felt the drops trickling down his neck and back. He would have thrust his gleaming damp and wind-blotched hands, which protruded from the cuffs of his over-short sleeves, into the trouser pockets, but the trousers were near enough pocketless. Whenever, forgetting their parlous state, he put his hands inside, he could feel his own bare leg. It struck Paddy now that this placing of cold hand into trouser pocket and feeling leg was symbolic in its way, a sure-sign definition of poverty. The hole in the left shoe, which was now letting in water so he appeared to have a limp, was too common a thing, and not like the pocketless trousers as a symbol of being penniless. Paddy was sorely in need of money.

A certain business opportunity had arisen by which he could put this situation to rights. He debated the pros and cons of this business opportunity. At first, it had been rejected quite out of hand (or out of pocket), but on thinking it over later he had become a little less dismissive; although he never, even only as the basis of speculation, accepted it with anything like a whole and willing heart. That was the present state of his refusal of what had been suggested to him, and as he scurried along the street, he still recoiled from the idea of it. The new business opportunity was as old as Ireland: to become an informer. Clenching his chapped cold hands, he thought to himself that if he did succumb he would never be so poor and pocketless again. He could go to the sun for the good of his health. But he smiled in the rain at his own momentary flirtation with the idea of doing such a thing – in Ireland that was the secular version of the Sin Against the Holy Ghost. He had overcome it. He was staunch and true. Strong of will. He felt happy and good about his own sterling character. He saw the face of the man who had proposed this business opportunity to him as the face of . . . of what? . . . of something pathetic, a pathetic clown, and not, as he had previously appeared, as the Dark Seducer leading Paddy Kiernan to a high place.

By the time he reached the cumbersome block of the Electricity Supply Building at the corner of the Square, Paddy was almost running. Where the brightly-lit offices gave way to poverty-stricken houses, given over to flats shared by transitory students and bedsitting-rooms for the more permanent lonely, the street was dark. With his hopping gait, he crossed diagonally over Mount Street, cursing a car that came round the corner from Merrion Square nearly causing him an injury, then leaped up the slippery steps of a tall, run-down house. He banged on the peeling front door with the flat of one hand, ceasing only to step back impatiently every few seconds to glare at the ground-floor window where one naked light bulb glowed through the broad chinks between narrow, grimy curtains.

The door finally opened a crack, revealing darkness. From inside the gloom, a cheerful voice said, 'You're come at last, then, Paddy? You took your time.'

Paddy pushed his way in, shutting the door behind him. The other man, Sean Cafferty, was short, with a broad face and a bald head that

12

had once been full of red-gold curls. Sean turned on the light. The single unshaded bulb of low power swung high in a dirty, intricately wrought ceiling. On the floor a narrow strip of carpet laid over the brown linoleum reflected the light from a veneer of ingrained grease.

'Good God,' Paddy said, 'What a tip.' His own home was two rooms in a Corporation block of flats on the North Side. 'Look at the state of that carpet.' There was the smell, too, of damp, cooked cabbage, and escaping gas.

'You're late. What took you this long?' Sean said.

'I had to wait for the phone to come free,' he said. Paddy stood dripping rainwater on the bit of old carpet nailed to the hall floor. 'There was an old biddy on it talking it dry of electricity. And then I took a minute to pay a call of nature, and there was another old biddy had taken over where the other one left off.'

This was one of Paddy's stories. The smaller man looked up smiling. 'Talking it dry of electricity, that's good,' he said.

'Then I had to go again, and coming back was another old biddy jabbering sixteen to the dozen down the line.'

Sean was preparing his face to smile, although he could see the story was tragic as well, on account of Paddy Kiernan's kidneys. Paddy had been a strong healthy lad when they started. He drove the car for Sean the first time Sean had ever shot a man. Afterwards they had done a lot of campaigns together.

'They must've been working shifts,' Paddy said of the old women monopolising the pay-phone in the National Gallery. 'Brendan will've been going mad down at Shannon trying to get through.'

'Well, you're here now,' the other man said. 'And he's here as well. Liam O'Tomas himself.'

'Ireland's own Lionel Thompson, you mean?'

'Will you hush that talk. He'll hear you,' Sean said. 'You go in now, and keep a stop on that tongue of yours.'

Sean Cafferty was afraid of the Englishman, Paddy could see that.

Paddy pushed the door open on the right of the hall and went into the room where the man he had called Lionel Thompson sat reading a newspaper. From behind Paddy Sean said, 'Liam, here's Paddy now. He had to wait for the telephone to come free.'

13

The Englishman who called himself Liam O'Tomas looked up from the newspaper. He did not look at all Irish. He had one of those long English faces, with too little chin and receding, long, pallid hair. He was quick-witted, and had a sharp manner. Rude without knowing it, in the English way, Paddy thought. The Englishman was about twenty-seven, and women thought him handsome, often giving him a hurried second look in the street. Sean thought that was why Paddy disliked Liam, although maybe he did not need an excuse. Paddy had done a lot of work, most of it dangerous, handling high explosives sometimes, too, although he was best at driving a car and shooting when he had to. The Irish cops had got him once coming back over the Border, but they didn't hold him. Otherwise his record was clean, but the men in charge must have thought him too old for the quick stuff up North. And, of course, Sean thought, he's ill. You could see that just looking at him. First he joked about it, saying it was quim, or the lack of quim. Now he didn't joke but said it was his health. At the same time you always needed cunt. Paddy was too poor to have any women, unless a patriotic whore took pity on him. Sean himself went to whores, but paid them properly with good money.

Sean went out into the little kitchen under the stairs in the hallway and put the kettle on for a cup of tea. In the room they could hear him swilling hot water about in the teapot.

'He's a proper little housewife,' Liam said. Paddy looked away. He could see nothing through the filthy window, but he could hear the rain drumming on the roofs of the cars parked outside. He sat down on the edge of a broken chair and watched the Englishman reading the newspaper. He'll fuck us all up sooner or later, Paddy thought. He doesn't get along with any of us, none of the Irish except that thin stick of a girl he's got over in Ranelagh. Except, of course, he's fucking her up, too. He'd be more actual use if he was killed or captured, to show that there were even Englishmen prepared to die for the Irish cause.

'There,' Sean said coming in with the tea, 'and there'll be enough for a second brew if we give it time to draw.'

Paddy saw Sean suddenly look glum, a puzzled frown on his broad face. Then, with a big grin like a conjuror producing a rabbit from a top-hat, the little man reached back and drew a spoon from his hip pocket and started shovelling sugar into his mug of tea.

'One or two, Liam?' he asked.

'No sugar,' the Englishman said. Then he said something under his breath that Paddy didn't hear. Another fucking snotty English remark, Paddy thought.

'Here it is now, nice hot tea,' Sean said. It was an irritating, fussy, old-woman's manner Sean had, Paddy thought, and it made the bullying Englishman go for him all the more.

'Haven't you any milk?' Liam said in what Paddy thought was a very English voice. His master's voice, Paddy thought. If it were only this Englishman to consider, there would be hardly anything now standing in the way of that 'new business opportunity'. But there was Sean and then there was Brendan, who was even more comic and defenceless than Sean.

Will you listen to this now? Paddy said to himself, hearing Liam complaining about the lack of milk seemingly unaware of the effect his voice had. Paddy had seen strangers hear it and give him a curious look. They suspected he might be making fun of them. Paddy watched him now looking down his long English nose at Sean. No, Paddy thought, he doesn't like the Irish very much. That was strange. So why did he come over here to fight? Must be something psychological. Mother didn't pay him enough attention. Something like that. It always was, they said. He was supposedly fearless. Shove a bomb up a London bobby's trouser leg if you asked him. He did a job on the mainland a couple of years ago. A job that left real Irish workingmen in gaol right now in England, Paddy thought. Arrested all together on a train. Innocent until proved Irish, right enough. Irish men are doing time while Liam O'Tomas sat here complaining about no milk for his tea. Does he ever fret at all? It was a strange cruel world, with no justice in it. Three years those men had been in a British prison. Did he ever feel any guilt? From the working class, too, and Liam such a big Red; he made enough speeches to them about it.

Sean started a long Irish explanation about weather conditions and their effect on unrefrigerated milk. Paddy threw back his head and laughed.

Liam O'Tomas turned.

15

'If you've something to say,' he said to Paddy in that school-mistressy voice, 'say it.'

Paddy hesitated. He was the possessor of tremendous tidings. He had been waiting for some formal manner of questioning. Liam was the chief of the operation after all, he should ask questions.

'She's arrived,' Paddy said. 'At Shannon Airport.'

'She's here at last,' Liam said. 'The time has come.'

Paddy heard the phoney Irish inflexion in the Englishman's voice. He turned away embarrassed.

'You're sure it's her?'

Paddy nodded. 'Brendan was at the airport,' he said.

'In his little trilby hat,' Sean said, making a joke.

Liam gave Sean a look. 'And it was just like the plan?' he asked Paddy. 'You spoke with Brendan?'

'It was as they said,' Paddy said. 'She was booked through to Paris but she got off.'

'If we get this wrong,' Liam said. 'Christ, if we get this wrong.'

'I know that,' Paddy said; and he thought to himself, God save us from Englishmen turned Irish patriots. He also thought that if they had got this wrong, it would be worth it to see what Mr Flynn would do to Liam.

Liam got up. He held a black leather jacket over one arm. 'There's things to do,' he said.

Paddy watched him, wondering what had made him turn so irrevocably against his own kind. To plant bombs in your own cities, blow up your own people. If he did love Ireland, he did not love Irishmen. Look at the way he treated Sean just now. He was not sympathetic with them, although there was always that Irish girl who was in love with him. There never was any accounting for a woman's taste in men. He'll probably be going there now. To get some, what is it Sean calls it, quim. Get some quim while we're stuck here with our fingers up our own arses dreaming of a united Ireland.

Paddy asked: 'What do we do now, Liam?'

'Wait. Bloody go on waiting. And keep in touch with your great friend Brendan with his trilby hat. He doesn't need telling to stay with her, I hope?'

'Oh,' Paddy said, 'you don't have to worry about Brendan. He'll stay with her all right.'

16

'We'll remember this moment when we're old men,' Liam suddenly said. The other two turned and stared for a moment at the sentimental Englishman, and then looked away. Liam put on the leather jacket, and left the room without another word. They waited to hear the front door slam, but it closed quietly. They listened to the footsteps quickly merge with the sound of the rain.

'Whatever did Mr Flynn see in a man like that?' Sean said.

'Maybe Fat Siobhan took a fancy to him,' Paddy said. 'A woman like that's a weakness in a man, even Mr Flynn.'

'Some weakness, built like the rock of Gibraltar,' Sean said. 'You think Mr Flynn thought Liam might provide a diversion, do you?'

'Mr Flynn's not a man to value the love of a good woman.'

'Nor's Liam. They have that in common.'

'Lionel Thompson,' Paddy said. 'Leo the Lion and Liam the Lionel.' He laughed. 'I don't know what the cause of Ireland's coming to. Do you ever think of getting out?'

'I like it here,' Sean said, looking round the cluttered, dirty room. 'If I only had someone to clean it again, it would be fine for me.'

Paddy knew he meant his mother, who was recently dead.

'No, no,' Paddy said, 'I mean Ireland.'

'What about Ireland?'

'Leave Ireland. Go away altogether somewhere warm. To America or Canada.'

'It can be cold in Canada.'

'South Africa, then. We could go to South Africa or Australia. We could go together. Brendan too.'

'I'll tell you what, I'll go to the bar with you,' Sean said. 'It's warm enough there for me. And we'll have one for Brendan, forced to keep an eagle eye on Miss Kitty O'Shea.'

He was putting on his anorak, pulling a cap from the pocket.

'I hope she brings more luck to Ireland,' he said, 'than the last one did.'

'Australia's a fine warm place,' Paddy said as they went out together into the murky evening and turned towards Baggot Street.

'Australia, a fine place. I've heard that,' Sean said. 'We'll go to the upstairs bar,' he said. 'We can watch the television there. I don't know what's on.'

'Does it ever matter what's on?' Paddy said. He stood head and shoulders above Sean. 'You know,' he said, 'I was listening to Liam talking there, and I was thinking of those men they say's in English gaols for what he did.'

'Me too,' Sean said.

'I suppose the English think there's some practical justice in it,' Paddy said. 'Them being Irish. But it's like taking hostages.' He paused and put his hand on Sean's shoulder. 'Never mind what's on the telly,' he said. 'If we don't like what's on, we can sing a few songs.'

'Yes,' Sean said, 'we'll have a few jars and sing some songs.'

Then they both laughed, knowing that certainly they would have too much to drink and end up singing songs.'

3

The great tragic landscape of Ireland lay all around her in the rain. As though on cue, the pale towers of a castle, symbol of past oppression, dominated the road from a high hillside. There were several old women by the roadside selling postcards and souvenirs. They protected their wares with large black umbrellas tilted against the wind-driven rain. Kitty stopped the car and got out.

'What is this place?' she asked one of the old women. Then the oddest thing happened. The old woman started talking but Kitty could not understand her. It was as though the old lady were speaking a foreign language. Was this Gaelic? Kitty thought. But no, she leaned forward and heard that it was English.

'Sure, 'tis Bunratty Castle, so 'tis,' the old woman was saying. Kitty puzzled over the strange archaic speech. She had only heard anything like it before with people making fun and using words like Begorrah.

'Why, 'tis a famous place,' the woman said. ''Tis history.'

With a sinking heart, Kitty gazed at the gaudy brochures advertising medieval dinners and costume balls in the castle. Was this dreadful tourist trap the real enchanted island?

The old woman, observing the puzzled frown, attempted to explain. 'Feasts for the tourists,' she said. 'So's they can eat with their fingers like in the old days,' she said, 'before they had the knife, the fork, or the spoon.'

Kitty bought a postcard from the old woman. It showed the medieval hall of the castle. The colours were too bright. They seemed unreal. There were couples dressed in gaudy casual clothes seated at a banqueting table, hideous unnatural grins on their faces as they were caught turning to the camera with some sort of mock medieval drinking goblets held daintily in their hands.

19

''Tis a good likeness,' the old woman said, 'or so they say, for to tell the truth, I've never been inside myself. Too cold and damp for me,' she said, 'I leave that to the tourists.'

Kitty thought there was a terrible pathos about the old woman selling postcards in the rain. She watched the crone's dry fingers digging in a bright, red plastic purse for change. The bright red thing had a cluster of window-pockets for credit cards. One of the windows held a cheap cloth medallion of the Sacred Heart of Jesus. The others were empty. The old woman followed Kitty's gaze.

''Tis American,' she said.

Kitty listened to the unfamiliar accent, with the stage-Irish ''tis', then she smiled a smile of lonely sympathy for the poor woman.

'I got it in Gary, Indiana,' the old woman said. 'Outside Chicago. When I was there last year on a visit, so.'

'Yes,' Kitty said, amazed. 'Chicago.' Kitty had never been there. 'Chicago,' the woman said, laughing. 'The Windy City, Al Capone.'

She pronounced the final 'e' of Capone, as an Italian would do.

'There's a lot of Sheehys there, in Chicago,' the old woman said. Sheehy was obviously her family name. 'And in Gary, Indiana, and in San Francisco where I was last summer.'

Kitty had never been to San Francisco either. She looked with interest at the old woman, and saw that she was only middle-aged.

''Tis a grand country, America, so 'tis,' the woman said. She pronounced it Amer-ee-ca.

'Yes,' Kitty said. 'I'm O'Shea. And my mother was Flynn.'

'Like Errol Flynn from Hollywood in the pictures,' the woman said. 'They're Irish names enough,' she said, 'unless they were changed from Spaghetti.' The woman laughed at her own satire. She was obviously a character. She had dull white plastic teeth and large spectacles framed in plastic of a modern design. Her glasses looked like two television screens showing close-up pictures of the human eye. Brooks's mother had eye-glasses like that. Kitty wondered why she had ever thought of this postcard woman as old. She must have been expecting something quaint in shawls, she thought, and that's what she saw. There was nothing quaint about the postcard seller. Everything she wore was composed of man-made fibre. She was completely contemporary, and hideous; except, of course, she didn't have any credit cards, and she also had that accent, but then Kitty wondered if she might not be putting that on for the tourist.

Kitty walked slowly back to her car. The rain was easing, though the wind jumped up at her back.

Across the road, she saw the dark head of the man who had helped with her luggage at the airport. He was sitting smoking a cigarette behind the wheel of a grey car. She would have to get used to what a small country Ireland was, she thought. He was staring up at the Castle, and did not see when she waved at him.

She drove off towards Dublin. The rain had stopped. A rather tearful sun, given an occasional chance to peer through the wonderfully tumbling clouds chasing across the sky, turned a glittering spotlight on the wet roof of a croft or a green patch of trees. It was the best thing in the world feeling the damp fresh air on her face through the open window of the car. An old woman sat wrapped in a shawl on a stool by a cottage door. Kitty waved to her, and to a young man standing by the roadside staring at the mechanics of a muddy tractor. The young man's heavy trousers were picturesquely tied at the ankles with twine. And out on the roadside were many miniature houses, with pocket-handkerchieves of fields behind them sparkling in the sun. She had never realised, she thought, how many shades of green there were.

She was like a showy bantam among those draggled old hens, Falk thought. Trivial, garish, vulgar creatures full of pus, the lot of them.

An unscheduled stop, surely? She was like all the rest, true to type, like all the other colonialist tourists patronising the natives. Probably thought it part of her cover, if she had the sense even to know what she was doing. Will you look at that walk. They must teach them that, in their whore schools. Unnatural, that's what it was. And the old crone with the postcards laughing with her neighbour, shaking her head. Bitches, all full of secrets and dark places full of deceit.

She's seen me, then. But she doesn't realise. Arrogant thing, without a thought beyond her own self. I'll give her thoughts to think about.

4

Liam O'Tomas, the Englishman turned Irish patriot, left the dingy room of Sean Cafferty and walked hurriedly in the rain and the encroaching dark down Upper Mount Street, his head bent forward lost in thought. Turning right at the Canal he strode down the towpath taking long steps towards Ranelagh. O'Tomas, with his long blond English hair swept back from his forehead, loomed in the half-light head and shoulders above the homeward-scurrying Irishmen, who looked to him darker and more subterranean than usual. Some few of them did not seem to mind the rain. These idly sauntering people were walking unhappy-looking dogs. The animals' wet ears were flattened against the wind and rain, and they gazed about with anxious mongrel eyes, as though the world of the towpath was utterly new to them, although they must, all of them, have walked it a hundred times.

He could not stop walking. Ideas raged in his head. Close to Ranelagh Bridge he turned and pounded back along the towpath the way he had come.

The job in hand should have been occupying his thoughts. The American courier had come with the money. He should be thinking only of that, not allowing his mind to reel with a dozen other things in such a ferment of excitement that he might become ill again with asthma brought on, the doctor said, by nervous tension and stress.

The business with the American money was, he told himself, only the start of many wonderful things to come. He imagined himself sitting at a council of war somewhere in some secret room, with important men listening to him; he heard himself saying, 'We have bombed King Billy out of Belfast and now we'll bomb the Pope out of Dublin.' In his mind, this melodramatic pronouncement was taken most seriously. But who were the important men seated with him round the table at the council of war in the secret room? With resentment, he knew he could not give them faces because he knew no one – with, of course, the possible exception of Flynn. Mr Flynn was the only one he knew who might be important enough to be there. That would all change after this great coup of the American money. Liam O'Tomas would become a man to be reckoned with then. Even Flynn would have to give him some respect then.

Now, however, he could picture only Flynn, who, for some reason, everyone always referred to as 'Mister' Flynn. Was Flynn even his real name? Mr Flynn was not a true revolutionary, Liam thought. No, he was a cheap little Irish gangster who was making a good few bob out of the Troubles. How was it that the others did not see through Mr Flynn, who dressed like a broken-down Irish horse trader and would sell his grandmother for a price? And he had that fat woman mooning about him, too. Fat Siobhan, she was called behind her back; 'Mister' Flynn himself called her Fat Siobhan, as though she were only his housekeeper, or some sort of mildly diverting servant. Liam wondered if Flynn and the woman might possibly be married. She was besotted with the man. It was a wonder he wasn't ashamed to be seen in public with a great slug of a woman like that. As Liam himself disliked being seen in the street or the bar with Niamh, who was thin like Siobhan was fat.

The thought of Niamh reminded him that he was walking in the wrong direction. He stopped in his tracks. Two teenage Irish girls went by, giggling as they stepped round him. He saw them smile and heard their laughter. They whispered about him. 'He's got nice eyes,' one of them said. She did not care if he heard her. It was as though he were an inanimate object. Dirty little Irish Catholic teases, Liam thought. Their minds, all of them, young and old, were filled with furtive sex. It was the superstition of their sick religion that did it. The Protestants in the North were just as bad in their own way, with the smell of disinfectant everywhere about them. To hell with them all. A Red Ireland, free of religion, would stand defiantly off the shores of England – of all of Europe – like Fidel Castro's Cuba stood off the shores of America.

How far had he come in the wrong direction? Liam glanced up at the Carrolls building. In his mind's eye, he saw it reduced to a distorted, blackened, smouldering ruin, stinking of smoke. Now, with the American money, they would be able to attack anything, wouldn't they? The new ground-to-air rockets would knock helicopters, and jets, too, out of the sky. There could conceivably be a time when there would be no commercial flights in or out of Ireland. And no building would be safe, no building whatsoever. Everything could, in such circumstances, be brought to a standstill. Then he would be among the leaders of the rebirth of these humble downtrodden people whose plight was now his cause. He stopped his furious walk, took a cigarette from a packet, put it between his lips and lit it. Often revolutionaries over-estimated the time it would take to create the revolution. Lenin in Zurich thought he would not live to see the revolution. And Trotsky himself was in New York and had been taken completely by surprise by the suddenness of events.

'Yous got twenty pence for a tea?'

Liam had not seen the man approach him. There were often drunks on the towpath. The government should do something about it, he thought. It was a disgrace. This one tugged at Liam's sleeve.

'God!' Liam shouted, full of exasperation. He turned and walked quickly back the way he came, striding back towards Ranelagh to see the woman Niamh who, he knew, loved him as Fat Siobhan loved Mr Flynn.

Liam, in return, loved her love of him. Of course he despised her for it, and often it was a great nuisance, her fawning over him, but she was always there. He was able to push her from his mind. He could go for days, for weeks, without seeing her, but for some reason this only increased her devotion to him. He was free, and that was what made it possible to accept her love.

There was another woman who loved him like that, but she was his mother. His mother's love, undemanding and automatic, repelled him as well. Every Monday that silly suburban woman, in her frilly high-necked blouse and a skirt with silly pleats she worried about creasing (was it the same skirt and blouse, or had she a closet full of them?), sat down in the neat lower middle-class terraced house in Croydon, in which she had spent her entire married life with that twisted old soldier, his father, to write to Lionel, her only son, who wished that she was dead. He hardly ever read all of the letters. They arrived, addressed to 'Lionel Thompson', with a Thornton Heath postmark. That was how those Irish has-beens, Paddy Kiernan and

24

Sean Cafferty, had learned his English name. Liam thought of Paddy and Sean as old men. He was one of those young men who could never guess the ages of men or women older than himself. Paddy was a mere ten years older than Liam, and Sean perhaps a dozen years his senior, but Liam thought of them as relics, and would perhaps not have been really all that much amazed to be told they had been in the Post Office that Easter – as boys, of course.

He, anyway, sneered in a superior modern fashion at their pathetic romantic nationalism. They had, he thought, visions of themselves as old IRA men in jodhpurs and green shirts facing the Black and Tans with Thompson guns, like in the old song they sang when they were one over the eight. 'With the green on the green and the rattle of a Thompson gun.' Something like that, it went. They were fools to themselves. They knew his name, but at least they knew nothing else about him, about the work he had done, for example, on the mainland, which had gone very well. It could not, in fact, have been better. Those stupid Micks were imprisoned. Everyone knew they were innocent. There had been a documentary film about them on British television. (Liam had watched it. Unblinking, he liked to think he had been. He saw himself as a steely-eyed fellow.) Some Labour MPs had asked questions in the House of Commons. There had been long, unreadable articles in those soft British liberal newspapers. Some other bleeding heart, a television personality and author, was writing a book about what a miscarriage of justice it was.

Those fool Irishmen had been undone by their superstitious religion. When they were arrested on the train, the police found Mass cards in their pockets. They were on their way to Derry to the funeral of a former colleague who'd blown himself up with one of his own bombs, and, of course, they'd paid to have a Mass said for the repose of his soul. Praying for the dead seemed to Liam a very weird primitive notion the Roman Catholics had. The idea of their praying for the soul of the dead bomber had, of course, filled all the English Protestants with loathing. That was enough to make them guilty in English eyes. At the same time, what fools the English were. They couldn't get Liam O'Tomas, but they had to have someone.

Niamh lived just off the Canal, in a flat above a newsagent's shop. When he was not in a hurry, and there was some sentimental festival at hand, Liam liked to loiter in the shop and watch the ugly

25

stick-insect teenagers buying cards for 'The Best Mum in the World'. There were those worn-out housewives, too, choosing satin hearts and bells for wedding anniversaries. He tried to tell Niamh about them, but she had no sense of humour and did not laugh.

He rang Niamh's doorbell. He caught the eye of the shopkeeper, an oaf who probably dreamed of Niamh at nights; at least Liam knew he regaled his customers with tales of what Liam and Niamh did together in bed. He said he could 'hear the thumping' of the bed on the floor, pounding on the ceiling of his store room in the back. It was good for trade, telling these stories, Niamh said. She thought it was very funny, she told Liam when he got angry about it. Then she said she was sorry for the shopkeeper because he didn't have anyone himself.

Irritated by this memory, Liam kicked at the door which led up the stairs to Niamh's flat. It opened with a bang. He ran up the dark passage, taking the stairs two at a time.

'Who's that?' he heard her call. 'Who's there?'

She came to the head of the stairs above him, a towel wrapped round her head. She did not move aside when he reached her, pushing out her pale face to be kissed.

'Who'd you think it was?' he said sulkily. 'What's that muck on your face?'

She followed him into the kitchen, pulling the belt of her blue wool dressing gown tighter round her thin waist.

'You could've rung,' she said. 'Then I'd have been ready.' He was in a bad mood. She must be careful not to inflame him, or he'd be ranting and raving at her for hours, calling her all sorts of dirty names. But here he was again. Without having told her he was coming. She hadn't seen or heard from him for ten whole days.

She began to rub her hair, bending forward, pretending to be unconcerned by him suddenly being there, and hiding her face because she knew she looked all soft and daft at him, she was always so glad to see him back. He stalked round the living-room like a complete stranger, like a burglar looking to see what he could possibly steal in such a humble place. Her hair tumbled so black it looked blue where the light caught it. So long as he didn't start raving, either with one of those political things of his, or against her and some of her personal habits, but there was something awfully exciting about the way he burst in and looked at her as if he had never seen her before.

Her long dark hair was beautiful, but Liam preferred blondes. She was of course too thin. At first she had made him feel very manly standing beside her, but now he found her merely pathetic.

'Do you want coffee?' she asked, looking up with her head bent over. He could see only one eye through the black curtain of hair; she reeked of the steam from the bath, like coming into a hot house full of potted plants.

'Only if it's instant. I can't stand all that grinding business. But at least it smells good. How come when you take a bath you stink up the whole place?'

'It's no trouble with the real coffee.'

'No, no, for Heaven's sake, dry your bloody self. That's why you've always got the sniffles. If you could see yourself with that dripping nose. What do you think that's like for me?' He was off again. He was forgetting to speak in what he supposed was an Irish accent. You could hear the Englishness in his voice, and she wished he'd just shut up and take her, like that, with her all open after a nice long hot bath.

'And the red blotches all over your neck. How old are you, and you can't dry yourself properly?'

He walked across the living-room. She had drawn the curtains against the raw weather, and lit the table lamp. He grimaced at the bourgeois image she had created, with the imitation leather three-piece suite and the Victorian picture of little children and a kitten. Liam threw himself down on the settee, stretching his long, thin legs towards the mock flames of the gas fire in the chimney-place.

Niamh, her dark hair hanging damp on her shoulders, brought in the instant coffee, in cups, with saucers. She worried that this would irritate Liam. Sometimes he was irritated when she served him tea or coffee in mugs, calling it 'micky'. But then if she used proper cups and saucers he would accuse her of trying to be bourgeois and 'nice', which he pronounced 'naice', twisting his lips round in a parody of prissy pretentiousness.

She knelt on the bright hairy rug, and allowed the blue dressing gown to fall away from one breast.

27

Irish prick-tease, he thought, and looked away.

She spoke his name but he did not answer. She touched his hand. Liam stood up, knocking her sideways.

'Cover yourself up. You're not decent,' he said. 'You're to do me a favour.'

She was lying back on the rug with her arms raised to him. He looked away from her. She didn't know how much that gesture made him want to hurt her.

'I'll need to bring someone here for a few days,' he said. 'She's only just arrived in Shannon.'

'She? Another woman?' Niamh sat up.

'Of course a woman. Do you think if it was a man I'd have to bring him to a dump like this? A woman from America.'

'Are you putting me up for something?'

'Oh, for Christ's sake. This isn't cunt stuff. But if you won't help out . . .' He shrugged, and stood up to go.

'Don't go, I'm sorry. Of course I'll help.' She got up and stood close to him, raising her long arms and putting them on his shoulders, with her fingers in the blond soft hair at the back of his neck. Her arms had long blue veins. Liam put them away, as though taking off a necktie which didn't suit him.

'Get me a beer, then. I can't stand the sight of these cups and saucers.'

He watched her walk into the kitchen to fetch beer and a glass. She had thin thighs, but he liked the sight of her narrow hips with the dressing gown pulled tight.

'Hurry up, will you,' he said. 'I haven't got all day.'

Nothing more would be said about the American woman now. He could bring her here. Niamh would make no trouble.

Sometimes he stayed all night at Niamh's flat, putting up with her because it made a change from his attic on the North Side of the city, where there were never any buses, and the cries and screams of the caged animals in the Zoo filled the silent nights with weird noises. But at the same time, Liam found something magical about the night Zoo noises. They didn't get on his nerves, as they did on some people's. If he had to be away for some time, perhaps up in the six counties on a job (one of those jobs only a young man could do, and which made the old has-beens jealous), he'd begin to miss the sound of the animals. He could hear the lion roaring at night. When that happened he would keep awake as long as he could, shaking his head to throw off sleep. He had had a dream there one night that he liked a lot. He had dreamed that he was a hunter or explorer far off in the green hills and yellow plains of Africa. But that, he thought, looking at Niamh in her blue dressing gown, was childish.

Besides, he had only ever had one of those beautiful green African dreams, only once. There had been a beautiful woman in it. Sometimes he remembered her as being very black, shiny like ebony; other times he remembered that the woman in the African dream was a white woman, a blonde, with a long, lovely, curving jaw and high cheekbones, with her hair pushed back from a broad forehead. She had stood before him without any clothes on, standing in her naked skin that she wore as unselfconsciously as a suit of clothes. He had never encountered anything like that in real life.

But the point of the woman in the dream was that she spoke in a kind voice, saying as she came to him, 'Do not alarm yourself', touching him on the shoulder with her warm naked hand. How could one dream like that have been so real, and so important? He laughed at himself.

'What is it?' Niamh asked.

'Nothing.'

Niamh opened the beer, and handed it to him with the glass to pour for himself in case she did it wrong.

'Turn on the TV, will you,' he said. 'It's time for the news.'

She reached over and switched on the set.

'Oh,' she said, 'it was about Irish bombers asking for an appeal. But we've missed it.' Niamh put her head on his shoulder. Her hair smelled of medicated shampoo.

'I hope and pray they'll let them go,' she said.

'Who, for Christ's sake?'

'The men they put in prison for the bombings.'

'Whatever for? This way the whole world can see capitalist justice.' He was very careful the way he said 'capitalist', instead of 'British', which is what one of the Irish nationalists like Paddy Kiernan would have said.

'But the poor men are innocent.'

'Yes, they are. And that's what shows up their filthy system. They're martyrs.'

'Unwilling ones,' Niamh said. She wasn't sexually excited anymore, the way she had been when he came up the stairs. It seemed as if they had been seated like this in front of the TV set squabbling for years, and nothing ever changed, like an old married couple, except that's all right for them, the married couples, they have other things, being married, like children. But she and Liam were not married, and never would be by the looks of things. She wondered what he'd do if she put two fingers in her mouth and then reached down with them and started to work herself off. Don't be silly, he'd probably say. Something like that, and here she was, not getting any younger.

She was sitting on the floor at his knee, with her thin legs sprawling out before her. He could see the line of one thin hip curved out. 'Turn it off,' he said. She rolled over, on her hands and knees, reaching out an arm to switch off the TV. 'Now,' he said, 'don't move.'

'Oh, Liam,' she said, 'there's the whole of the big bed in the bedroom.' That's what married couples did, she thought. 'Don't speak,' he said, pushing her head down, kneeling behind her where she couldn't see, and unbuckling his trousers. She could hear the buckle and his zip.

'Here,' she said, moving her shoulders, 'I'll take this off.'

Niamh could feel the leather of his black jacket touching her backside where he had lifted the skirts of her dressing gown. She wanted the feel of the leather over all her back as he bent over her. But it was too late to stop.

'Leave it on, you bitch,' he said, 'and don't speak. Don't say a word and don't move.' He lifted the long skirt of the blue wool gown and revealed her thin, pale buttocks like a young girl's. He saw her look up over her shoulder at him. How could she understand so little? He felt like cuffing her across the face; as he had often done, even drawing blood. But she'd just look at him and say, What did I do?

'Oh, that's nice and lovely, Niamh,' he said. 'And now just reach down between your legs and give me a hand.'

'It's so dry,' she said, but it wasn't at all. He liked that though, she thought, shoving that great big thing in when he thought it might hurt her.

30

'I told you, don't speak. Say nothing.'

With his trousers down, Liam was gazing in admiration at his erection, wondering if he should fuck it in her face and listen to her gasping for breath. Afterwards she never had a word of complaint, although her thin jaws must have been sore.

'What are you thinking, you randy whore?'

'Oh, Liam, I can't think at all. Not with you inside me like this.'

He could easily be a Brit, she thought. An undercover man. He hits me once too often, I'll shop him, him and his dirty talk, treating me like a whore. God, wouldn't that be something if I did. Him up here mounting me like a dog in the road, and all the time I'd know the boys were waiting for him downstairs to march him off to a ditch somewhere. That would be something for a woman to know that was coming to her lover while he was rummaging at her like a great hound from behind, all cock and gasping for breath.

'Niamh,' he said, 'that's beautiful and tight, like a young Irish Catholic nun's pussy.'

Oh, God, she thought, he's started that nun stuff again. Why does he have to talk?

'She likes it, you see, the nun does. Better than being a Bride of Christ.' (Oh, Jaysus, Niamh thought, there he goes again, and me about to explode.) 'Better than the Mother Superior licking her cunt for her. I'll get you a nun's outfit. You'd like that, wouldn't you? Don't move, keep still. I'll move you so it won't come out. Now you can move, you bitch. And reach down a hand and grab my balls like a proper little whore nun. Do you love it?'

'Oh, Liam.' At least he doesn't want me to gab away pretending to be Sister Bernadette or anything sacrilegious about Brides of Christ.

'And we'll do it again in twenty minutes,' he said. 'We will, won't we, because you'll suck me up?'

But, he thought, we never do. She doesn't know the arts of the proper whore. Then, besides, he always just pushed her away, unable to bear the touch of her hand afterwards. When all the time now he couldn't get enough of that hot red cunt a mile up inside.

They moved together like true lovers for some time, with Liam giving her some sweet loving strokes that made her feel all so full of love.

Then he was banging and thumping against her backside like a good belting and there was no time and no breath, and then the lights exploded in her head and there were no words.

'Oh, Liam, that was marvellous love you made to me,' she said, lying there smoking a cigarette.

'It was?' He felt good, his head very clear, now, about the job with the American woman.

'Oh, yes. I came and came.'

'You didn't,' he said. 'You don't have to be a come-faker for me.'

'No, no. Look at my legs shaking. I suppose you learned that from those English nurses.'

'What English nurses?'

He was pulling up his jeans. Getting away from her as fast as he could, that was it. He would never let her hold him afterwards. He was one of those men who could only ever come once. It was probably his asthma. He always gave a dry little cough, like signalling the end, just after he'd come off. He couldn't be much of a secret agent with asthma like that, she thought.

'The nurses you told me about. That time you were studying to be a doctor. At the medical school. The nurses in their stiff white starched dresses,' she said, only laughing a little at him. 'Having to lie still while you fucked them so the patients wouldn't hear you give it to them in the hospital wards.'

'Oh, them,' he said, looking down as he buckled his belt. Fancy her remembering that, he thought. A medical student, even a failed medical student, would be a feather in her cap. Something to tell her friends.

She got up and stood beside him, wanting to hold him, he was so sweet really. She knew better than to try kissing him, because he might get really cranky and shout or hit her.

Liam let her put her thin arms round him for a moment. When the American woman came, he would have Niamh go out, perhaps send her away somewhere for a few days. Not that he would have much time for such things.

Still, it was nice to think what a fool she was and the different things he could do to her. He could have the American woman right here in the flat, with Niamh in the other room. Why not?

There was nothing to stop him. And the American woman would be drawn to an Irish rebel. All women were fascinated by violence. They all wanted to know if he had ever killed and if he ever had, had he killed up close with a knife or a gun or with his bare hands. Sometimes he invented some nice stories for Niamh and watched her eyes cloud over full of shuddering violent thoughts as he whispered to her, that always turned them on.

5

Kitty, driving into Limerick, thought that the smug face of the town offered stone-slab evidence of the rule of nun. The first thing she saw was a sober grey church, and, at this time of day (it was late afternoon by the time she motored in), a line of virtuous women in sombre shades, and with joyless, prim looks upon their thin lips, trailing in and out of it. There was something depressing, too, Kitty saw right off, about the brown paint on the windows of otherwise neon-lit bars overlooking the main road coming in from the open country. The painted windows provided a 'modesty board' protecting the prying pious eyes of the prudish – or what might they not have seen – men laughing? Or, something dark and mean, men sprawled drunk across the bar in long, heavy silences, broken only by sudden outbursts of despair. (Middle-class Kitty's educated imagination owed a definite debt to the stage directions of Eugene O'Neill.)

Hunger dispelled these fantasies and anthropological speculations. She had been enjoying that sense of freedom that comes from being in transit, and had not wished to stop to eat, but now she was hungry. She would buy something to have in a little picnic for one by the side of the road (the rain had not returned) in a picturesque spot.

She slowed, turned up a residential street and parked the car off the main road, thinking she would buy some bread and cheese, and perhaps a solitary apple, but then she saw a bookshop, and thoughts of playing the literary tourist returned to her. She would buy *Ulysses* to use as a travel guide to Dublin.

It looked a nice old-fashioned bookshop and there was even a jangling bell as she opened the door and entered. Kitty felt right at home. The shop lacked the order of Romeo's in South Hadley, or the academic clutter of the Hampshire Bookshop in Northampton

(Kitty had prepped at Miss Davenport's school in Northampton, Mass.), but it was familiar ground.

A tall young man of thirty-six or so in bookish tweeds was standing in the shop. And how marvellous was that extraordinarily-cut cloth, Kitty thought, looking as though it had been cut not with scissors but with a knife and fork; quite unlike the new-car finish of the ex-Brooksie Lawrence's Brooks Brothers tweeds. And just look at the man, standing there reading a book with his half-moon horn-rimmed specs pushed down his Irish beak of a nose. How European it was. No one at home, she thought, would dare to be so eccentric in such a studied manner. His hair was flecked with grey and unkempt. One lace of one big brown full-brogue shoe, she noticed, was undone. Here she was at last in another thrilling world.

'Do you have James Joyce's *Ulysses*?' she asked the man.

'I accept no other brand. Although there is a Homer's *Odyssey*, for the older crowd.'

He was a character. Kitty could see that. He also smelled of whiskey.

'I'll take one,' she said.

'Just the one?'

'Just the one. Why ever should I want more?'

'They all say that,' the man said. 'But the next thing you know one leads to another, and then –' He gestured with his right hand. In his left hand he had the book he had been peering at when she entered the shop, one of those slim volumes of verse, in paperback. Kitty saw the title, *Spring Harvest*.

'It's down here, I think,' the man said, sticking *Spring Harvest* into the already bulging pocket of his wonderful tweed coat.

He was not so young, Kitty saw. There was white stubble on his cheek where he had shaved that morning in a haphazard fashion. (Sidney's beard was now flecked with grey. It was her Peter Pan complex, Sidney said, that made her search for a dad. Sidney said he was a father figure himself to her. She thought for a moment about Sidney, who was Jewish, and said most Catholics mistakenly thought they didn't need a shrink.)

The man in the wonderful suit was walking head bent among the shelves at the rear. 'They've still got Joyce stuck out of sight,' he said, turning about with a smile. He kneeled, looking at the lower shelves.

No, not young, not even still in his thirties, she thought.

'You couldn't get him at all until a few years ago,' the man said, 'not legally at least. James Joyce and ah . . . rubber . . . goods.'

Kitty observed a blush spreading across the extraordinary man's face.

'I'm sorry,' he said. He was obviously embarrassed about something. 'What was it exactly you were looking for?'

Yes, the man was drunk. She could smell it on him. Kitty smiled. This, she thought, was so typically Irish. She could tell Sidney about the amusing bookshop man who'd been squiffy.

'James Joyce,' she said.

'That's the fella,' the man said.

Kitty laughed.

'That's good,' the man said. 'Laughter is good. It unravels the –'

'That's sleep.'

'I knew it was something.' He produced the book. 'Here it is,' he said, 'do you want me to sign it?'

'Not really.'

'What a shame. I'll sign this one for you.' He pulled the paperback from his pocket.

'Here, take it,' he said. 'And Joyce, unsigned, a gift.'

'But I must pay.'

'Nonsense.'

'But –'

'It is a custom of the shop.'

'Am I the millionth customer or something?'

'I could not have put it better myself.'

'Extraordinary.'

'It is.'

'Well, thank you. Thank you very much, Mister –?'

'MacBride.'

'Mr MacBride.'

'Just MacBride.'

'I'm O'Shea. I'm very Irish, too, you see.'

'And you've come from rootless America in search of your roots?'

'By Jove, Holmes.'

'Elementary, O'Shea.'

36

'I think you're crazy.'

Kitty was smiling as she left the bookshop. She was smiling as she bought bread and cheese in a little corner shop like something out of a folk museum, and still smiling as she walked back up the street looking for a likely picnic spot.

Falk stretched long knotted legs under the driving wheel. He lit a cigarette. It was very quiet. He could hear the mutter of the car engine as it cooled. He would need petrol. What kind of an American stopped in a place like this? There were those modern hotels you can't tell apart all over the place now. That's where Americans went. She would feel at home there. Why stop in this little suburban street?

No fear of losing her, though. Not with the sight and the sound of her like a beacon light among the rest, great tall girl that she was. Falk, cold-eyed, watched the shop door open. She must not see him this time, and start waving at him again. Too much of a coincidence altogether, even for her who thought all human life revolved round her. He drew in a great sigh of cigarette smoke as he watched her walk away, past her parked car. He climbed stiffly out of his driving seat, flicking the cigarette into the gutter. A big tabby cat scavenging there spat at him and ran away.

She had bought books and food; she would find somewhere to eat that. Probably guide books; scenic Ireland. Tourist mentality. Even if she wasn't a real tourist at all. He knew what she would do, knew her mind. Hatred fed Falk's intuition. And, anyway, he knew her sort. She wouldn't want crumbs in the car, even a hired one. And she was in that kind of sentimental daze they always had when they came to Ireland. The bookshop was in the main street, with lots of customers going in and out. Falk thought she would not have done business there. The man in the shop had his photograph in the window on a card, with his name printed under it and the name of some book he was signing. MacBride? Could dig with either foot with a name like that. Hard to tell with some of them. There was something about the man in the picture in the window. A West Briton, maybe. A Protestant on Horseback. That was a good few years ago that photograph in the window was taken. At his first Communion, great Papist pansy writing books. And a good few drinks, too, had gone down the hatch since then, by the looks of it. An agriculturalist, was he? *Spring Harvest*. Looked more like some kind of nance than a farmer. Probably something to do with the EEC, pack of pen-pushers. Look at the smile she gave him. Dirty little whore. Can't leave them alone, even some drunken hayseed. Plant him somewhere to feed the weeds, if there was time. Maybe I'll come back and do it. What would Tyler say? But you can't save Ulster talking.

Kitty leaned over the parapet of the bridge where she had eaten her picnic; just a few bites of the strange cheese, she had bought much too much. She tossed pieces of bread into the river below, and watched seagulls swoop to scoop them out of the water. She thought how pretty it must be here in summer, with warm sun on the grey stone, and perhaps a few bright splashes of colour among the passers-by who, dressed for the blustery wind of early spring, looked universally drab.

'Sure, it's sometimes hard to thank the Good Lord for His great gifts,' a cheerful voice at her elbow said. She had not noticed a stocky little man in a felt hat of very bright tan, tilted on top of his head, as he came up beside her. He leaned over against the parapet, his legs well short of the ground as he looked down at the muddy river.

She wondered if she should offer him her extra cheese, but hesitated in case she should insult him. His tan trilby was stained. It would have been cheap and nasty anyway, even when new. The man's trousers were also too short, and showed off bright blue and yellow nylon socks which were nearly as shiny as his cheap plastic shoes, which had some sort of yellow medal ornament. The medal thing on his left shoe was broken. The man was looking out over the water, not looking at her, but he was saying something out of the side of his mouth. She could not make out a word of it. She nodded politely, wondering if he could tell, and all the while looking at his poor clothing and the general wretchedness of the way he had been put together by both God and his mass-produced tailoring, and she thought, too, how little contact she had had with the common folk. Sidney had claimed to be the first working-class man she had had any contact with. She had laughed, but she knew he was right.

The wind tossed Kitty's black hair across her cheek. The little man turned so he was facing her; he grinned. A happy leprechaun,

Kitty thought, if ever there was one. If he wasn't smiling, he was laughing.

She pushed her hair back, and leaned down to hear what he was saying. There was a nasty odour about him. The wind blew his words away. A heavy lorry braked on the bridge with a great gasp of escaping air. Kitty turned to tell the man she had not heard what he said, but he was gone. Once, as she walked back to her car, she thought she saw the gruesome little hat bobbing across the road, through the traffic, among a crowd of yet more of the common people.

It was already growing dark. The road map in the car said it was not all that much of a long way to Tipperary. She would go there and stay in some desperately modern 'Americanised' hotel that would be sinfully expensive. She would dine alone. An intellectual lady, head bent over James Joyce.

He had him now, Falk thought. The drunken agriculturalist with his photo in the window of the bookshop had been a possible, but not likely. No, the little tan hat, a fussy little item of headwear. Very Pape. And he was at the airport. He had ducked away quick enough, but that face of hers was beaming at him like the best of pals. They use the older men down here. The young ones were up North or blowing things up in England.

There she is, swanking to her car. A poor little specimen of a motor car, she must think that, after the great big piece of ostentation she would have at home in Chicago. And all that goes with a big car like that. Only care for money, that type. Once they're sexually aroused, they start spending it. A good man's money. Want everything new then. New carpets on the floor, new clothes on their deceiving backs.

Whore.

6

In the murky light of the early April evening, Paddy Kiernan and
Sean Cafferty went to Neary's bar. This was often a good place, on
a rainy night, to find lonely visitors to the City hoping to mix with
the natives. Full of greedy malice, Paddy and Sean were more than
willing to feed them tales of the pity of Ireland's history in exchange
for free drinks, vying with each other in fantastical challenges upon
the foreigner's credulity.

Tonight, though, there was a show at the Gaiety Theatre, and most of
the drinkers at Neary's long bar were musicians in the Gaiety orchestra.
They rushed in and out through the connecting door between the stage
and the bar for a drink before they had to take up their instruments. The
musicians kept tally of the bars of music, timing with a careful count
when they must leave their drinks and return to the theatre. This elaborate business irritated Paddy, who had seen it many times before.

Sean recognised Paddy's mood. It's his poor health, he thought.
And the money he owes.

They went out of Neary's and walked to Davy Byrne's in Duke
Street, but it was full of Trinity students, so they moved on to the
Old Stand, then to Mooney's, and from there, dodging the traffic
in front of the Bank of Ireland, to the Pearl Bar in Fleet Street across
the way from the offices of the *Irish Times*, where there was always,
Paddy said, being very sarcastic, a drunken journalist prepared to buy
a round to keep in touch with the common man. But the talk in the
Pearl was all about extradition.

It was still early and they were hungry. They sat in a fish and chip
cafe in O'Connell Street. An anorexic waitress, in a short orange
shift with a grubby white apron, and a great burden of dyed black
backcombed hair above a chalk-white face, brought them plates of
food, egg and chips the colour of neon.

Paddy told Sean she reminded him of Liam's Niamh, only more bad-tempered. 'No wonder she looks so bad-tempered, with her shoes at least two sizes too big for her rubbing the blisters on her heels,' Sean said.

'You're too good for this world, Sean,' Paddy said.

Sean squirted ketchup across his eggs. In the powerful strip lights, Sean looked an unhealthy yellow, Paddy thought. Paddy could see his own face in the mirrors printed with scenes of palm trees and canary-coloured suns which lined the walls above the tables. His face was etched with hollows and deep shadowed gouges.

Across the cafe, amongst congealing plates of limp chips and greasy fish bones long abandoned, an old man sat alone at one of the tables the waitress was too lazy to clear. At the tables nearest the glass front of the cafe, with the buses flashing past their heads in the street outside, a group of teenagers shouted at each other above the din of the juke box. They were sprawled across the formica-topped table, and fondled each other openly, and, as far as Paddy could see, indiscriminately.

'Jaysus,' Paddy said, 'don't you sometimes wonder?'

'And what's that you wonder, Paddy?' Sean said.

Paddy looked round the cafe. 'Is this the Ireland we want?' he said sourly. 'A place to be proud of, is it? And everything about it as English as a football hooligan. The junk culture. Do you remember Devlin, the crazy American from San Francisco?'

'Sure I remember him. How could I forget him? A great trans-planted Irish patriot. Why remember him, anyway, poor fellow?'

'He told me,' Paddy said, 'he came to Ireland because it was all Disneyland in America. That's what decided him.'

'Is that so? Well, Disneyland'll look good to him now, all right, from where he's sitting in Wormwood Scrubs.'

'This new Ireland's worse than Disneyland,' Paddy said.

His fingers slipped on the table top as he tried to get a grip to pull himself upright. The plastic salt container fell over, and they both scrabbled to pinch some up and throw it over their shoulders. It stuck to their greasy fingers.

'Unlucky,' Sean said, rubbing his hand on the sleeve of his anorak.

'Now here am I,' Paddy said, looking very intense and serious,

41

'nearly forty years old, and nothing to show. Not even the price of a drink. And my own countrymen after me. I mean the duns and the debt collectors.'

Sean shook his head. He could not help it, but he could not share Paddy's mood; he was full of good cheer. It had been his idea of a perfect evening, good drink, good food, and a bed to go home to, all in the company of his best friend who knew him so well there was no need for pretence.

'You'll not be worrying over a few pounds for the horses, Paddy? If you're short, there'll be the money coming to pay us. For this job,' he bent forward and spoke in a whisper, 'with the American woman.'

'It's more serious than that,' Paddy said. 'Much more than a few quid this time. My luck's out.'

Sean did not understand Paddy's passion for gambling.

'This isn't like you,' he said. 'There's no need to spoil a good night out worrying about things you can't change. If it's money that's bothering you, that's very simple. When we get paid, you can have what's coming to me. To pay off your debts. That way we'll be back to normal.'

He would give up the money for me, Paddy thought. Even though he thinks I'm all kinds of an eejit, he'd give me his money. But it wouldn't be enough. Paddy forced himself to smile. He could see his own smile looking ugly, looking more like a snarl where it was reflected through a blade in a palm tree in the cafe mirror. It doesn't look too convincing, he thought. Paddy said:

'Keep your money, you old eejit. But if you're so set on giving it away, what about another jar?' And, Paddy thought, I'm not even grateful. In fact, I think he's soft.

They went out of the cafe and back the way they had come towards St Stephen's Green. The traffic raced round the corner at the bottom of Nassau Street, and they dithered on the pavement.

'We're getting old, Paddy,' Sean said. 'That's the top and bottom of it. We're old.'

'Jaysus, Sean, I need a piss,' Paddy said, when they had finally crossed to the other side of Nassau Street. 'I should have gone before we left.'

They hurried up Dawson Street. There were people on the streets, but the buildings were dark, silent, unlit offices and shops. The ragged black outline of trees on the Green was etched against an indigo sky. On Stephen's Green, outside the Shelbourne Hotel, a group in evening dress were getting out of taxis. The taxi driver, unable to stop close to the kerb because of the densely packed parked cars, leaned across to take his money, ignoring snarled traffic behind him.

'I can't wait,' Paddy said. He was sprinting up the hotel steps saying, 'Wait there, Sean, I shan't be long,' when the uniformed doorman, who had been helping the people out of the taxi, suddenly turned and gripped Paddy by the arm.

'You can't go in there,' the doorman said.

'What's this?' one of the women in evening dress said. They were smiling, watching Paddy and the doorman.

He thinks Paddy's down and out, Sean thought.

'This is no establishment for the likes of you,' the doorman said, trying to keep his voice down because he had shouted too loudly when he first grabbed Paddy, and now he was embarrassed because the people in evening dress were standing there watching him.

'For Christ's sake, man,' Paddy said, 'it's let me in or I swear I'll water your ornamental flower pot this very minute.'

Sean could see Paddy was attempting to make a joke of it but wasn't succeeding.

'Is it your tip you're afraid for,' Sean said in a loud voice, trying to be comic. Sean turned towards the group in evening dress, who were waiting, watching the drama of Paddy and the doorman, while one of their number argued with the taxi driver about the fare.

The lights from within the hotel illuminated an arc of pavement. Sean broke into song, a spirited but unrecognisable tune. At the same time, he shuffled among the people on the pavement, holding out his hands cupped for money. 'For the relief of the kidneys,' he said.

One of the men laughed.

'Are they buskers?' a woman asked.

'No, no,' the man said. 'Just drunk.'

The doorman, still holding Paddy, turned to Sean as though Sean was the responsible man.

The woman dropped some coins into Sean's hand.

'I'll have no alternative but to call the Gardai,' the doorman said to

Sean. He smiled as the smart group pushed past him. ''Tis a diabolical and cacophanous onslaught,' the doorman said to Sean.

Sean repeated the phrase.

'What is he saying?' one of the women in evening gowns asked.

'He said, "it's a diabolical and cacophanous onslaught"', the man with her said.

'Good Lord! Isn't that marvellous?' the woman said.

'He doesn't like my singing,' Sean said. 'Or what is he talking about?'

Sean turned away. He saw a tall man in a dark double-breasted suit striding along as though he thought he was marching with a troop of men. The soldierly figure glanced at the scene between Paddy and the doorman and stopped. He's a copper all right, Sean thought. Now we'll all get arrested.

But the man said: 'Mr Kiernan, isn't it?' The man was speaking to Paddy. 'What a coincidence!' the man in the suit said, 'I was only thinking of getting in touch with you.'

Must be some mistake, Sean thought. Then he looked at Paddy, who looked as if he were stricken with some awful news.

Maybe he's a bookmaker, Sean thought.

Then the doorman, who might have been seeing Paddy and Sean for the first time, suddenly said: 'Good evening, Mr Doyle, gentlemen. Will you be coming in for a drink? Clement weather for the season, Mr Doyle,' he said to the man in the suit.

Paddy stood on the steps looking, Sean thought, as if he weren't really there.

'We've time for one more,' Sean said.

'Were you going in?' Doyle asked.

He spoke in a precise voice, Sean thought. Not used to being talked back to. Big, too. Tall, real old-time Dublin peeler.

'We're on our way home,' Paddy said.

What about that piss he had to take? Sean thought. He was practically jigging for the want of one. With his kidneys.

'You won't change your mind?' Doyle asked. 'I usually go into the Shelbourne bar this time of a night for a quick one.'

Paddy shook his head. 'Another time, Mr Doyle,' he said. 'This isn't our kind of place.' The doorman pulled a comic face full of mock surprise at that.

44

But the man touched the brim of his soft felt hat in a military manner and walked away up the steps of the hotel with the metal tips to his heels beating time, as though he was picking out a tune. Maybe he was something in the military from the Red House, Sean thought. No reason why Paddy shouldn't know an old soldier.

Paddy took Sean's arm and pushed him towards Baggot Street.

Paddy said, 'Sell my soul! Kowtowin' to monkeys to get inside the Shelbourne is too high a price for me.' He walked away.

Sean wandered unsteadily after Paddy, who was hurrying again.

'What's the hurry?'

'I still need a piss.'

'Oh, so we're back to that again,' Sean said.

'Yes,' Paddy said. 'And when ever don't I want to?' But he was shaken by the encounter with the would-be benefactor. And right in front of Sean, too, he said to himself. And what if someone sharp like Liam O'Tomas had been there? It was different on the telephone. The crazy man Devlin had been betrayed like that, over the phone; although the police tried to make it look like great detective work.

The two men did not speak until they were back in Sean's room.

'I'll make the tea,' Sean said.

'You stay where you are,' Paddy said. 'I'll put the kettle on.'

Outside the door of his room, under the stairs leading to the next floor of the house, Sean had a small kitchen, with a hideously stained sink and a gas ring caked with old cooking. Paddy urinated in the sink, and turned the single cold tap on full to flush it. He filled the kettle and lit the gas, which flared and then settled to a tiny blue flame. Paddy left it to heat, and returned to Sean.

'Jaysus, Sean, it's some time since this place saw a woman's touch,' he said.

'It suits me well enough,' Sean said. 'It's very convenient.'

'It's disgusting,' Paddy said angrily. 'And the lavatory on the second floor, for God's sake.'

Paddy was bad-tempered. Money on his mind, Sean thought.

'Who was that man?' Sean said. 'Do you owe him money? He looked like a fellow in a bank. Or a peeler.'

Paddy looked at Sean. 'No, no, he's a man wanted me to do a job for him,' he said.

Sean was about to ask what kind of job, but then he thought better not. 'I didn't like the looks of him at all,' Sean said. He meant this as an expression of loyalty.

'No,' Paddy said. 'I don't either.'

It was very cold in the room. From outside in the street, they could hear drunks shouting. Paddy took a blanket off Sean's bed and pulled it round his shoulders, then went across the room and sat in the old broken armchair. Sean stood looking at him. Every few moments Sean cocked his head, listening to hear the kettle boil.

'If we had enough money,' Paddy said, 'we could get out of this.' He stared at the window. Outside there was still the sound of drunks clashing among the dustbins. 'What wouldn't you do to get enough money for that?'

'Pigs might fly,' Sean said.

'What's to keep us?' Paddy said. 'What's Ireland ever going to be? It's not even what it was, and that was bad enough. Did you ever ask yourself what difference would a United Ireland make? When all's said and done? All the world wants burgers and Disneyland?'

'That's Devlin talking,' Sean said. 'You got that from Devlin. You'll feel better for a cup of tea.' But the mood was hard to shift. Paddy bit his lower lip, huddled under the old blanket.

'And who is Liam O'Tomas to tell us what to do? Lionel Thompson, from Croydon, Surrey. He's not one of us.' Paddy's voice was raised. He was getting angry in a melodramatic way; like someone on the stage in the theatre, Sean thought. Sean stood by the open door, with his hand on the broken knob.

'You'd better stop that talk,' Sean said. 'It doesn't matter where a man was born. He's one of us. It's because he's young you don't like him. If you were young, you'd be up in the North. Or over in England. But don't take it out on Ireland that you're not young anymore.'

Paddy ignored this. 'Proved it, has he? By making martyrs of innocent Irishmen. Liam's a Trotskyite. We don't need no Trotsky to show us the system don't work. Not when all history shows us that the system don't work. Haven't we fought for that? And our fathers before us? A long time before there ever was a Trotsky. Ireland don't need no Jewboy Russian Trotsky.'

He sounds the same as Liam making a speech, Sean thought, same theatricals anyway, and having a good time losing his temper.

46

'He comes in here with no history at all and thinks he can do better than men like our fathers?' said Paddy, whose father, Sean knew, had been a dustman. 'Daniel O'Connell wasn't no fucking Trotsky,' Paddy said, 'And who's to say he's what he says he is? Someone betrayed that fucker Devlin, and Liam hates Yanks. All those Trots hate Yanks, that's a proven fact.'

'That's not a funny thing to say,' Sean said. He could hear the kettle sing. He hesitated in the doorway. 'That's a terrible thing to say. You have to trust the men you work with, you know that.'

'I was just thinking,' Paddy said.

Paddy thought Sean was not what he had been. In the beginning Sean had taken Paddy under his wing. Sean was quite a different character in those days – they both were. Paddy had driven the car. Sean could not drive a car; he exhibited many such 'little womanish' failings, like the fussing in the kitchen now for the tea. Paddy drove the car and pulled up just on time, as the man himself, a big noise in the RUC, was stepping from his house with the wife and little ones framed in the doorway, most domestic, like an advert 'What happens to them if something happens to you?' – X marks the spot, the strength of the Halifax around you. Sean, leaning out of the car window, shot him in the face.

Afterwards they met up by chance, and Sean said 'Fancy meeting you here!' just like that, and all at once Paddy saw it had been Sean's first time, where, at least, he had pulled the trigger into another man's face and him looking right at you. Before it had been just nail bombs – they didn't have the real proper stuff. Not like now. Mother of God, it was surface-to-air missiles now, with Liam O'Tomas ready to take on the whole fuckin' RAF.

'I'll be going now,' Paddy said to Sean. He would not wait for the tea.

'All the way back to Balbriggan?' Sean asked. Paddy lived several miles out of the City.

'I wish it were further,' Paddy said.

7

Night had fallen. From the shadows a church, a broad sweep of road, a series of small shops, all appeared briefly in the headlamps of Kitty's car and were then swallowed in the blackness of the night. This sturdy market town was the first after many miles of road with no more than an occasional scattering of dwellings along the route.

In the broadest part of the road stood a hotel of grandiose promise, all glowing yellow windows and ivied walls in the otherwise dark street. Kitty turned off the highway to join other cars parked head-on to the kerb outside this welcoming frontage.

She heard a jangle of voices through the open window of the hotel bar; sudden shouts of laughter, loud protests followed by more cheerful sounds. Kitty leaned against the car, easing her legs. The air was damp and cool. She caught the smell of pipe tobacco smoke and beer; and then the wonderful homey smell of wet dogs. She paused for another moment, gazed at the stars, and felt very happy.

There was no one to be seen in the street; but where she had thought the darkness complete, she could now make out the silhouettes of children in the windows above the little shops that stood opposite the grand-looking inn. Against drawn curtains, she could see the blue flicker of television sets. From somewhere up the street, the cheerful proletarian din of an Irish showband, accompanied by a male singer on the verge of ironic Celtic tears, came to her and made her smile. Kitty felt excluded, as alien as a visitor from another planet spying on a scene of astonishing ordinariness.

There was no traffic through the town. A car had pulled off the road and parked further up the street. Its headlamps lighted Kitty's way as she went inside the hotel.

In contrast to the outside charm of the ivied walls, the inside of the hotel was stark. The light in the hallway was dim. Kitty tripped

48

over some cracked linoleum and caught hold of a table to stop herself falling, overturning as she did so a bunch of plastic daffodils thrust into a vase.

'Just as well they're not the real thing. There'd be water everywhere,' said a woman in carpet slippers and a lime green nylon overall, who had suddenly appeared from a door behind a high counter. She brought with her the odour of wrung-out dishcloths and bleach.

There was only one room available, she said, and then was moderately insulted when Kitty asked to see it.

'Please yourself, but you'll not get me climbing those stairs with my legs in the state they are,' the woman said. 'But I can tell you for nothing,' she went on, looking Kitty up and down in a suspicious narrow-eyed manner, 'you'll not find another room between here and Dublin with the races at the Curragh tomorrow. I've only the one room left because it's –' the woman in lime nylon halted. She really did not wish to speculate on why the room was free. 'The window is broken,' she said. 'At least, there is no curtain. Someone pulled it down.'

'Well, I guess I'll take it anyway,' Kitty said, a little taken aback by such casual service. 'Is this building very old?' (The American tourist was hoping for some historical frisson by association with a famous Irish personage.)

'That it is not,' the woman said. 'It is modernised continuously.'

Kitty turned her head away, trying not to laugh.

Upstairs the bedroom smelled of being shut up for a long time and when Kitty opened the window it looked out on a narrow alley. The bed took up most of the floor space; that, and a spindly table with a panel of mirror tiles glued to the wall above it, was all the furniture there was. A crudely painted crucifix hung over the bed, which was covered by a shiny purple sateen eiderdown just reeking, Kitty thought, of menace to moth; and the sheets, when she turned them back, had spent years under the dictatorship of starch.

Kitty had taken only an overnight bag from the car. She pulled out her washbag, and, like all real Americans, she went to have a bath.

She walked down a long corridor of huge blue wallpaper roses into an old-fashioned ice cavern where, jutting precariously over one end of a giant cast-iron bathtub, was a grotesque piece of Dickensian ironmongery that, she realised, must heat the water. Kitty had turned on both big handles of the ancient tub and was already undressed before she tested the water coming from the brass taps. It was stone cold. She peered at the vast machine and saw that it must first be switched on. 'Oh, hell,' she said aloud, 'there's no way I'm going to turn this damned thing on without blowing us all back to Tipperary.'

Kitty closed her eyes tight and sat rigid in the icy water thinking how terrific it would feel afterwards.

She leaped from the bath. Then she stood looking at herself in the mirror. It crossed her mind that it might be nice to find some absolutely straight man to share a bit of straight sex. She had brought condoms with her. She had been looking forward to a French lover in Paris. Now here she was all kitted out for l'amour toujours in Paris, France, and she had to get off the bus in the Old Sod. She wondered if Irishmen fuck; she rather thought they didn't.

Falk, the gooseflesh on his neck rough against his turned-up collar, leaned against the delivery door of a shop, a darker shadow against the dark alley wall. His foot slipped in something soft amongst the rubbish in the doorway. He pawed the pavement with his shoe to remove it. Damn the woman. What was her game? Driving here, there and everywhere around the countryside, without rhyme or reason. And yet the leaked information from the writhing squealer with his kneecaps drilled and expecting (he wasn't disappointed) the bullet in the back of his head, had been quite specific. This was the one, definitely. Everything fitted, even if she was more like bloody Miss America than the grim, tight-lipped harridan he'd expected. Bloody amateurs, using a woman who looked like this one, with clothes to swank around in like a Hollywood film star when she should be the soul of discretion.

Falk had seen her going into the hotel by the light of his headlamps as he parked his car. And now it was luck the light had come on just above his head where he could watch her. There were no other lights on that side of the building above street level. A little later he saw another light come on in the hotel further down the alley. There was the sound of a rushing of water, and then, Falk, looking up at the further lighted window, swallowed.

50

All the whole white length of her jay-naked, the shape of her just blurred against the glass, as though on a television with bad reception.

Falk stared. He moved away from the doorway, blood thumping in his bony temples. He shifted his weight to rest his left leg. The damned weather in this benighted country always made the old pain worse. Falk in wet weather limped; he had in his youth exchanged fire with an armed enemy far off in the snow of Korea, and lived to plant a sign there, 'You Are Crossing The 38th Parallel Courtesy of the Royal Ulster Rifles.' Falk had been in his youth a man among men. Damned woman, putting him, a man of his years, in this draughty alley in the back of beyond with the filth of the street blowing round his feet and his eyes running with the raw cold. Falk, pale-skinned and waxen in the shadows, black-coated, stood invisible, the weight on his right foot where he could feel the ridge of something vile still stuck to his sole.

Above his head, the light in the room went off, and a few moments later, another light shed its yellow beam against the wall above him from an uncurtained window.

The sound of footsteps drew his attention to the front entrance of the hotel. It was the same man, wasn't it? The man in the bookshop. Walking into the hotel as large as life and with a further skinful in him by the looks of it. A coincidence? A big turn-up when he'd have sworn that fellow in the trilby was his man.

Above Falk's head, the light in the uncurtained room went off.

Kitty, dressed in college widow's black with a plain gold chain about her neck, descended to the warm heart of the hotel, to the noisy bar where a huge fire burned under a great arched chimney with enough room for a man to stand upright in it.

There was a rowdy crowd of racing men and farmers gathered there. They beamed wind-burned, friendly smiles at one another, men of the turf and the plough, they talked of horses, dogs, and the price of things, which were going up. There was, in an instant, a dreadful silence as Kitty made her entrance. The dark stranger, emissary of free and easy womanhood, cast a chill over the house. All the manly eyes looked, then looked away. There was another moment, just the merest moment in time, in which to clear the throat, then the masculine hum began again. Only the publican himself, behind the bar, greeted the lone woman in a civilised fashion. Could such a jolly fellow be husband to the sour nylon woman at the reception desk? But that creature herself seemed better-tempered when she served Kitty a meal at a table by the fire, with some young men getting up 'to let the lady tourist from America sit down in comfort'. She was 'only an American', the word went round the room, and made her appearance tolerable if not completely correct.

After she had picked at her food in best visiting-American fashion, Kitty sat on with a brandy and soda, gazing into the flames, and thinking how wonderful it was that she was all alone, for the first time – since when? whenever had she last been all alone? – with no one having any notion about where she was. The bar was full, but no one came to take up the empty places at her table. Again she saw herself as an alien visitor watching the curious creatures of another planet. No, they were like people out of time. The clock was set back decades.

Sidney the Shrink would laugh to see her now, sitting there with her arms crossed in spite of the heat of the fire, and flushed with an enjoyable embarrassment as the centre of all eyes. Of course, she made these Irish farmers shy. They weren't used to brazen, bold-faced girls in such a place, let alone one that looked like the sort who came in one of those magazines the government banned from entering the country; only fully clad, of course.

Voices were blurring into the drowsy buzz of bees in the heat of the fire, soothing as a summer's day the sound of it was as Kitty thought of Sidney, who had been married (Daisy née Bernstein, South Orange, New Jersey, B.U. class of '78), who had two sons (Bob and Ted, seven and eight), and who was now unhappily divorced. ('She was so pretty,' Sidney said. 'Dark, with beautiful eyes. A beautiful nose job. A beautiful chin job, too. Also, I'm almost certain her breasts were too wonderful to be merely God-given. An absolute Jewish-American Princess, and not a brain in her head. At twenty-three, that is a young man's dream of home.')

'Well, hallo again. Are you waiting for someone? Or just nodding off by the fire on your own?'

Kitty started, looking up from the flames. There was a psychedelic effect on her vision, for the eyes of the man standing by her table expanded into violet strobes, and his teeth flashed theatrically like trick photography.

'Oh, my,' she said, holding one hand up, shielding her eyes. 'I can't see you.'

A once beautiful man, slightly tousled, as though it had been a long time since he last checked his appearance in a mirror, stood smiling at her, holding a glass of whiskey in one hand.

'You're the man who owns the bookshop,' she said.

'I don't own a bookshop. Whatever gave you that idea?'

'You mean you were a customer too? And you stole those books?'

'Exactly.'

'You are mad.'

'I certainly hope so. May I sit down?'

'Please, for God's sake, yes. I seem to have broken some weird Celtic taboo coming in here, a woman alone.'

'Is that the reason you've come to Ireland? To break taboos?'

'I'm looking for my roots,' she said, smiling her big white smile to pre-empt the mockery she knew was coming.

'Ah, yes, you said. You're a narrowback. You're in for a rude awakening.'

'What do you mean, narrowback?'

'You're a narrowback.'

'Am I?'

'What is that noxious stuff you're drinking?'

'Brandy and soda. My ex-husband used to drink it. He liked to think he was like those respectable old men with white moustaches at the Tavern Club. That's a Boston club. A very Bostonian club.'

'And was he?'

'No, not yet. He will be some day. So what is a narrowback?'

'Well, the first Irishmen who went to America had broad backs and the generations of Irish-Americans, who came after them, stood on those broad-shouldered forefathers of theirs but now only have narrow backs.'

'Sounds kind of a tortured metaphor.'

'You're not insulted?'

53

'Not in the least. And what do you do, Mr MacBride?'

'MacBride.'

'MacBride, when you're not stealing books?'

'Have a decent drink.'

'I can see that.'

'I mean you. Have a whiskey. Have a Bushmills. It's a Protestant whiskey, but any Republican would grab any chance to drink it.'

'What a terribly complicated life you do all live here. Is there a Catholic whiskey?'

'There is, Paddy's Irish, and I can drink that myself without choking to death.'

'Why should it choke you?'

'Oh, I'm a Protestant, you see.'

'No, I didn't realise. I assumed –'

'Well, there you are. I'm from the North. We can usually tell at a glance.'

'How extraordinary.'

'It is.'

He rose and went to the bar. He's steady enough on his feet, Kitty thought. It was his general manner, she suspected, that was akin to drunken nonchalance. He looked tall and rather dashing standing at the bar. A knight in a rumpled tweed suit.

'Here you are, O'Shea,' he said, returning with glasses of whiskey. 'I am a poet.'

'Did that rhyme? I hadn't noticed.'

'That book of verse. It was mine. The one I gave you. The signed one.'

'Good Heavens. How rude of me. I didn't look at it. Do you make lots of money, writing poetry?'

'What an American question.'

'I'm afraid so. But I meant, do you have to supplement your income stealing books from shops? How do Mrs MacBride and the little MacBrides live? Does your verse provide for them?'

'They, alas, do not exist.'

'I feel sorry for them.'

'Another whiskey?'

'Why, MacBride, you say the cutest things. Let me get it.' He's full of banter, Kitty thought; like a homosexual interior decorator back

54

home. Perhaps that flip talk was defensive. He should be married. Or at least divorced. He didn't look gay, but perhaps it was harder to tell in Ireland.

'No, no,' he said. 'I'll buy.'

He was old-fashioned about that, then, she thought.

'I teach at Queen's University, Belfast,' MacBride said when he returned from the bar. 'I was down here at Cork University giving them hell and I'm on my way back, with a lecture at Trinity College, Dublin, to give in passing. And you?'

'I'm an absolute parasite, I'm afraid. I was married just out of college, and I've done nothing much since.'

'No little O'Sheas? Is O'Shea your married name?'

Well, if he's gay, he's an awful tease to ask a question like that, Kitty thought. 'No to both. We were not, as they say, blessed, myself and Brooks Acton Lawrence, boy legal-eagle specialising in securities and stenos with big tits.'

A pause.

'Is *Spring Harvest* a terribly tragic poem?' she asked.

'Oh, Christ, in the midst of life we are in death. Tell me more about yourself and Brooks and the steno with the . . . It sounds very grand, all those names of his. I'll get us another drink.'

'No, I couldn't.'

'One for the road?'

'Is it long?'

'Endless.'

'All right, then.'

The bar started to empty. The fire had settled to a dull red glow. Kitty's eyes were focussed only on MacBride and his baggy tweed coat, and it seemed more difficult to keep up the lively talk – college banter, she called it in her head. Besides, she could see he was a middle-aged man who didn't have any sort of real sex life. When a woman was getting plenty of sex, like Kitty was with Sidney and others – especially after one of those dreadful stereotype marriages – she began to see the rather awesome power she had over a certain type of man. They were usually virgin kids, or ageing married men, or a longtime bachelor like MacBride. In books, she thought, it's always the demon male who awakens the woman, but that was because in the past, men wrote those books. In real life, it was the dried stick of a man who was awakened, when he ran up against a piece of hot female stuff who wasn't afraid to take what she wanted.

'You know,' she said, 'this evening with you is the first time since I arrived in Ireland that I haven't felt like some kind of a freak.'

'You –'

'They look at me in a funny way. There's one weird-looking grey guy in a plain grey car I keep seeing. I think he must be following me. Isn't that paranoid?'

'Why? I'd follow you.'

'How far?'

'To the ends of the earth. Except tomorrow I'm going to the races with a friend. I've got an idea I'm going to lose really big tomorrow. At least all next year's royalties for the old *Spring Harvest*.'

'Why does everything you say sound as though it's written in code?'

'Spoken. Do you know Princeton University?'

'Of course. Frank was there.'

'Frank?'

'My brother. Why Princeton?'

'Why Princeton? Oh, they asked me. Somebody did. If I'd like to be the poet in residence for a year.'

'You must be a very famous man.'

'I don't think so. I think it's because I write about the Troubles in Northern Ireland, and they think it would be rather trendy to have the poet of the petrol bomb in their midst, making verse seem up-to-the-minute and significant.'

'So you are a terribly serious person. And you let me chatter on as though I hadn't a thought in my head.' Except, she thought, that he'd run screaming if he knew the thoughts that were really running through her head that moment. She crossed her legs and leaned forward. Sidney would have recognised the look in her eyes. 'Are you staying at this hotel?'

'Unfortunately. Isn't it a dump?'

'My window has no curtain, shade, nor blind.'

'No curtain, shade, nor blind?'

'That's exactly the way I'd put it myself, MacBride.'

'Let's have one for the road.'

'For the stairs, you mean. But I think they're actually, basically closing this joint.'

'Fear not, Mary –'

'Kitty.'

'Fear not, Kitty. I possess the MacBride family bottle in my room.'

Well, that's that, O'Shea, Kitty said to herself.

'Ditto a curtain for the window. We MacBrides come prepared.'

'The O'Sheas as well,' she said, but she was sure he had no idea what she meant. Poor Sidney, she thought, he had predicted this, but of course, he envisaged a dark and romantic Frenchman.

Falk huddled in his car, holding his black coat tightly wrapped across his chest. He had reclined the seat, and had to crane his neck slightly to see through the windscreen. The faint smell of fat and vinegar lingered from his supper. He felt slightly sick. At first, he kept wiping the fog of condensation from inside the windows as they misted over with his breath and cigarette smoke, but when the lights in the hotel bar finally went out, he no longer bothered. He would see when the upstairs light cast its yellow beam against the alley wall. Then he could sleep.

The locals had come out and driven off noisily in their cars. A taxi stopped; he must have been called specially. A man came out, but not the one Falk was waiting for. He was drunk, staggering down the steps to the car as though he'd been knifed. Another whiskey patriot. His name will be blotted from the book of life. He looked like the man in the Limerick bookshop, though it was hard to tell. Falk discounted him. He was the sort of man those well-brought-up kind of women went for. He'd seen her himself, hadn't he, with his own eyes seen her touch herself lecherously? Dirty bitch, like a cat in heat. Practising her whore's tricks. Nothing else. He was sure of it. She hadn't passed anything over yet, wherever she had it hidden.

Falk closed his eyes and dozed. The wind, strengthening in the early hours, rocked the car. Falk started awake, then dozed again. It grew very cold, and in the cold, he hugged the jacket closely round his body, his hands clutching at the material like a dreaming dog as he slept.

In the curious light cast through a red velvet shade, the long legs of the trousers of MacBride's tweed suit were draped over an armchair, with the broad, green-felt straps of the dangling braces looking like a surgical apparatus. His room was bigger than Kitty's, nearly as high as it was wide. Except for the brown double bed, all the furniture was pushed into one corner as though to leave room for a camera crew booked to record whatever action was to take place on the shiny plum-coloured eiderdown. But no, Kitty thought, not the setting for a blue movie. Not with the crucifix above the bed, and St Teresa, patron-saint of gardens, in winsome, rather than tortured mood, holding a purple blossom. (It was a bloom of the narcissus family, known in Renaissance Italy and now extinct. This Kitty, who minored in botany at Mount Holyoke, and who could rattle off extinct blossoms, noticed. She would remember that all right, she thought.)

As she would certainly remember the heavy blood-coloured wallpaper of the room, patterned with plush like the inside of a jewel case. She took off her clothes, letting them fall just anywhere to be polite so he'd think she was carried away by passion, and not the sort of cold bitch who would neatly fold them before. It was not polite.

She looked at him naked, with no hair on his chest. He had good shoulders on him – and a waist. He was not erect but getting there for when he held her she could feel it rising against her thigh. All those condoms. MacBride said she could have been stopped at Customs.

By the time they had made it to the bed, MacBride was ready for her.

'Oh!' MacBride said, stretching up as though in pain.

'Keep it like that,' Kitty said. She could tell it had been a long time since he had done it. She didn't want him coming off too soon. When they first go in is the best thing, she thought, then clasping on tight for dear life because the pleasure always seems elusive. Afterwards, she thought, there were of course the skills ('schooled in the arts of the courtesan, O'Shea,' Sidney said, 'Did Daddy's Kitten learn that at Miss Davenport's?') but nothing was quite like the first time as a new man entered you. Any which way was just great when you started. Poor MacBride's struggling.

'Do you want me to get on top?'

'Oh, yes,' he said. 'I'm forty-three.'

Old as that. They always apologise, the nice ones do. Old ones like this, and the young ones saying Sorry, meaning they think they came too soon for you.

'You just lie there. I'll get on top, lovely MacBride, you ancient man.'

See that a lot in Sidney's porno flicks on the video because they see less of the man and more of the woman that way. No real man wants to watch another man's hairy ass banging up and down. They like a girl in full view with her long hair swishing about and her holding on like a cowgirl on a bronc. But it's hard work.

'Thank God, MacBride,' she said, 'I'm not a man, it's such hard work. What you men do for us, with your great pricks and muscles.' Did he like that sort of talk? Sidney said she was a slut talking the way she thought men liked. Not with poor Brooksie though. The stenos must have given him the dirty talk.

'You've beautiful hands,' MacBride said. 'Such little fingers.'

He's romantic, Kitty thought. Doesn't like dirty talk. And he is beautiful, turning me over and mounting once more, with renewed vigour, all red shadows in the red room in the moonlight. When they come in to you like that, it's as though there's nothing else in the whole world. 'Oh, MacBride, on your knees like that, thrusting into me, you are beautiful. I can feel your sweat dropping on me. Like that, MacBride. Keep that up, just there, like that. Oh, none of them has made love to me like this, not Brooks, not Sidney, not like that.' That ought to please him. But he's going wild. My little Irish virgin. Must have been years since he's had it. I should never have believed this. Just coming off all the time. Could they all be like this? Perhaps that's why they never get anything done here.

'MacBride, I don't know what to say.'

'It's because I haven't had a woman in such a time.'

'Well, you had this one, beautiful MacBride.'

'What beautiful hands,' he said. 'And lovely narrow feet.'

'What? My feet now? MacBride, you're obsessed.'

'Just to lie here,' she said, 'in this old-fashioned room. How mysterious it all is. Do you suppose I could roam Ireland in that little Dinky hire-car and do this each and every night? In an old hotel with a new MacBride?' He was laughing now, she saw, and wasn't so terribly sad-looking. 'Or are you a completely unique, one-off MacBride?'

'I am,' he said, laughing.

'I was afraid of that,' she said.

8

Kitty was a moment remembering where she was, and then she thought how stupid it was not to be waking in Paris, but to be here in Ireland searching for her roots. Was meeting MacBride and a night of rumbustious sex really worth the trip? Kitty stretched out in the sordid sheets and thought that most likely it was. Here's to you, dirty old love, she thought.

Rising, she hurried across the bare floorboards (the room's one six-by-four red, blue and green turkey carpet was still scrunched in a corner where, all naked arms and legs, she had had her wicked way with MacBride on the floor) to the mirror fixed on the wall of the love nest above a dressing table. She wished MacBride had not gone away so soon. He had risen early, kissed her gently, then had gone out to the front of the hotel to wait for the friend who was going with him to the races. Kitty, lying in that early morning slightly edgy but still blissful state, after a night and dawn of secret sex with a total stranger, had heard MacBride's friend's car on the gravel and then MacBride's voice, footsteps, and the slamming of the door.

'What a man!' she said to herself with her bruised mouth in the cracked mirror. She looked at herself and saw her own face subtly changed, softened, as though her reflected self knew a secret she did not know. Romantic gush. That comes from fucking a poet. Who would have thunk it! A poet. Now she felt like calling her mother on the phone. Hey, Ma, it's me, and I'm in love again. Haven't been in love since don't know when. How wonderful life was. Fate had brought her to Ireland to find true love, had it? Could she believe that? It couldn't be true. Well, it could be true.

She went down the blue rose-papered corridor to her own room, feeling very good about everything. There she changed her clothes and stared into the mirror some more, trying to analyse signs of happiness, before going downstairs to where the nylon woman, wearing a yellow morning overall, served her breakfast in a corner of the bar.

Through the window, thrown open wide to disperse the lingering smell of smoke and stale beer from last night's festivities of the racing men, a soft, deceitfully warm wind filled the room with the scent of bruised grass and wet leaves. The air in motion mischievously scattered ash as the nylon woman, lips folded firmly against Nature, emptied cigarette butts from the ashtrays into a black plastic sack. Kitty asked her if she had any hotel stationery. The woman made a great business out of bringing her two grubby sheets and a cheap envelope. Kitty started to write to Sidney, all the time feeling very wicked because every orifice in her body was filled with the scent and the sight and the sound of MacBride.

The nylon woman's husband, last night's friendly barman, his shirtsleeves rolled up on brown muscular arms, brought in a bale of peat bricks, which he threw down with a dusty thump beside the still-glowing ashes.

'Travelling, are you?' he asked Kitty, straightening his back slowly.

The woman sniffed and spoke to her husband in what should have been a whisper. 'She's one of those Americans looking for origins,' she said.

'I know that,' the man said, 'you told me that last night.'

Kitty laughed.

'You must see a lot like me,' she said to the man when he came over to look, for a moment, out on the beautiful morning from the open window by Kitty's table. 'Though I suppose your tourists are mostly English.'

He rubbed together big red hands which had stiffened round the heavy bale of peat. 'A fair few of them are,' he said, 'but the price of petrol puts them off. English tourists always expect Ireland to be cheap, because it's a poor country itself.'

The nylon woman butted in. 'As if we can afford to be cheap, with the troubles we have here.' She gave Kitty a very disapproving look.

'It must be terrible,' Kitty agreed, smiling at her. 'I read in one of the papers back home that statistically there's not a single Catholic

62

family in the Republic that hasn't lost a relative or close friend in the violence. Since 1969,' she added.

The man took up a towel and began to polish glasses, putting them away on shelves behind the bar. 'Well, a lot of the young people go across the water to find work all right,' he said.

He had, she saw, completely misunderstood her.

'It's economics,' the man said. 'I don't know what we'd do without the Americans here for their roots,' he continued, breathing on a cloudy glass and rubbing vigorously. He was obviously getting at his wife in some husband and wife married way.

'So,' Kitty said cheerfully,' you tell me what I should do today, something that's really typically Irish. Something really authentic.'

'If it's shopping you want, there's the best shops in Dublin,' the woman said, stacking Kitty's dishes with fussy impatience.

A large tabby cat, that had been curled in a shaft of sunlight on a window sill, stretched, leaped down and stalked across the bar floor through a dusty beam of sunlight to the table, hoping for bacon rind. The woman pushed it aside with a slippered foot.

'There's the racing today at the Curragh,' the man said.

'What would the likes of her want with a place like that?' the woman said scornfully, glancing at Kitty's silk blouse and white linen trousers.

'It's as good a way as any of spending money,' the husband said.

'Oh, and don't I know that well enough, with the proof of that you've given me. Him and his races,' she said to Kitty. 'Why don't you go,' she said to the man. 'You'll only be mooning all day if you don't.'

'Maybe I will, too.'

They began to argue. Kitty left them to it. Her day was made already, in anticipation of seeing again the poet MacBride in Dublin that evening at the Shelbourne bar. The intervening hours must fly past in a dream. It was years since she had looked forward to seeing someone like this. What was MacBride's first name? She didn't even know that. The book of poems was in the car. With Brooks, of course, for years it had been like this until they were married, and something mysterious but dreadful seemed to have happened to them, which was probably not mysterious at all, but only marriage. Also, for a time, with Sidney she used to skip through the leaves that beautiful New England Indian summer to the tennis court by the medical centre, to watch him in his white shorts and his beard, playing a game all lobs and spin – 'Most rabbinical, don't you think?' Sidney said of his tennis. But that hadn't lasted forever. Then there was the other, the third lover, the one before Sidney, which was just so shameful that she simply did not wish to think about it. Betrayal. How much better it was to be betrayed oneself. MacBride was an ageing decadent with a drink problem, and she couldn't wait to be with him again. He wasn't that old. Only forty-three. Thirteen years. Sidney was younger, but much older, so to speak.

Outside in the street, it was warmer than in the hotel. The day's sunshine turned to colour what yesterday had been monochrome. A group of beautiful old men sat in comfortable contented silence on a broad low stone wall, occasionally spitting with marvellous neatness into the gutter. On a telephone wire above their heads, a group of starlings sat similarly hunched, merrily chattering like happy old wives. The old men held gnarled hands to their eyes to shield them against the light as they watched Kitty walk to her car.

'What a lovely day!' she called to them, offering a great white smile. But they dropped their eyes. There was something too open and sensual about her long-striding walk in the flashing white trousers; she might as well have been naked.

In spite of them, she did not feel embarrassed. She opened the door of the car, and reached over for MacBride's book of verse in the back-seat. George Albert MacBride, that was his name. She opened the slim volume and gazed at some lines.

Spring Harvest

In the Fall we planted those fields of petrol bombs
They'll rise and flower again at Easter time.

Kitty turned the page, and another title caught her eye.

A Terrible Beauty is Borneo

The daughter of Houlihan is brave,
Brave as the painted savage is brave,
And all Kathleen ni Houlihan's men.
'All changed. Changed' and begun again.

She could make little of it, except she recognised a line of Yeats,
(who, in her American way, she insisted on calling Sir William
Butler: and East Coast liberal Kitty wondered if that crack about
painted ethnics might not be racist). She would read G.A. MacBride,
with a jug of wine and a loaf of bread, at lunch.

She drove slowly along quiet roads. Through the windscreen the
sun was warm as high summer. Two children playing hopscotch
outside a roadside cabin returned her wave; a farmer on a tractor
hurling great clods of mud from its tyres on to the road smiled at
her as she carefully passed him. She turned off the main road to
follow her nose. Once she was forced to back up a track between
steep cowslip-covered banks. Mount Holyoke botany minor Kitty
observed much flora and some fauna, when a herd of mud-crusted
black-and-white Friesian cows forced her into the hedge.

One lane led to a river bank where she tried to turn and found her
wheels spinning helplessly for a moment before they caught. That
scared her. Had the tyres not found sudden purchase, she might have
been stranded for hours in such a lonely place. (Kitty, for all her
knowledge of botany, was frightened by the great outdoors.) She
returned to the main road.

Through the open car windows, she heard the music of a brass
band, the sound ebbing and flowing on the wind, the brass sharp
against blurred drum beats.

Away to her left, across a broad belt of grassland, she saw a scene
of festival, laid out like a child's painting. She could see a marquee,
crowds, bright colours, the sun glinting on the roofs of distant cars
covering the grass like metallic daisies. This must be MacBride's race
meeting.

She followed a stream of cars off the main road down a narrow
track across the great grass plain. Women in bright dresses, making
the most of the sun, laughed as their high heels sank in the soft

65

turf. Coloured pennants fluttered above the white tents, while from loudspeakers slung, wires trailing, from any precarious high perch, the brass band played a distorted fast-forward march.

Kitty joined the drift of the crowd, engulfed in the steamy, beery warmth of people, catching the excitement and boisterous goodwill. Pushed forward by the great cheerful human torrent, she was finally tossed against a paddock rail, and clung there. The horses parading round the ring stepped out, heads high, posing like film stars. It was so beautiful. They walked round the gravelled track, their grooms leaning into their necks to hold them on line, talking to them low and intimate, like lovers on a stroll. Above the smell of the crowd, of crushed grass and beer, rose the sharper, wild odour of excited horses.

'Oh, how beautiful!' she said.

'Take a closer look,' said a man standing at her elbow, handing her his binoculars. 'And many's the good man has ruined himself for the likes of those creatures.'

The man wore a tan trilby. 'I'm sorry,' she said, 'I was miles away. I've seen you before. Weren't you in Limerick? On the bridge?'

'Indeed I was, have no fear of that,' the man said.

She studied the gleaming horses, then, thanking the little man in the hat, gave him back his binoculars and went in pursuit of MacBride. She thought she knew where he would be. Kitty followed a considerable group, all male, all seemingly dressed alike in brown suits and polished brown shoes of varying age, who were hurrying to a large tent already packed with drinkers.

But MacBride was not there. She turned away from the hubbub in the beer tent and moved away, her heels sinking in the soft ground, forcing her to walk with slow elaborate care as she returned to the paddock rail, and the company of the gleaming, dancing horses.

Falk had not realised he was grinding his teeth. Two young men, strangers, heard the sound, and looked at each other in a startled manner, then turned and looked at Falk. He recoiled from their notice, slipping away among the many milling bystanders. Grinding his teeth was a habit he thought he had defeated during the daylight hours. Occasionally the noise woke him in the night to a sense of unspecified rage and hatred.

He felt out of sorts now in the bright sunlight. Falk was not a great believer in the sun. It hurt his eyes. Sunlight made his pale, washed-out eyes melt and overflow in stinging tears, leaving him marooned, blinking, in the bright light. His black coat and tallow face attracted glances here among the bright colours and red cheeks of these Papist hoydens and their booze-sodden menfolk. Falk felt out of place among all this boisterous laughter.

Over the loudspeaker, some sottish fool was reading the names of the runners and riders. Through the crackling, the odd name he heard served to underline the frivolity of this godless place. 'Latin Lover', 'Abbot's Choice', 'Secret Seducer', 'Daemon Fairy', 'Gay Deceiver'. Shameless, with their light thoughts and venal mockery. And her, the American woman, just look at her. Skipping in the mud, all glowing and abandoned after the debaucheries of the night. Glued together, she and that pen-pusher, in the sweat of their carnal conjunction, to look at the face on her, with the lips drawn back and her wanton hair blowing and her eyes all alight. Pointing her finger and sucking her thumb over those beasts, and the jockeys on their backs. Putting money into the cupped hands of the bookmakers. Vulgar, brash. A disgrace even to them, the terrorists who call her sister.

Falk wandered out of it, back to the car park. He sat in his car, waiting. It would not be long before the American whore came back all smiles to her car, parked in front of his, and found it would not start. He could just see the corner of the rotor arm that he had carefully removed from the engine of her hire-car, revealing a bit of itself under the wheel of a van parked next to him. And soon enough there she was walking up the slight slope in that stiff-legged way tarts have. When he was a child, he'd seen them walking just that way down the alley by the docks after they'd been with the sailors in the dark. He had watched them as a boy, with the glass in the bedroom window steaming up in front of his eyes, and the sounds of his brothers and sisters restlessly asleep together in the big bed in the room behind his back. Filthy little whores, those girls who went with the sailors. Creatures beyond the pale. His mother had told him. Cast out utterly.

Still drawn to that stewpot of levity? Look at her turning back, not wanting to leave, as though drawn by the power of evil. Wants to pick up another partner in illicit pleasure already. No. Still satiated with last night. 'Have you had yours today? Yes. That's why I walk this way, dum dum.' She's turning the ignition. Nothing. Puzzled, aren't you? Try again. Nothing. Opening the window won't help you, whore. Now get out of the car. That's right, now the bonnet? She can't open the bonnet. Frown all you like. Fiddle. Rub your silly fingers. Black marks on your pure white trousers, too. More than biological washing powder to . . . Oho, a little temper. Spoiled Yank brat. Slam the door as though the car can feel it. Just like a woman. Well, it's not the car's fault. It's I who has it, I have what you want. Not take your temper out on me, you won't.

What do I do now, Kitty thought. She thought of MacBride waiting for her in the bar of the hotel, expecting her, and then, with the second or third whiskey, deciding that she'd stood him up. He'd probably feel uncomfortable enough in the bar of a famous hotel like that, in that bummy tweed suit of his among the swells. Or would he? He might. Then he'd go and find somewhere more congenial, and cheaper, poor poet, to drink. No, it isn't funny. Would he even bother wondering why she did not come? Probably not; just another case of . . . She must get there. She could not even find the lever to release the catch on the hood. She felt like crying. Perhaps MacBride and his friend were still around? But how could she find them now, with the lines of cars stretching for miles on either side? And everyone else still over there watching the last race. It wouldn't be easy to drag anyone away from the horses and the betting to help her start her damned car. Well, she'd simply have to wait.

Cigarette smoke? Gawd, couldn't she do with a smoke now, even if it did mean she'd break her three-months record since she last had a cigarette, having taken it up, along with lovers, when the marriage went sour. She'd never smoked until she started to sin in earnest. There didn't seem to be anyone around that she could see, but someone had lit a cigarette. Yes, in the grey car, in the line behind. A man sitting behind the wheel. Oh, please God, please let him be good with cars.

Falk's pale eyes watched the begging smile as she came, wagging like a fawning dog. Used to using it to get her way. That kind starts early, making up to their fathers. Listen to it, please, and if you would, and all the thank yous. A token inspection. A fine kind of a secret undercover operator, can't open the bonnet of a Ford. Huge eyes watching, begging to know what's the verdict. As if I didn't know. She's almost dim-witted. All her brains down there, jumbled up after a night pleasuring in her own sweat. Almost panting now, with her please pleases, playing helpless. Must get to Dublin. Not a chance in that car. Pleased to escort, you, ma'am. Where 'ere you walk, take you there meself. On my way. I'm to Dublin, same as you. Luggage, don't forget the luggage, and all those books.

What with the great outdoors and one thing and another, the poet MacBride was feeling a bit fuzzy. Funny, he thought, the girl in that car that just bumped off down the track to the road at a great rate of knots looked extremely like Kitty O'Shea. Perhaps those last two quick ones in the tent were a mistake. Eyes a bit unfocussed. He was not, he had to admit, in any condition to be a reliable witness. And anyway, he'd got that woman on the brain. For the first time in years of peaceful absence of passion. (MacBride, thrice-stung by lovers, limited himself to one-night stands with eager co-eds.) But he could not get the American out of his mind. So young and strong. Junoesque? Or Artemisian? No, that made her sound like water in a well. It wasn't a wonder if he was seeing things after a night like that. She hadn't asked to come to the races with him, thank God. Women and racing don't mix. But MacBride gazed at the dust settling across the grass plain where the car had passed, and felt, through the haze of many drinks, a small excitement at the suspicion that the beautiful American might have come to the races because she knew he would be there. But her car was red. He had seen it outside the hotel, with *Spring Harvest* lying on the back-seat. What would she be doing in a strange grey car with a strange grey man?

PART TWO

A DROP OF THE HARD STUFF

9

A Saturday night crowd was already milling outside the arched Front Gate of Trinity College, the undergraduates spilling out of the college entrance on to the pavement causing homeward-bound Dubliners, who were hurrying for the bus stop in Nassau Street, to step off the pavement into the busy traffic. There was much honking of car horns and shouted abuse. There was an odd quality about the evening sky. Unusually for April, it was lighter than it had been in the afternoon. There was a queer pale glimmering belt of sky drawing an opal line of sunlight between the heavy grey cloud and the dark roofs of the imposing buildings in College Green. The light made everything look unreal, as though an artificial setting on a stage.

Paddy Kiernan, wearing his old blue serge suit which had gone shiny now with wear at the knees as well as the seat, and with a not really clean white nylon shirt buttoned at the collar, but with no necktie, felt uncomfortable and out of place once he had crossed Nassau Street, walked through College Green, and found himself inside the Trinity railings among the milling undergraduates. A poster outside the porters' lodge advertised a performance that evening at the Players' Theatre.

As he walked through the vaulted, stone-slabbed entrance, he found himself walking beside a tall young girl. The girl had long blonde hair and wore boots, and a red and black shawl wrapped about her shoulders. Turning her head in an animated fashion while she walked with long-legged strides, she appeared almost to be speaking to Paddy when she suddenly said, 'All revolution is essentially romantic.'

Her clear voice, fierce with a sort of endearing naivety, ricocheted off the crumbling, ancient walls of the building. For a moment when the beautiful girl had turned her head towards him Paddy Kiernan had felt very young and shy, as if, he thought, she had spied him pulling himself off or doing something equally shameful. But then he watched the girl stride past him on long, booted legs, her face, smiling broadly, turned up to an extremely tall student who was himself most theatrical-looking, with long, dramatic hair, all curly at the back of the neck where it sprayed out over a snowy white collar. This tall student wore a navy blue cape of an old-time military style. The two of them looked like figures in light opera.

'That's all very well, darling,' the tall student said, 'as long as you don't imagine all revolutionaries are romantic. Take it from one who knows –' But his voice was lost, they were now so far ahead of Paddy, heading, with many others, to the Players' Theatre.

What was he listening to that for? Paddy said to himself. Those two might be Irish, but they were a race apart from him. They send them up to that Trinity College to learn them how to talk like Englishmen. In his own mind, he was talking to Brendan, who would enjoy that crack about the Trinity swells aping the English. Except, Paddy thought, Brendan was dead. Was he in Hell? In eternal damnation? Killing in a war was different. Brendan was in Purgatory. All nonsense, except he believed Brendan was up there somewhere watching him. And if you believed that, then there must be a place for the really evil bastards to go to.

Paddy paused and looked at the poster for the play that was on that night. *The Possessed.* Brendan didn't possess anything anymore.

Paddy had spoken on the telephone not twenty minutes before with a boy with a County Monaghan accent; breathless with excitement the boy had been, telling Paddy that the American woman, Kitty O'Shea, had been snatched and then, almost as a by-the-way, that Brendan was dead – his skull dashed in with a heavy object. Brendan had been seated in his car and an attempt had been made to set the car alight. The County Monaghan boy said the fire had gone out before it destroyed the evidence of Brendan's battered skull. Paddy understood then why the boy was so breathless on the phone. He had seen Brendan's body and was not being so terribly offhand about Brendan but only thought the kidnapping of the American girl was more important in the big scheme of things.

Of course it is, Paddy thought. The poor bitch. A real looker, too, Brendan had said. A glamour puss, he'd said. An old-time expression, glamour puss. She'd not be much older than one of these Trinity student girls, Paddy thought, and she'd come all that way for the cause of Ireland, a country she'd most likely never seen. They'd kill her, of course, once she gave them the money. A sad business, but she wasn't like Brendan, one of their own, no matter what the services rendered or the call of blood over the generations.

Across the slippery cobbles, groups of young and pretty girls were coming and going through the Front Gate, stopping to glance at the notices of the various schools, or to wait about for friends. They were mostly Irish girls, born and bred, who would flee sooner than dream of doing what the American girl did willingly for their country. Kitty O'Shea was Irish, naturally, but it would not be the girl's real name. Paddy wondered at the odd choice of the name of the woman who had brought down Parnell. He didn't know enough, or the cause of Ireland was perhaps too real and immediate, for him to see the name as both romantic and comic. His sense of irony was much earthier than that.

At the narrow entrance to the Players' Theatre, no more than a stairwell, the play was about to start. The man on the door stopped Paddy, and asked him if he had a ticket. A group of students, acting as ushers, chatted quietly outside the closed door. Paddy felt uncomfortable again among the students. Bunch of swells, he said to himself. When he tried to attract the attention of a girl who looked friendly, she appeared not to hear him. Then a tall boy, with a lot of hair and large round glasses, slipped round the door out of the auditorium. 'Yes?' the tall boy asked. 'May I help you?'

Paddy recognised the voice. It was the student in the cape who'd been talking like an English sissy to the pretty girl at the College entrance. Now Paddy saw that the young man was a 'character', with the round spectacles and a long, humorous face. A West-Brit, Paddy thought. Insulted if you didn't call him an Irishman. Well, he probably was.

'I've come to see a fella,' Paddy said. 'Liam O'Tomas, the maintenance man. And electrician, doing the business here tonight. There's been a terrible death in his family. I've come to tell him.'

The tall student looked down intently as Paddy spoke, as though he were hard of hearing or attempting to memorise what Paddy was saying. Then he said he'd find Liam, and left Paddy standing by the door, beyond which he could hear the play already going on inside.

Liam worked as a casual labourer at the university, doing maintenance, cutting the grass in the Provost's garden and the like. Not over-serious work, Paddy thought, but a decent cover. When he had something to do, Liam called in sick. He said he had asthma attacks. They probably thought him just another drunk malingering. And Liam did have the asthma to make it look authentic. Paddy had heard him wheezing often enough. He could imitate it down at the pub, doing it along with the phoney accent of the Englishman talking Irish. Then Paddy suddenly thought of Liam in bed with Niamh, with her beautiful dark head of hair. Wheezing into her ear, he'd be. There's a fella, Paddy thought, in the Six Counties right now could give you a cure for the asthma, Liam O'Tomas. A slit throat would end the wheezing, sure as the bashed-in skull ended Brendan's troubles. Must be good to catch Brendan unawares. Not much to look at, but he was an old soldier. Brendan had been in the Congo with the Irish Army for the UN. Of course that Congo caper was a few years back, but Brendan could tell some stories about the ghoolie darkies. Long swords, they had. And human meat hanging up for sale outside the village shops away up country in the jungle round Katanga. Cannibals, they were. No fooling, Brendan said. Sounded romantic. Brendan was like Sanders of the River, one of those old explorers – Stanley hunting Livingstone, or Bring 'Em Back Alive Frank Buck. A taste for adventure there in Africa for the UNO. But they didn't call it UNO anymore, only UN. For some reason it made a big difference, like calling them Provos. What a lot of shite it all was, committees, squabbling over names. Liam O'Tomas was a great one for that.

The tall student came back out of the theatre, walking with that long, looping stride. Paddy thought maybe he was a bit of a comedian. Or daft, Paddy thought. But of course not, he was a student. Still, it was said that genius and madness were tough to tell apart sometimes.

The tall student stood by Paddy and then, taking a deep breath, as though collecting his thoughts before delivering a most complicated message, 'Well,' he finally said, 'he says he has no family. You said

76

there was a death in his family and he says he has no family.' The tall student looked more amused than suspicious.

'Oh, for Christ's sake,' Paddy said, 'tell him it's Paddy Kiernan says his brother Brendan is dead in a car crash and his sister Kitty O'Shea from America is missing. That ought to be enough tragedy to jog his memory.'

The tall student did not seem the least put out by running messages. He went off, and left Paddy listening to an actor on the stage, sounding off about revolution. Liam's kind of talk, Paddy thought, all talk and theory.

The tall student came back. 'Is his brother really dead?' he asked.

'My brother it was,' Paddy said, sounding bitter.

'I'm sorry,' the tall student said, 'I didn't understand. Anyway, Liam says he'll be out directly.' He put Paddy down as drunk. First the maintenance man's brother and his sister, now his own brother. You'd think even a drunk could get that right.

Liam came out, leaving the door ajar. Paddy could see the actors on the stage. They were bathed in an unnatural white light that made them look like corpses, or, because they were standing, like the dead arising in a religious picture. Liam, pale and gasping for breath, leaned against the wall with his arms up and his head resting, like a runner after a race. Paddy was afraid his wheezing would attract attention, and pulled him out of the entrance into the open air.

'What is it you said?' Liam asked, and Paddy could hear him trying to get his breath. Paddy felt no pity for him. He thought Liam's asthma had some psychological cause, he'd heard a lot about that on TV.

'Brendan's dead,' Paddy said.

'Jesus,' Liam said, and the asthmatic wheeze made it sound like a foreign word.

'And the girl's taken,' Paddy said. He could see Liam going pale.

'Oh, Christ. The Gardai?'

'No,' Paddy said. 'The other side.'

'That's torn it,' Liam said. He was short of breath and had to gulp for air.

'We've got to tell Flynn,' Paddy said.

'We'll tell him.' Liam could barely speak.

'You should go see Flynn,' Paddy said. 'You can explain. It was your job.'

'Brendan wasn't mine.'

'Brendan was a good man.'

'Not all that good.'

'You never mind about Brendan,' Paddy said, 'you think about Flynn.'

'I've got to,' Liam started to say and then he turned away from the wall and looked as though he was about to fall. 'Sit down,' he said.

'Well,' Paddy said, 'you sit down then and think about what you're going to say to Flynn, and never mind Brendan who's dead and can't defend himself.'

Good Christ, Paddy thought, this English bastard would go and tell Flynn he couldn't work with the old broken-down gobshites like Brendan who gets himself kilt and that Paddy Kiernan's an old drunk. Liam was the boss, and said Brendan should do the job alone. He's the one said there was no need for another man, and Flynn'd better be made to realise that.

The tall student with his long face and round spectacles came out from the theatre entrance and said, 'Is everything all right?'

'I'll have to get him home,' Paddy said.

'I thought you said it was your brother, not his.'

'They were very close,' Paddy said.

'So I see,' the tall student said. 'Shall I call a taxi?'

'Liam has a van,' Paddy said. 'If you can just limp him round while I get it, I'll meet you outside the Front Gate.'

The tall student helped Liam out of the Front Gate and stood there waiting for the van, holding Liam by the elbow. When Paddy drove up in the van, Liam was breathing much better, but he was still a bad colour. After they got him in the passenger seat, Paddy set out for Ranelagh, where Liam's girl, Niamh, could deal with him. Beside him in the passenger seat, every time Liam turned to say something to Paddy, he would shake his head as if either the effort to speak was too much or the catastrophe that had overtaken them was too great for words. Either way it seemed unsatisfactory to Paddy, who was thinking of his friend Brendan, who had kept the cannibals in the Congo from eating each other, who had performed many daring deeds for the old cause, and was worth many times the value of Lionel Thompson, the ersatz Irishman. Looking out of the car window at the quiet streets with the lights on in the houses, he thought, too, of the brave American girl, whoever she really was when she was at home. He wondered if there would be anyone to miss her, and sound the alarm at her disappearance.

They had brought out the whiskey in celebration, but Detective Sergeant Byrne was saying: 'She's a hard-faced little bitch, that Kitty O'Shea, with all that red hair. Face like a weasel and hardly more than five foot tall. She gave me an awful bite on the hand.' Byrne held up his hand with the bite mark on it. They had all seen it already. 'I wouldn't have minded so much,' he said, but she called me a fucking Brit and an Englishman.'

Doyle laughed.

He leaned over and poured whiskey into the glasses of the policemen seated round his desk.

Detective Sergeant Byrne said: 'I had quite a job convincing her I was a genuine Irish pig and not an English one. Kitty O'Shea would appear to be lacking in a knowledge of the basic geography of her motherland.' The Detective Sergeant held out his glass again to Doyle.

'Well,' Doyle said, 'that's that anyway. We've stopped those bastards getting their hands on all that money. Now,' he said ironically, 'I suppose we have to wait for all the bank robberies to start, to make up the deficit.'

They were all a bit subdued about the celebration because they were not announcing it to the Press. And indeed, maybe they never would.

The policemen laughed at Doyle's irony.

'With the funds dried up, they'll be back at the armed robbery, so there's no rest for the likes of us,' Doyle said. Still, he felt good. They had arrested the American courier with the loot intact, and outside the open window, a balmy breeze stirred the leaves of the pot plants on the window ledge.

'Spring is here,' Doyle said, looking at the soft evening light with that special quality it had after rain. He opened his desk drawer and took out a necktie full of red dots on a bright yellow background.

Doyle removed the dark tie he had been wearing and started putting on the polka-dotted one.

'I guess it is,' Detective Sergeant Byrne said, looking at the red-spotted yellow tie.

'A time of rebirth,' Doyle said. He didn't look like a policeman anymore, even in the same old dark grey suit he always wore. The red-spotted yellow tie, especially as it was wrinkled and slightly grubby, made Doyle look like a middle-aged lounge lizard, or an unlucky racing man, Detective Sergeant Byrne thought. Then he thought that Doyle had got his man, or his woman, anyway, but he was the one the little red-haired Yankee bitch had bitten. And, he thought, they had not got any of the men supposed to contact Kitty O'Shea. They should have scooped them up. But at least Doyle had got the American, and that without any troublesome nonsense about going back and forth across the Border.

'Are you off now?' Byrne said to Doyle. What with the suede brogues and the yellow tie, Byrne knew Doyle was set for the Shelbourne Bar. 'It's a fine thing to be a bachelor,' he said to Doyle and Doyle laughed. Byrne wondered if Doyle was lonely. Byrne was a religious man who had wanted to be a priest, married now, and with two little boys, and a detective sergeant and still only twenty-eight years old. He remained religious, though, and it bothered him sometimes when Doyle got particularly anti-clerical or even downright atheistical. It was the cynicism Byrne found shocking. Sometimes he thought it was put on and then Doyle would say something that showed Byrne it wasn't put on at all. It would make him feel better about Doyle's cynical atheism if he thought Doyle was lonely.

Doyle took his old brown felt hat from the peg and turned at the door to wave goodnight. Downstairs, he stepped into the warm embrace of the April evening, and walked in a slow and casual way, with both hands thrust deep into the pockets of his comfortable old suit, his soft brown hat tipped at an angle. After the rain, the air smelled fresh.

The pavements were crowded with others promenading, like himself, in the soft evening. Daffodils swayed gently on a patch of bright grass, and for the first time that year, women walked out on a Saturday night in bright dresses, their coats over their arms.

Doyle felt quite irresponsible, freed for a few hours from the burden of the constant battle against villainy. He strolled towards the Front Gate of Trinity College, pausing to read on a notice board attached to the railings that the Macabi X1 were to play a limited overs friendly match against a TCD X1 in the College grounds that Sunday. That's tomorrow. The cricket season already, Doyle thought. He'd said Spring had arrived. And that very night, at the Players' Theatre, the students were giving a one-night only performance – a 'world premier' no less – of Jim Parsons' adaptation of Fydor Dostoyevsky's *The Possessed*.

Doyle watched as a tall Trinity student with large round spectacles showed a drunkard the door. He was pushing him into a small van. The van driver had got out to help, and, Doyle saw, that driver was Paddy Kiernan. How that man kept turning up, Doyle thought, asking himself what would that bogman be doing in the halls of Academe? And the fellow with him green with drink. It's a mad world: a Jewish X1 playing cricket on a Sunday in Dublin; Paddy Kiernan and Dostoyevsky at Trinity. And Kitty O'Shea, carrot-haired offshoot of some bog-trotting horse thief, deprived of her million-dollar donation to the cause of old Ireland, safe now she was in the basement facilities, with the taste of the interrogatory right-hand index finger of probing Detective Sergeant Patrick Byrne in her mouth while he, Michael John Doyle, the Great Detective, was off to enjoy himself in the highly salubrious surroundings of the Shelbourne Hotel. A short life, he thought, but a merry one.

Every time he heard a female American voice in the crowd around him at the Shelbourne Bar, George Albert MacBride, the poet of the petrol bomb, thought it was her. And each time, as he turned to see, he would find that the sound of his new American sweetheart was issuing from a middle-aged blue-rinsed harridan or from a precocious brat of either sex, or someone equally inappropriate. As far as MacBride was concerned, all American females sounded the same. It was a sorry thing for a lover to contemplate, staring on a double whiskey at the bar. Especially, he thought, they all sounded the same after you had been sitting for two hours drinking large measures of expensive drinks and waiting for what he now most definitely thought of as his own true love. He realised, in a fleeting moment of clear-sightedness, that he might just possibly be about ready to get horribly and perhaps uncontrollably intoxicated when lines from the poems of G.A.MacBride started whispering themselves inside his head. That was always a danger sign. Why this should be, he did not know, but he could recall some fairly disastrous nights which began with The Voice speaking the poetry with hideous persistence.

At first, MacBride had sat in a leather chair in the lobby of the hotel, gazing at the doorman in his long coat outside on the steps, and the taxis and cars dropping people off. They came through the revolving door, with its shiny glass and polished dark wood, men and women spinning into the foyer with that sudden smiling look of expectancy that people have coming into a grand and imposing place when they want to give the impression they are quite at home. MacBride had been sitting there for close on half an hour, in the hope of being somewhat sober for his new girl, when he began to feel that he had been sitting there for hours. He looked, he knew, as though he had been stood up. He went into the bar where he sat in a big chair facing the door for about twenty minutes, until he decided he'd been sitting like that for hours, and moved to another chair which definitely did not face the door. Now he was drunk and had the poetry in his head, which was very annoying, even if it was his own stuff, and perhaps particularly because it was his own stuff.

He went to stand at the bar, looking at what was a not over-familiar face reflected back at him in the bar mirror. The suit was familiar, and he was pleased to see his reflection was wearing a clean shirt, but the sudden grin of recognition on the reflection's face looked silly to MacBride. He sat down on a stool.

Some American ladies came in, talking about the doorman.

'Did you hear what he said?'

'I couldn't make a word of sense.'

'I said "isn't it a lovely evening?", and he said "April is a perpetricious month indeed, ladies". Now what in Heaven's name does that mean?'

'Oh,' the other said, 'it must be an archaic use of "perpetrate". But isn't that what we came to Dublin for? To hear how they use the language?'

MacBride was about to go over and tell the American women how terrific he thought that was, and ask them if they knew Kitty O'Shea, even if that was a long shot. He had a great desire to speak Kitty's name, but then the American women left without having a drink.

Inside MacBride's head, the singing of a hymn from his childhood, 'All Things Bright and Beautiful', replaced the recitation of his own poetry. He noticed that there was a brown felt hat, battered, but once having seen better days, lying on the bar. For a moment he thought it must be his own similarly battered but once good brown felt hat which, along with an overcoat and several umbrellas, he had lost years before, now restored through happy chance. But then a large middle-aged man in a grubby yellow tie with red spots on it, reached out, saying, 'I'll get this out of your way', and moved the hat.

'I had a hat,' MacBride said.

'But not when you came in,' the man said.

MacBride laughed.

'What'll you have?' the man asked.

'Oh,' MacBride said, 'just the one.'

'Better make it a large one, then,' the man said.

MacBride laughed again. 'That's a good one,' he said.

'It always was,' the man said.

'I had a hat when I came in,' MacBride said. 'I hung it on the wall.'

'Did you?'

'No. I had a girl when I came in.'

'You don't want to go hanging girls on the wall,' the man said.

'You would this one,' MacBride said. 'She's pretty as a picture.'

The man laughed. 'Doyle,' he said.

'MacBride.'

'I'd like to see her, MacBride, the girl pretty enough to hang on the wall.'

'I'd like to see her too, Doyle, but she's stood me up. That's why I'm drinking.'

Doyle laughed. 'I got my girl,' he said. 'That's why I'm drinking.'

'Me too,' MacBride said. 'My girl, that's to say, the young woman who has been rude enough to leave me standing stood up, is an American young woman.'

'Snap,' said Doyle.

'A Miss Kitty O'Shea,' MacBride said.

'What?' Doyle said. 'What did you say her name was? Kitty O'Shea?'

'The girl who has not arrived here today, this evening, hours ago.'

'What did you say the name was?'

'MacBride. George Albert MacBride. George after my father's brother, my Uncle George, and Albert after someone or other else.'

'This woman of yours.'

'O'Shea. Kitty O'Shea.'

'It's a common enough name,' Doyle said. 'I suppose in America with Irish roots and all that, there'd be a lot of them. Is she usually on time?' Doyle said, not thinking it was so much of a coincidence anymore and attempting to be pleasant.

MacBride shook his head. 'That I can't tell you,' he said. 'I only met her yesterday.' He raised his hand to stop Doyle from speaking. 'Don't say it. I know what you're going to say. But time doesn't count.'

'So,' Doyle said, still feeling better about the coincidence of the names. 'You only met her yesterday?'

'Yes,' MacBride said. He was very drunk now. 'Yesterday. How about you? One for the road? Same again, barman,' he said. He turned to Doyle and said, 'She flew into and out of the saga which is the life of G.A. MacBride. At Shannon.'

'You met her at Shannon?'

'No.'

'But you said –'

'You ask questions like a cop. Come to think of it, you look like a cop as well as ask questions like one.'

'Where did you meet her, if it wasn't Shannon?' Doyle asked.

'Kitty O'Shea? Oh, in the bar at the hotel in the town where I spent the night. Then I went to the races. You know, I thought I saw her at the races. But then I was seeing her everywhere. Everything reminds me of Kitty O'Shea. In fact, Doyle, you have just reminded me of Kitty O'Shea, have you not?'

Doyle flinched, hearing the name.

'Don't be like that, Doyle,' MacBride said. 'I don't mean you look like her, although at the races, at the Curragh, I saw one looked exactly like her.'

'A horse?' The man was just drunk, Doyle thought. He might be respectable and well-educated, but you could tell he liked a drink. He'd be a bachelor like himself, and just a bit lonely but not enough to really want to get involved.

MacBride laughed. 'A horse? Don't be silly,' he said. 'A girl. With dark hair.'

'Dark hair? Not red?'

'No, no, dark hair. I thought I saw her at the Curragh. She was sitting there with her eyes opened wide and her mouth open, like in the painting.'

'What painting?'

'Painting by a man with a name like a fish. "The Scream". I have this image of Kitty O'Shea sitting in a car screaming. You know, I even get this vision in my mind's eye that she was screaming as she was being driven off.'

'You saw this other girl, who looked like your girl, screaming?'

'Yes, like in the painting.'

'Jesus,' said Doyle.

'Yes,' MacBride said, 'it was haunting. The man's name is Munch, the painter with the name like a fish.'

Doyle said: 'You think she was being driven away? Against her will?'

'You do sound like a policeman.'

'I am,' Doyle said.

'You know, I thought you did. I thought you sounded like a policeman.'

'And what do you do, George?'

'I never liked the name George. I'm a . . . this is worse than being a policeman. I mean, it's more dishonest. I write poetry.'

'Do you make a living out of that, MacBride?'

'Thanks. No. Unfortunately I am forced to descend to depths even lower and more obscene than poetry or policing. I teach.'

'In the North?'

'You noticed? Was it the George or the Albert that decided you?'

'They helped.'

'Alas, we are ever damned and divided by our very names into barbaric tribalism. I suppose you, too, have names, Doyle.'

'Michael John,' Doyle said. He edged close to MacBride in

a confidential manner and said, 'I don't want to worry you, MacBride, but if you think something has happened to this girl of yours. Something serious.'

'Worse than standing a man up?'

'Exactly,' Doyle said. He reached into the inside pocket of his old suit coat and brought out a card which he gave to MacBride. 'There's day or night numbers,' he said. 'It's best to be safe. The way things are today. Still, I'm sure there's a good reason. But it's best to be safe.'

'My family motto, Doyle. Safety First.'

Not long after that, Doyle left and MacBride realised that Kitty would not come, nor even telephone. It was getting late. Some students had come in. One of them was a tall comic-looking man with large round spectacles. He stood at the bar alongside MacBride. He was telling the other students, who had been acting in a play that evening, a funny story about a man who came and dragged the stage electrician off so the tall student had to do the lighting himself.

MacBride lost all sense of time, but he suddenly found himself talking to a pretty girl with long blonde hair, with a red shawl wrapped round her shoulders like someone playing a gypsy beauty in a comic opera. The girl with them had once heard him at a poetry reading. MacBride said something which must have been very rude to her, for the barman, who had been eyeing MacBride all evening, said, 'None of that now,' and the next thing MacBride knew he was outside in the street with the tall student and others including the gypsy beauty and they were all being friends together. The tall bespectacled student was telling MacBride about the play, based on Dostoyevsky's *The Possessed* which he had adapted and which had had its first and last night that evening. The young dramatist said he had, of course, seen his own play at all the rehearsals, but he had missed most of it that night because of this Irish character who'd come round and stolen the electrician with some cock and bull tale about the electrician's brother being killed in a car crash, and then it was this fellow's own brother who was killed. And then the electrician had turned out to be drunk or dying, and he'd had to help him into a van to be rid of him. There was also a girl in this story but MacBride couldn't quite figure out where she came in. MacBride was only aware of being out in the cool air of a brightly illuminated street, with trees in leaf overhead, and this talkative tall student telling him this boring story, and then they were in a room and the gypsy beauty girl was asking him to recite some poetry. Then he said he would and she said, 'You didn't write that, that's a hymn.' MacBride was rather disappointed that she failed to see how funny it was him reciting 'All Things Bright and Beautiful' like that, and that was the last thing he remembered.

How beautiful Niamh was, Paddy Kiernan thought, with the history of Ireland written in her pale face under that dark hair. Without ever knowing, he thought, a girl could be that, the embodiment of her race. Like they say 'an English rose', or 'Miss America', but a Yankee girl Miss America standing there in her swim-suit and crown, holding a tin sceptre, she knows. But a simple Irish girl like Niamh just has it without knowing.

Niamh was leaning over the bannister looking down at them in the hallway when Paddy led Liam in and saw her with her face looking very white under the blue-black hair, gazing down at them. No, he thought, not us. Him. She only had eyes for this wheezing English gobshite.

'What's happened?' she said. 'Is he hurt?'

She came down the stairs, stooping with urgency, with the blue dressing gown fallen open and her breasts showing. Paddy turned his face away, blushing, then looked again and saw that she was completely unaware of his eyes or of her two beautiful breasts hanging loose from the low neck of the gown.

'He's had nothing to drink,' Paddy said. Listen to that, he said to himself, defending the man. The freemasonry of the male, sticking together. Women the common foe.

'It's his poor asthma,' Niamh said.

His poor fucking asthma, Paddy thought. Stuff the gobshite and his poor asthma. She was like the rest of them, wants to mother. At the same time she think's he's the pirate bold. She must know what he does. Have an idea, anyway. Can't really keep it secret. Talking in sleep, that kind of thing. They get to know. Also, she would get to know he was no good. Should have got herself an Irishman.

The television set was on in the neat little flat. Nice place, Paddy thought. What a nice place. Liam was breathing normally now, and the colour had come back to his cheeks. If he'd had a girl like that, Paddy thought, with a nice homey place. Well, what wouldn't he do? Go to Mass on a Sunday with the wife and kids.

She was fixing up her hair now that the crisis was over. Her man safe at home. Paddy watched her. She was mindful of her tits showing, clutching the robe to her. The glamour of an Englishman. They probably gave themselves to the shipwrecked Spaniards, too, when they came dragging their handsome selves ashore, all earrings and flashing teeth after the Armada. Breathless they would be, too, after the swim. But she'd find herself more at home with one of her own after the glamour wore off. The poor asthma. Beautiful tits on a slim body. Paddy had a friendly whore called Maeve from Tallaght who was nice to him sometimes, but she was forty-three and had great rolls of fat down her back and round her middle. 'Made for comfort,' Maeve called herself, and Paddy laughed, but she wasn't.

'The van's outside,' Paddy told Niamh, handing her the keys.

'I know,' Liam said. He took the keys. He was being the boss again. He'd figured out what to tell Flynn, Paddy thought, about Brendan being alone and fucking up enough to get himself killed.

'Oh, it speaks now, does it?' Paddy said, trying to make a joke. Niamh laughed.

'I'll call him,' Liam said. 'I'll call Flynn,' but he didn't move from the sofa.

'He can't go out,' Niamh said. 'There's no phone here.'

'Wouldn't use it if there was,' Liam said.

'You rest yourself,' Paddy said, 'I'll phone him.'

He left them in the cozy flat and went out into the deserted street, thinking how he would give the bad tidings to Flynn; and then he thought about the brave American woman – a stranger, really, as much or more a stranger in her own way as Liam O'Tomas – and he wondered if she was not in fact dead now, buried in some misbegotten forlorn spot that would be forever Chicago or Philadelphia.

10

It must be like this to be blind, she thought. Frightening, not being sure what was going on. No way of proving anything, without the evidence of the eyes. Hours ago, the man had put on the blindfold and tied up her hands behind her back and shoved a cloth into her mouth so she couldn't scream, or even breathe and bundled her on to the floor in the back of the car. Then he turned off the tarmac road and drove right up into the hills, with the motor climbing with its engine labouring, jolting and bumping where there was no more than a track, that was bad enough, thinking any time he'd start the rape. They kill women after.

Now, at least, with the blindfold quite loose there was a sense of light. Then he'd stopped the car, and she'd thought: is the rape business going to start? And they like to sodomise women too, some of them. The papers are full of what they do. His hands were rough, getting tangled in her hair. Was he taking the bandage off? Bandage! she thought, as though it was a wound, not a blindfold shutting out the light. He'd tightened it, that was all, with the lovely clean smell of adhesive tape over the stench of his breath. But that was the end of the light, and the power of rational thought just seemed to disappear without sight. All she could think was, please God, no knife.

He'd taken her out of the back of the car, hitting her hard across the back of her head, and marched her into some building with a rough floor, and tripped her up so she lay on the floor waiting for him to start. And all the time, she thought, what comes after?

But then as time passed, thinking came back. She thought, it's got very cold all of a sudden and she remembered it used to be like that at all-night parties in the early morning, or after making love till dawn, that sudden cold. About that time there was the sound of birds. It must be dawn for them to be singing like that, full of joy, they sound, but they're only hungry, still they are not afraid, that means there aren't any people about. Those aren't alarm calls, only just the fledglings demanding to be fed. But something was moving. Some kind of animals.

Now she listened to the animal sound. It was quite close, the sound of movement. Not human. An animal. Whoever or whatever this is, it's not aware of where it's going, just wandering aimlessly. Not worried at all about men being about. A sound of tearing, too, like ripping a piece of old cloth into strips. And breathing. Heavy breathing, quite frightening. Sheep. Of course, it's sheep, grazing. There'd been sheep huddled by the roadside all over on that ghastly drive. She'd seen the sheep when the headlights of the car had picked them out. They'd looked like boulders at the side of the track. That drive was the worst time she'd ever had in her life. Worse than anything that had ever happened to her, or to anyone she knew. Artie Biggs, a black boy from Dwight Street where the poor people lived, he'd bled to death on the floor of a helicopter in Vietnam. He used to mow the lawn. And Mr Gleasman had been shot dead by a Puerto Rican drug addict in Gleasman's Drug Store. Someone from home – there was a picture of her in the *Evening Telegram* – had been hi-jacked by Arab terrorists but they let her go, and she, Mrs Rosen or Rose, continued her holiday and sent telegrams to all her friends as though nothing had happened.

But things did happen. The man in the car never said a word. Before he'd hit her she knew it was all something strange and had asked him to take her back. She'd pleaded with him. She'd got angry. She'd even tried to reason with him, saying he was sick and not to blame, and she'd make sure he got the right psychiatric help he needed, because there were a lot of inadequate men like that, about his age and everything, who had problems relating to women. They really thought nothing of it in America, they'd gotten so sophisticated about anything to do with human inter-relating. It was something she knew about. She certainly should, after going out for so long with Sidney, who was a well-known psychiatrist, and was bound to be able to put him in touch with a good man over here. Sidney had patients who were much worse off than him – really grotesque, sometimes. But Sidney said nearly everyone could be helped, however gross their problem, if they really wanted to be. She blamed herself too, she had to admit, because she had dismissed the first thought she'd had at the airport when she thought he might be sexually attracted to her. And then later, when she'd seen him again, she should have been warned to be more careful. Well, all that must have sounded the most terrible drivel. Paperback book psychology. Could a person imagine a woman saying that to a mad man?

And he'd never said a single word. Not one. Just sat there driving. He hadn't even tried to touch her, either. That of course, made it worse. There'd been a point when she found she was even more frightened to think he wasn't a sex maniac than to know that he was. That was before he'd stopped the car and got out. He hadn't moved away. And then another car stopped behind, and he'd moved. There'd been a scuffling sound, and she should have run then, when he was out of the car. God, why hadn't she run? It was the most stupid thing. But she'd just looked out of the car window at all the dark, and been afraid. There'd been a funny smell, gasolene. She thought she was going to be sick. He was paranoid. Persecution mania, Sidney called it, it was clearly something like that. But he was back in the car by the time she'd realised he had just killed a man, and set the man's car on fire. It was horrible.

If it wasn't sex he wanted, then, what was it? Once they'd arrived here, with the very tight blindfold on so she could no longer make out forms blocking the light, she could tell there were other men. A whole gang, by the sound of their breathing and their smell and what little talking they did. They must be after a ransom, she thought. But how would they know she was Brooksie's wife when she used her maiden name? Her passport was in her bag with her married name still in it. And she was Judge O'Shea's daughter. There was money, mother still had some money. She'd pay, and Brooks, too, he'd pay. Of course the FBI didn't like it, but anyone would pay the ransom if they could, so it was just a question of having to wait and endure and see it as a blessing that he hadn't been the mad rapist. The blindfold was for the best too because it was better not to be able to identify them, if it ever came to that. Except for the man like a crow. The blindfold meant they didn't intend murder.

There seemed to be two men and the crazy one from the airport and the car. Why had he killed that man? Was it a policeman? Or

MacBride? She'd turned and shouted to him on the racetrack. He hadn't noticed. So why'd he come after her and get himself killed? The other two men spoke quite freely, as though they thought someone who was blindfolded was brain-damaged. There was a foreign one, who sounded very young, and his accent was definitely European. From Germany, it seemed from what they said. He spoke English poorly. Not that the other spoke it all that well, with his accent so thick and grating she could hardly understand a word. He sounded almost respectable. He gave orders to the kidnapper, whom he called by a short name she could not catch, as though he was a flunkey, so however terrible he was, he didn't have the sort of status you'd expect from someone directing a kidnapping.

The German once called the older man, who seemed to be the boss, 'Tyler'. She'd heard that. He had a hideous voice, and said, 'Shut your mouth with names, Karl.' But for that she could understand very little of what he said. The man who'd brought her said nothing. But twice they called him a name that was like a crow's call. Then he seemed to go away because there was the sound of a car and Tyler was shouting at the young German, telling him to stop meddling with . . . whatever the name was, like Hawk or Talk or, Fook or Falk. Tyler spoke about him in a way she knew he wouldn't have done if the man had been within hearing. Then Karl said, 'I think Lucas Falk is crazy in the head,' and she realised the name was Falk because the non-English speaker pronounced it more properly than the Irishman did.

Falk, grey as a shadow against the bare stone wall of the room, pulled the blanket closer round his shoulders. He'd had a few hours' sleep. Tired after the drive. Now it must be nearly dawn. The others were still asleep. No way of telling about the woman; she was tied up too tight to move much, and the gag meant she couldn't snore, if a fancy woman like that did snore. Probably awake. The German, on the other hand, should have his adenoids fixed, snoring like that. They had an operation, and a rich spoiled brat like that, his father could have afforded it. And now he was a public nuisance keeping the world from sleep. His face, though, when he first saw the whore. The German boy looked like he hadn't dared hope. Pretty as any of the naked whores in his magazines. And Tyler had got angry about the Fenian he'd killed on the road. Falk had to tell Tyler. 'Not on our own doorstep,' Tyler had said. Falk had tried to make a little joke about the Papists loving to die, to meet the angels, but Tyler wouldn't have it. It was true though, it was a religion in love with death, but every one of them was a coward in the face of it. The little fellow had been a spunky sort, a fighting bantam, they called that kind of Mick. He fell for it, though, thought she was alone in the car. Men take it for granted, the bladder's imperative, the call of nature for another man. Thought he could take advantage of a slash in the woods to snatch her back. Tyler called it crazy, killing him. As if Popery ever responded to words.

Falk eased his leg against the hard earth. They were the same as Tyler, some of them, in Korea. Didn't want to upset the Chinamen. 'Come on, Corporal Falk,' the toffee-nosed English captain used to say, 'Let's you and me go out on the q.t. and get some Laundrymen.' Slipping across at night to do in the Chinamen. Against regulations. Rear echelon wanted a truce. Don't get the Laundrymen cross. Bloody nonsense. The captain knew. 'Come on, Corporal, we'll bag a brace of Laundrymen.' You could smell them in the dark. They were supposed to be able to see in the dark, the Chinamen, but they smelled. Now the reek of the American whore's scents was in his nostrils. A sickly stink.

Still as death, the shape of her. The storm lantern's turned down low, it's running out of fuel. Karl's got an itch for her. Not a fairy, after all, thought for sure he was a nancy boy. Likes to see things hurt.

Moving carefully, making no sound, Falk slipped out of the room into the cool dawn. He lit a cigarette and leaned against a dry stone wall staring across the desolate hillside as the first pale light of dawn opened the gap between earth and sky, thinking of the splendid dawns he had seen when he was a young soldier in far off lands. Nothing now was like it was then.

Kitty, her arms and legs, beyond cramp, grown numb, heard the men begin to move around. It must be light outside now. She heard Tyler say, 'Oh, there you are, Falk. We're about to eat.' The foreign boy coughed and complained about smoke. Tyler told him to shut up, and if he'd brought dry wood instead of the green rubbish he'd gathered, they wouldn't have trouble with smoke. Falk still didn't say anything as far as Kitty could hear. She heard one of them say, 'Should we have a fire?'

'Oh, we have to have a fire for the eats.' That was Tyler's voice. So the one who was worried about smoke was Falk, the mad killer from the car who had hit and punched her, and tied her so tight she couldn't feel anything in her hands anymore.

God, she thought, there were places where they used to bury women underground. They must have thought that too, in Ancient Egypt, in the tomb, or were they raised to it? All part of their religion. But would they be able just to accept when it came to it? Pray for us now, and at the hour of our death, amen. Just absolutely rattling them off as a kid. Ten decades. One hundred and forty-four days off Purgatory, and then, looking on the calendar and seeing what day it was, what saint's day. Like Saint Edward, the patron saint of bald men. Louise La France at Miss Davenport's in Hamp, she was a Catholic, too, and knew all the funny saints. It was like living in the past, with those medieval tales to bring to mind when everything around was so loud and modern. How happy it was then. Louise had a nickname. Was it Frenchie? There was something hanging down, something loose, soft, and quite warm, clinging. For God's sake. A spider's web, that's all, don't scream. Stretching out the feet, touching something hard, knobbly, same all round, stones, stone walls, the kind without cement the Irish have all over the place.

How cold it is! The human body draws the damp out of the earth floor. Chattering teeth, even with the gag, a muted sound like that woman working the knitting machine, where was that? Some place twee, a cottage industry in some quaint village in Vermont. Sidney had laughed about what she was knitting: a sweater with something like 'I Love Elvis' written on it. Something ridiculous. Imagine remembering that.

She could hear the men moving. Somebody dropped something, or knocked it over. He cursed. It was the foreign boy, Karl, grumbling, said they didn't need to get up so early, did they? Tyler muttered something, and Karl making a kind of whooping noise, and said he'd forgotten that, and he'd wake the prisoner so they could get on with it.

Kitty heard a loud crack, which was a door catch opening. Then

94

she could tell there was a shaft of light. She could see nothing. But the blindfold was coming loose, all those tears having an effect. Rough hands sliding on the silk of her sleeves pulled her towards the light. Tears ran down her face as she wept, a flood of tears flowing out from under the blindfold. The light did not come from outside, she could tell, but from a storm lantern. She could smell kerosene. There was heat from the fire, too. They were hiding out. Afraid someone would see them. It was Karl holding her elbows from behind. He had a smell of his own. Fresh sweat, not like the stink of Falk.

Smoke was billowing from the fire of green wood she'd heard them mention. The blindfold was loose enough to see the men's feet; and the smoke from the fire floated about white like beer foam. There were the three of them now. She could smell Falk. Karl, behind and to one side of her, wore Dr Marten's boots with criss-cross fancy laces. The dangling trouser bottoms and dirty, cheap, white socks were Falk's. The shoes went with the rest of him. Large busted black shoes, more boots than shoes. The shoelaces, having snapped, were tied in two places on the right shoe and one, two, three places on the left. He had shoes like a mad wino you might see muttering in the street.

Tyler and Falk. Scotch-Irish names, the same people as the Rednecks back home who hated the blacks and the New York Jews, Catholics, too, for that matter. All the stuff in the papers over the years about Ulster and the people there made them out like a different breed, and they turn out to be so familiar after all. But then, all her favourite writers had names like that, too. William Faulkner and Flannery O'Connor and Carson McCullers. Maybe not Flannery O'Connor. She might be 'one of us'. One of us. Like marching off with Louise La France and the four or five other Catholic girls to the local Catholic church for Mass on Sunday in Northampton. Tribalism when you came down to it – tribalism? How could she and Louise La France be of the same tribe? – but when it was your own, you never thought of it like that. Anyway, could any sane person identify this cold place, full of rain, with visions of the smokey Deep South of William Faulkner, full of dusty roads and mules like the opening of *Light in August*? Except there were the Negroes they called them and a vicious hatred jumped out of the pages (and was very confusing reading on a snowy winter evening in perhaps slightly smug New England).

A rush of cold air meant that the door had opened. There was light, and the heavy layers of wood smoke stirred as in a stately dance routine and then reformed across the bare floor. She could see Tyler's big red face emerge through the smoke as he stopped to peer at her. Large, with greying reddish hair and stubble like verdigris on his beefy veined cheeks, he righted himself and she could see only his trouser bottoms. The blindfold slipping allowed a narrow, restricted view. They were in a primitive cottage or hut, no curtains, just a window with boards nailed clumsily across. The breeze when the door was open stirred the dust on the earth floor. This had been cut up recently, chunks of dried mud prised from the surface, and she knew that that was her, kicking out with her feet, which were not properly tied when they had brought her in.

The lower half of Tyler moved forward like a ghost out of the smoke.

'Take her outside,' he said. 'She's got to go to the lavatory.'

When he spoke she could not understand what he said at first, and only several seconds later did she grasp it. 'I don't know,' Karl said. 'Good if she messes herself. Good tactics?'

'And we live with it?' Tyler said. He was laughing at the German. 'This is not a pigsty,' he said. 'Just do what you're told.'

Tyler undid the rope round her ankles and Karl pulled her up. Someone shoved her and she went outside. There was a rocky hillside steep behind the stone cabin, and barren dark hills all round, with purple scrub and slaty scree. No trees, no cover, nowhere to hide if she ran. The sun, scarcely climbed above the hilltop on the right, was partly hidden by swirls of dark grey cloud. A patch of short-cropped green grass outside the door, starred with a familiar little flower. It had some Latin name, but everyone called it Scottish thrift. Someone had given her, years and years ago when she was a little girl, a small curiously-sided coin, a threepence piece from Britain, with Scottish thrift on the reverse side, and the Queen of England on the other. Perhaps they called it Irish thrift here, or did one of Falk's great-great-grandmas bring the little flower from Scotland?

From several feet away, the smell of the chemical toilet was powerful. Her feet scrabbled feebly on the rough ground as the blood began to return to her legs. The lavatory was a lean-to at the side of the cabin, the wooden roof overgrown with grass. Karl's grip was tight on her arms. If she could break away, he was the one who would come after her. Falk had a slight limp; Tyler was a fat man. He'd tie her even tighter after she'd been to the women's room. But he'd have to untie her hands first. She'd scratch his eyes out, then they'd be equal and she could pull off the blindfold and run.

But when he did, her hands were useless.

His hands were small, with long thin white fingers. He was tall and pale, with a hyperactive Adam's apple protruding like a huge moonstone jewel from the open neck of a Scotch plaid shirt. Crush their Adam's apple, and they die, she thought. She'd heard that. The back of the hand across it. But she went into the shed. The rounded toecaps of his Dr Marten's were plain to see under the gap of the shed door.

'What you doing in there, goddammit?' he asked, as if she could answer him.

He was impatient when she came out, pushing her round to retie her hands.

Then he cried out, 'Murdering bitch!' and fell back screaming like a girl which brought the others running.

'Good Lord,' Tyler said, smacking her full in the face with his fist so she sat down hard.

She could see Karl sitting on the grass cursing in German, holding on to his face where she had got him with her nails, missing his eyes. The dark chemical stuff seeped through his fingers.

'My God, man,' Tyler said, like a schoolmaster to a boy, 'what's that all over your face?'

'What you think it is. She scratched me goddam it.'

Falk pulled her to her feet, holding her, and twisting the soft flesh above the elbows. He didn't say a word, just harsh breath hot against her ear with a rotten smell. No sign of it coming, he just turned and kicked, right in the stomach, like someone kicking a dog without any sign of anger, merely to teach it a lesson.

She was out, unconscious, and awoke hearing Tyler saying, 'That's good time wasted. She's all right now.'

Kitty did not understand the questions about money. They'll pay a ransom, she told them, her family would, any reasonable amount. Of course they'd pay.

They didn't seem to want to hear that. They seemed to think she'd brought a large sum of money into the country, but she could not understand why they thought any sensible person would do a thing like that. Karl went through the suitcases, ripping the lining, smashing bottles of make-up. The scent of Arpege filled the air, smelling like a drug counter, and her clothes were everywhere.

'What's this, for the love of God?' Tyler said. There was the sound of shuffling paper. Tyler began to speak in a mocking voice, as full of frustration as it was of comic irony. '"Deep down all an erring gal's thoughts are of Sidney."' It was the letter to Sidney she had been writing in the morning in the hotel. '"How's the old tennis elbow?" Now what the hell's that?' Tyler asked.

'Code?' the German boy said.

'Don't be a fool,' Tyler said. She heard him crumple the paper and toss it aside. The man stamped about, full of rage. 'Jesus,' he shouted, 'where is it? I'll cut the cunt out of yous, you bitch.' Then she felt his boot kicking at her, swearing at her in that ugly voice that filled her with contempt. How low and vulgar he was, and stupid with his ugly shouting voice going out of control. Tyler began to use his broad leather farmer's belt on her, each blow like ice, and then turning very hot. When he grew tired, he gave the belt to Karl. She could see Karl's face very pale, raked with red scratches, where she'd gone for him. He got puffed out and sat down, angry. Kitty lay there feeling she would never be able to move again. Karl holding up a pair of black silk cami-knickers, expensive ones, bought for Paris.

'Sezy,' he said.

Only one hope, she thought. MacBride. Oh, MacBride, did you wait for me. Did you wonder what had happened, when wild horses wouldn't have kept me away? You're the only person in the world who might wonder or start an alarm. No one else would know for weeks. Oh, Mary, Mother of God . . . Surely the watch must have stopped. Can it be only 9.30 in the morning, Kitty thought, looking at the second hand turning on her slim, very expensive wristwatch.

11

MacBride regained a consciousness that was too painful to open his eyes and gaze upon. He slowly stretched out, feeling fingers, and wriggling toes in stockinged feet. He seemed to be lying in a coffin; someone else's coffin, to judge by the restrictions of length. He raised himself to a sitting position and opened his eyes. He was fully clad, except for shoes, coat and necktie, lying in a strange bathtub. The sun was streaming in, shining in a cruel fashion on garish brass and gleaming porcelain.

How he loved these moments, painful as they were physically. Such mornings were among the chief pleasures of his youth, when he had escaped the restrictions of childhood and school, Campbell College, the Eton of Ulster, and gone up to university here at Trinity. He recognised the bathroom, right down to the evil-looking face flannel draped over the edge of the bathtub, which might have been the flannel of his youth. If he were a character in Charles Dickens, he thought, he would start going on about the face flannel, like they do about Little Nell's shoe. Here he was, over forty, if not quite fifty, and still acting like an undergraduate.

He stood and stepped from the sun-filled, painful-to-the-eyes first-thing-in-the-morning bathtub and quickly felt for cash in his trouser pocket.

It was there still, some of it. Enough. No office called to him. He had no lecture to give. No wife fretted at home for him, with hungry kids clutching at her apron strings as she telephoned the police and hospitals to inquire about his fate. This was joy. A curative jar or two, and it would be pure joy, stretching out through what was left of the morning and into the long and sunny afternoon. He thought there was a reading – a poetry reading – that evening, somewhere in Dublin; he'd got it written down on a piece of paper he put somewhere safe, in his coat or trouser pocket, or, perhaps, between the pages of a book. There was plenty of time for that. The evening was a world away.

He remembered nothing of how he had got there, wherever in College he was. Even when he staggered out of the bathroom and into a small sitting-room full of heavy old-fashioned furniture and stacks of unruly books covering the floor, he could not recall what had happened. Nor did he recognise the tall smiling, red-cheeked young fellow who sat at a small table in the room writing furiously; except that MacBride had often enough awakened in just such a manner as this and strolled or staggered into an adjoining room to come upon many such strangers. It was familiar ground, and welcomed.

'Awake at last,' this person said, very friendly.

'Where am I?' MacBride said.

The tall student leapt to his feet and embarked upon a show of agitated solicitousness. The tall student wanted to be a playwright; MacBride was a published poet from the great outside world. The fact that MacBride was old enough to be the tall student's own father had only troubled the student at first the night before. When MacBride had been revealed as G.A. MacBride, the Ulster poet, drunk in the Shelbourne Bar, the tall student had thought this might be one of the great chance meetings of his life, which he would speak of, when he himself was famous, and would be written about by literary journalists in *Hibernia* and the English weeklies.

'I'm Jim Parsons,' the tall student said, 'these are my rooms in Trinity, in Dublin.'

MacBride laughed. He sat down heavily in one of the chairs.

Parsons asked, 'Want a drop of whiskey in the coffee?' He strode about, fussing. MacBride took the mug and poured the whiskey in himself.

'How did I get here?'

'You just came along and sort of stayed.'

'Oh,' MacBride said. He rose and walked carefully to the window and looked out. His head swam and he stepped backwards as he looked down at the people coming and going five floors beneath. They were in a rather grim barrack-like building behind Front Square. It hadn't changed much.

'That's Botany Bay,' Parsons said. Of course, MacBride thought, that's what they used to call it in his day, too.

'My God!' MacBride said. Botany, he thought, that reminds me. He remembered the American woman telling him she did something called minoring in botany. 'There's a girl,' MacBride said.

'You were on about a girl last night. You were really very amusing. Very funny about it. Beatrix thought it was a cat you were looking for, at first.'

'Beatrix?'

'The tall girl. With the shawl you wrapped yourself in, the shawl in the bath. When you climbed in the bath. You said you wanted to marry her, now this other woman was lost to you. We all laughed. At least, I did. Beatrix kept going on about her shawl. She's hopelessly middle class about possessions.'

Parsons poured whiskey into his coffee mug, smiling, and imagining the fine tales he could tell about being on a pub crawl in Dublin with G.A. MacBride.

'I've got to use a phone,' MacBride said. 'I've got to make sure she's not dead or dying in a foreign land.'

'We could kill two birds with one stone,' Parsons said, 'if we went to some suitable hotel, with a bar and a telephone.'

'Last night,' MacBride said, 'indeed, yesterday afternoon at the races at the Curragh, I wasn't as sober as I am now.'

'Oh, really?' Parsons said.

'Yes,' MacBride said, missing Parsons' comic irony, 'I saw her in a car, but being, well, having had a bit too much, I wasn't sure.'

'And now you are?'

'What?'

'Sure.'

'Yes. I think she's been abducted.'

'Whatever for?'

'Ransom. She has rich connections.'

'Oh,' Parsons said. He was disappointed. He had envisaged a day of poetry and the arts, not cops and robbers.

'The IRA,' MacBride said. 'They're always looking for money.'

Parsons looked down at his feet. He did not want to know about the IRA. His own large Anglo-Irish family, of ancient Protestant stock, lived in a big house far in the south, and had done so since before Cromwell. His grandfather had had some trouble with the Fenians in 1921 or 1922, a shot had been fired at the old man, and a few outbuildings burned down. But his grandfather had died in bed at ninety-three sometime in the 1970s. Ulster was a far-away country of whose people Jim Parsons knew very little.

'Of course,' MacBride said, 'she could be safe and sound in hospital. Well, not exactly sound, but as well as can be expected.'

'Yes,' Parsons said. 'And she could just have stood you up.'

'Indeed,' MacBride said, 'that is an explanation.'

Paddy Kiernan got to the bar in the sidestreet near Amiens Street Station before Doyle. The place was just opening for morning business, and it was empty except for Paddy and the barman. Paddy went to the bar and asked for a pint. Then he went to the gents. When he got back to the bar, Doyle still wasn't there. Paddy thought of leaving. But then he'd quite likely end up in a ditch with his kneecaps drilled.

Jesus, he thought, they use the drills you put the wheels on motor cars to do it. Christ, a bullet in the back of the head would be a blessing with the kneecaps gone that way. Paddy standing at the bar felt as though his legs were very thin and vulnerable inside his rough trousers. It's not 'they' drill the knees, he thought. It's us. Paddy sat down in a dark corner.

Once the door opened and Paddy looked round quickly, but it was only a local drunk. The barman paid no attention to the drunk, who sat against the wall by the only door. The drunk didn't order anything, or speak. He sat with his chin on his chest, gazing down at something that wasn't there.

Outside, the sun in the street failed to penetrate the bar. The dark room was meanly furnished with cheap plastic-topped tables and wooden stools. The bars in Communist countries were probably like this, Paddy thought, if they had bars there at all. Every now and then a train passed on the elevated section of the line to Belfast above the roofs of the mean blackened buildings in the street. It wasn't pleasant at all, even by Paddy's standards. The trains shook the beer in Paddy's glass. He wondered if he'd be able even to imagine a dirty little dive like this once he'd been out in the sun of Australia or South Africa for a while.

Brendan Walsh was dead. Paddy felt he was coming to the end of an era. Brendan was dead, and Sean was like a shuffling old woman, fussing about a warm teapot. Old, they all were now. It had come to that. Brendan was murdered. Whichever Orange bastard had actually done it, it was Liam's fault. Liam was the one who'd destroyed everything, with his talk of rockets and missiles and international financing deals with foreign terrorist groups with nothing at all to do with Ireland. And when Liam O'Tomas, the cold English fucker, learned Brendan was dead, all he could do was curse because he was afraid of what Flynn would say about the American woman. He'd try to wriggle out of it, but Mr O'Tomas was in dead lumber now with Mr Flynn, Paddy thought. Flynn, what could he do, with men like me and Sean and Brendan, not an able-bodied physical specimen among us, and all thick as two short planks.

Of course, the English bastard was right, they were past it. Must be, if an old stager like Brendan could get suckered. Still, how that poor girl Niamh could stand the man, Paddy would never know.

Paddy remembered the look on her face last night as she knelt there with nothing on at all under her dressing gown and stroked Liam's face. There was no understanding women, and best to keep away from them for anything important. That look on her face had been for the man who did everything but murder Brendan with his own hands, which said something about the truth of female emotions. Lovely white breasts, and the swaying of her arse moving inside the blue gown. There'd be girls with breasts brown from the sun in Australia. An Irishman who could handle his drink would get a job easy enough out there as a barman in one of those bars they have with no walls right on the beach.

He needed to piss now. He shifted on the seat. If Doyle came in while he was in the gents, he'd think he'd decided not to turn up. But what a cheerless place to wait for the man who was offering the business opportunity of a lifetime. Even so, it wasn't easy. But Sean would be better off in prison for a while. Otherwise he'd end up like Brendan. And it'd keep him off the booze.

Paddy started to take a swallow of beer and then, remembering he had no money for another pint, let it dribble back into the glass.

Jaysus, he needed a piss, but there was Doyle now. Not a clown any more, but once again the Seducer, leading Paddy Kiernan to a high place. Doyle loomed melodramatically huge against the brief light of the open door. Paddy gazed about the room. There was only the one other man in the place, and he sat leaning against the wall half dead.

Doyle stood at the bar buying drinks, then came to Paddy. 'It's good to see you again,' Doyle said. He wore a long unseasonal overcoat, almost to his ankles, which he took off and laid carefully across a neighbouring table. He looked funereal, in a dark suit, like someone in a bank.

'I haven't decided anything yet,' Paddy said. 'I'm still thinking,' he said.

'My offer still stands.' Doyle had a beautiful voice, like an actor. He didn't seem to care what Paddy did.

Doyle sat very still. Paddy kept waiting for him to move, but he didn't. Even Doyle's kind of a policeman, Paddy thought, must do the early years on the beat where they had to stand for hours. Or as a soldier, maybe, guarding the barrack gates at Gormanstown at night although no one ever dreamed in those years that they might need guarding for real. They must learn keeping still like that, Paddy thought. Might as well be made of plaster of Paris.

Paddy got up to go to the gents. When he returned Doyle seemed not to have moved a muscle, in spite of looking so uncomfortable on the plastic stool, a big man like that.

They talked carefully of other things. Doyle seemed to understand the dilemma he had created for Paddy. Doyle might have known Liam, too, the way he talked of the old days and how a new breed of fanatical psychopaths and Red Trotskyites were changing the old ways. Fanatical psychopaths, they were, and international Marxist terrorists. Must think I'm soft, Paddy thought, waving The Plough and the Stars like we'd been boys together at the Post Office.

'Have another?' Doyle said. He pulled out a wad of notes. 'Here,' Doyle said, 'to tide you over. While you make up your mind.' Doyle put three or four notes on the table, and quickly gathered the glasses. He spoke and smiled like an uncle with a favourite nephew.

'And if I don't do it?'

Doyle shrugged. 'I'll be able to lose it on the claim form, the much-maligned taxpayer will never know.'

Paddy put the money in the inside breast pocket of his jacket. Doyle was at the bar.

'Slainthe,' Doyle said, when he returned with the drinks.

They drank in silence. A train whistled. Then a scruffy girl of about twelve came through the door and pulled at the sleeve of the man slumped against the wall.

'Me Ma says the dinner's on the table,' the girl said, and already she had the voice of the mature nag. Doyle smiled, the smile of a man who knew he would never have children, and did not really regret it.

'Dinner,' Paddy said, 'I haven't even had breakfast yet.'

The barman shouted at the child.

Paddy's father had had to be begged home from bars often enough. But a man like Doyle, Paddy thought, no matter how much he might wander the backstreets, did not really know, not from first hand where it counted. Doyle had never been poor. He had been cared for and educated. He was a big man with wide shoulders and large hands, but he had had it easy. Paddy could tell. The real world would not rub off on him even in twenty-five years in that job of his.

Doyle offered Paddy a cigarette.

'Is that gin you're drinking?' Paddy asked.

'Tonic water,' Doyle said. 'I was on the sauce last night.'

'There's a woman,' Paddy said. It just came out like that. Like reading out a letter. It wasn't difficult. 'An American woman.' He stopped. Doyle was suddenly alert. He hadn't expected me to come out with it like that, Paddy said to himself. 'She's bringing money,' Paddy said, 'or access to money. Real money. To pay for rockets.' It was too easy, he thought. Once you started, the words just tumbled out. He hadn't intended to mention it yet.

He didn't look at Doyle. He spoke with his head down, talking into his drink. Doyle had to lean forward to hear him.

'A woman?' Doyle asked. 'What woman?'

'We saw her into Shannon Friday morning.'

'Wait a minute,' Doyle said. 'What woman?'

'An American woman,' Paddy said. 'She was on her way here, then yesterday afternoon she disappeared. They got her at the races.'

'What do you mean, the races?'

'At the Curragh. D'you credit it, she went to the races. On a job like hers. Do you know Brendan Walsh?'

'I know Brendan Walsh.'

'They got Brendan Walsh.'

'The RUC say it was a road accident,' Doyle said.

'It was no accident.'

'I didn't think so,' Doyle said. So, he thought, it isn't the money and the sunshine of Australia, it's the lost comrade. A sentimental Irishman after all.

Paddy said: 'She'll be in the North by now, the American. Our men are trying to find out where they're holding her. And the man organising things down here, he'll be in the North himself in a few hours' time. We're going up.'

'We?'

'Oh, him and me at least I hope, or the bastard'll drop me in it.'

'With Flynn?' Doyle asked.

'Yes,' Paddy said. 'Eammon Flynn. I don't know. I'll ring you from there.'

'I'll be here,' Doyle said.

'No one must know. We've got to make it look good,' Paddy said.

'We'll make it look good,' Doyle said, 'don't worry about that. We've done it lots before. You'd be surprised.'

He sat back.

Paddy looked at him. Doyle had odd eyes, when you looked at them, as though they'd been painted over. From all the years of giving nothing away, Paddy thought. But Doyle still seemed puzzled, Paddy could see that.

'This woman,' Doyle said. 'Who is she?'

'Kitty O'Shea, she calls herself.'

Doyle frowned. 'Kitty O'Shea?'

'It's a made-up name,' Paddy said.

'And you say your men had her?'

'She came Friday, like I said. From America. It was all fixed. And then she went to the Curragh and disappeared. She'll be over the Border now.'

Doyle looked very doubtful, as though he thought Paddy was making it up, or just building on a rumour, which is what his sort were always doing when they were anxious to show how good they were at being undercover agents. 'Kitty O'Shea?' Doyle asked.

'Kitty O'Shea was a kind of password,' Paddy said. 'We don't know her real name.'

The skinny half-starved bastard, Doyle said to himself, he's having me on. He wants to find out if the Gards had got Kitty O'Shea locked up. 'Do you have a description of this Kitty O'Shea? Do you know anything about her?'

'She hired a red Ford Escort from Ryans Car Hire at Shannon,' Paddy said. 'The car was found at the Curragh, with the rotor arm removed. She spent Friday night in a hotel on the road. With a man.'

'What man?' Doyle asked.

'Brendan Walsh,' Paddy said, 'was tailing her. She picked up a man at the hotel and went to his room.'

'Was this man the one who snatched her? What does Walsh say?'

'He don't say nothing. I told you, they killed him last night.'

'I mean what did he say?'

'He said she was a real looker, a glamour puss, he said. How do you like that, a glamour puss? And she picked up a man in the hotel bar, for loving.'

For loving, Doyle thought, how do you like that, for loving?

Doyle shook his head. What the hell is all this about, he asked himself. 'The man,' he said. 'What sort of man?'

'A man in the bar,' Paddy said. 'She was an holiday. She was pretending she was on holiday, at least. Get themselves fucked by strange men, that's what American women do on holiday, isn't it?'

Paddy stood up to go. Doyle did not move. I've got to get this right, he told himself. Make sure of the facts when you're involving the British security forces in the North. It wouldn't be the first time, he thought, they'd gone off half-cock up in the North on a tip from the Republic and finished up empty-handed.

'I'll ring,' Paddy said. They shook hands. Paddy went out. The sudden sunlight hurt his eyes. That hadn't been too hard, he thought. Too easy, almost. He was bursting for a piss again, but he could not go back in the bar now.

In the bar, Doyle looked with distaste at the glass of soda water. 'Whiskey, I think,' he said to the barman. Codename Kitty O'Shea, he said to himself, but they probably had a million Kitty O'Sheas in the United States of America.

12

Lucky birds, no wind to speak of, the hills are protection. No, stop that, that'll start the crying again. Don't ever cry, whatever happens. It must be Sunday afternoon.

Outside the hillside was purple and bright green in the streaming sunshine. A blue sky, with little white clouds high in the air.

The door was only half open. The blindfold had slipped down so the left eye could see. Surely they must know? A smell of dry straw, and dust. No one's lived here for years. Not even animals. The contents of the suitcases all strewn. Bottles broken. A ballpoint pen even snapped in two. A Nieman Marcus silk blouse torn. And the pants weren't cheap either. It's not possible to believe this could be the end. Death and eternal life are for other people. Her father may have died, but he was her father, and fathers do die. The floor was covered with litter. They've been here waiting, count the meals they've had to tell the days there's been someone here. The German boy looks just like anyone. Does he see he's being watched? His face all claw marks. Scratch his eyes out – it's said often enough. His library. Porno magazines. Girls with dildoes. They're Asian girls. Filipinos. Or Thais. Do anything for the money. Just like pieces of meat. That's what the Church teaches – taught – against in Pagan Rome. But they had all kinds of gods in Rome, too. Great big dildoes protruding, and those asinine grins to the camera. Poor things. But are they so poor? Making a living. Men like Brooks would. Sidney, too, on a scientific conference in Bangkok – to study The Psychosocial Aspects of Buddhism. My foot. Karl holding the magazine up. Written in German, but he's not reading. Wants to shock, knows he's being watched. Please God, as long as they're afraid of being identified, there's hope of being freed in the end.

Tyler said to Karl, 'Put it down.' Does he see the eye through the

108

blindfold watching? Falk could be identified. The blindfold because they don't want to see the eyes when they do it to a woman. They're nervous now. They smell different when they're scared, like animals. And the way they move. Playing cards now – perhaps that's what Tyler said to Karl, asking him to stop reading the magazine and play cards. Maybe Tyler doesn't know, but Karl held up the Asian girls with the giant dildo in the magazine.

The card players were on her blind side, and she dared not turn her head, but every time Karl played a card, she could hear him make a wet slapping sound, like an old man, with his lips. They were playing gin rummy.

Tyler doesn't like losing. What is it they want to know? Who's the woman? They keep going on about money, where it is. What kind of woman could get herself mixed up? They've been through everything in the cases, places no one in his right mind would think of. Never seen a Tampax before. Tyler the boss, no doubt of that. As if anyone would hold out against this, just for money. What do they want to know after they heard about Brooks? They know where to get Brooksie. He would pay. Against his principles, to trade with kidnappers, terrorists; supposed to be a lawyer, after all. But what else do people pay lawyers like Brooks for – taxman, corporation law – except to get round principles? A loophole – Brooks would find one so he could pay. Sidney might cough up. They must know by now there's no money here. What do they expect to make them believe it? If they hurt a woman really badly and she still doesn't say, then they would believe. That's what they'll do.

And the woman they obviously thought she was, how would she behave? Spit at them. Yell and scream. That kind of woman maybe didn't feel afraid like this. She'd expect it. She'd deserved it. Probably laugh if she knew, without an ounce of pity, she'd be like them. Wouldn't feel any guilt. There but for the grace of God, she'd think. She was a patriot, wasn't she? She lived to fight another day.

In Kitty's soul there was a lonely, alien feeling of something lost. Perhaps she was not really Irish. Not that her family ever bore any other names but Irish ones. But what made her Irish, after all? They had no relatives they knew of in Ireland. The O'Sheas did not even know from which county they came, which was usually a great boast among the Irish in America, who delighted in saying those simple but exotic names: Cork, Sligo, Mayo, Kerry, County Clare.

There were apparently O'Sheas everywhere, but she knew none of them. Her father had been Judge O'Shea. They had lived in Holford Park. The fact of her Irish name had never made a bit of difference to the way she felt or to the way other people treated her.

Sometimes, of course, when she was little – seven or eight years old with a camel hair coat with a brown velvet collar and her hair in braids – it was embarrassing going in a car past some low dive and seeing it called O'Shea's Bar and Grill, and a great schoolgirl wit like Prudence Brown or Mimi Vallard would point and say, 'I do believe that's Kitty's family's establishment.' Or else it would be a real low-class, neon funeral parlour, saying 'O'Shea's' and they'd say something else witty. But it had nothing to do with the O'Sheas of Judge O'Shea's family.

There wasn't any harm in schoolgirls making fun. Kitty was pretty and her family had money. No, there wasn't any harm in it at all. America was so full of different people; much more so than Ireland or any other place in Europe, except perhaps Russia.

And that other woman wouldn't know, anyway. No one knew. Only MacBride, and he didn't even know he knew. What kind of White Knight was that?

Tyler said something to Karl about the toolbox in the car. Karl got up from the table where they'd been playing cards. He shoved the chair back so roughly it tipped over. Nervous about something, Kitty thought. And Tyler walking about tight-lipped, grim, making some decision. They're going to use a knife, won't risk a gunshot being heard, they're very nervous. Or maybe it's just the car's broken down. Imagination runs away. The door opened wide, thank God for fresh air, if only he'd leave the door open wide like that all the time. Something is wrong with the car. Perhaps they've decided to leave. Does that mean it's over? Are they giving up? How to explain this to the police? Going over and over it. Just be glad to get away. Promise anything, and they're safe. Who would wait around while they went through the process of law? Out by the first plane.

The German boy back, looking very grim. And nervous. Karl put the toolbox on the table down among the playing cards. Tyler started rummaging through it, making a lot of noise and breathing hard. Falk's there, somewhere, Kitty thought, being silent.

What are they doing now? She could see Karl with a Stanley knife. He had a flat stone in his other hand. He looked very pale and young. She went to scream, but she couldn't with the gag in her mouth.

Falk watched, scarcely blinking. They would kill her, of course. The question was when. Look at them though, practically falling over themselves to touch her, making up to a dead thing. She knew. She was waiting. It showed in the way she held herself, the expectation of death. Tossing her head about trying to see. Falk could see her startled eye watching in horror through the gap in the blindfold. But not him, never a glance at him. He was almost invisible against the dark walls and dried-out earth of the floor, standing in a corner away from the light.

What was she thinking of, that brassy little mind of hers whirring? The Yank swank didn't last long. The Colleen Queen of the Holyoke St Patrick's Day Parade. Bunch of red-faced Mickies.

Falk looked away, full of bitter ironic day-dreams of the Irish-Americans parading through the streets of some far-off Massachusetts milltown. Then he turned again and watched the nervous German boy attempting to cut off her finger. Looked a bit different now, the Colleen Queen, black hair wild swishing like the tail of a dirty tinker's horse, white skin all swelled and red. Sins of the flesh under the scourge of judgement, except Tyler's soft. He doesn't like it. Needs the whiskey. Big mouth wet on the lip of the bottle. The Irish Kiss, big baby at the teat. And mother's boy, the German, too, some kind of tourist, over for the thrills, but his throat jerking like a metronome with that giant Adam's apple. Looks like a new-born rat. Shouldn't be here. A weak link. Surprised at Tyler allowing. What did he want with a creature spawned by a fat Hun cow probably sitting now in Frankfurt, wondering, What's young Karl doing now? Out with some nice American girl, studying anatomy. He'll probably vomit now the finger's off, very bloody, just the start. Tyler going white at the gills. Looks like he's going to tell her it hurt him more than it did her. Once a bloody publican, always a publican. Screaming inside that gag fit to raise the dead, but not the living, they don't hear.

111

13

A trick of light or trompe d'oeil threw up a sheer chalk cliff so it seemed to Paddy Kiernan that he saw a mighty citadel standing in the blurred sunlight. Beautiful, he thought, it's beautiful, like a picture book.

He and Liam in the old blue van were approaching Derry on the main Belfast road. What Paddy was seeing in the trick of light was the Creggan Estate, viewed from across the River Foyle. He saw now it was only a housing estate, but for a moment it had looked to be a natural phenomenon, a sheer rock face, a natural protection for a beleaguered people against marauders coming from the river.

Paddy drove down the road towards the bridge; the white-washed houses climbing up the slope of the far hill had returned to everyday life. It was an ordinary grubby and run-down patch of Corporation housing bisected by a stark and prominent straight road. A poor lookout, he thought, when a glorious patriotic symbol like that was simply a trick of light.

Liam sat beside him in the van. He still looked pale. They had scarcely spoken since they left Dublin. That was hours before. The old van was not built for speed.

Now that he had spoken to Doyle, Paddy was not keen about going with Liam to Derry to see Flynn. It was a trip he did not relish, but Liam O'Tomas would blame Paddy and Sean, and Brendan Walsh, too, of course, for the Orangemen getting the American woman. Christ, Paddy thought, if we'd brought Sean along Flynn'd see Liam's point all right. Also, he told himself, if he did not meet with Flynn, how then could he tell Doyle anything? Jesus, if they knew he'd spoken to Doyle. Paddy could feel the sweat in his armpits. He looked at Liam to see if the Englishman could see how frightened he was, but Liam was staring ahead, looking sorry for himself in what Paddy thought was a typically English way.

Paddy was going to duck the Derry trip but then Niamh had rung him on the communal phone at the bottom of the flights of stairs at the Corporation block on the North Side of Dublin where he lived. First thing in the morning, she'd called, but still she'd been lucky to catch him. He had a few quid from Doyle. He had half a mind to scarper then and there. Get to London. It wasn't Australia or the South Seas but Niamh told him she wanted Paddy to drive Liam to Derry. She was worried about his health. There was something forlorn in the girl's voice. The sound of her voice, a woman beseeching, touched Paddy. And then her money had run out on the phone, and it had been too late to make up an excuse not to go. It would have been easily done on the phone. Now his course as an informer was set. And in his heart of hearts, he had known ever since he accepted the business proposition that he would have to go. But Jesus, it was making him bust for a leak. The things they did to a squealer. The pliers on a fella's balls. And, of course, drilling the knees. They end up begging for the bullet. They were like men possessed by the devil, and Flynn the worst of them all. They said an animal, but animals never did that. They mean an animal has the same unblinking chewing on the still living piece of meat. The men who do it, what does it make them feel? Sean shooting the RUC man in the face. That was assassination, and, at least, Sean shook after it. Liam blowing up the English disco kids. Girls he might dance with if he ever did go dancing.

Paddy had never spent more than a few hurried minutes alone with Liam before this long ride from Dublin to Derry. These days, the man took up such a disproportionate part of his waking thoughts that Paddy had come to think of them as though they were seldom apart. But it wasn't so, of course. It was, he knew, his mind playing games. Liam didn't look himself. Very white, after the asthma, naturally – and it occurred to Paddy that the man was not at all the same person as the monster he himself had made of him. He was reduced. Oh, well, Paddy thought, it was too late now to try and find out what made him tick, or what a girl like Niamh could see in him. Paddy thought of her as a great beauty. In his mind, he endowed her with all the cheerful, friendly qualities of Maeve, the

patriotic whore of Tallaght, without Maeve's beefy red face and the
flabbiness of her large body, flab which rolled when she lay naked or
in the cheap armoury of backstreet whoredom, the black stockings
and the underwear, doing a charity fuck for Paddy Kiernan.

And what was he? Paddy asked himself. 'Scapegoat' Kiernan for
the likes of Liam. He'd get Liam for that, the bastard.

Now he broke the long silence. 'Where's Flynn's place?' he
asked.

They were crossing the bridge into the city centre, above a river
swelled and yellow with recent rain.

Liam unfolded a scrap of paper that he had held clasped in his
left hand throughout the journey, like a messenger boy with a note.
Paddy saw that the paper was limp and blotched from the sweat on
his palm.

'It's on the Creggan,' Liam said, peering to make out the words
where the ink had run.

He's falling apart, Paddy said to himself. If he went in like that,
Flynn'd shoot him on the spot.

Paddy tried to make conversation. 'Do you think his fancy woman
will be there?'

Liam didn't seem to know what Paddy was talking about.

'Fat Siobhan. You've heard of Fat Siobhan?'

'Oh, yes, her,' Liam said. 'She lives in Belfast, though. He has
a daughter here looks after him. A grown-up daughter. Yes, she's
grown-up. She keeps house for him.' He's shitting himself all right,
Paddy thought. He's shit scared.

The house was at the top of the hill on the Creggan Estate, where
the backs of the steep gardens behind the houses were on a level with
the bedroom windows. There were steps to the front door, and a
neglected patch of grass in front. Liam became quite talkative. He
smiled at Paddy. The colour had come back to the Englishman's
cheeks, and when he spoke he attempted to put some Irish into
his voice.

'There's something odd about these houses,' he said.

Paddy could see nothing odd about them.

'I know what it is,' Liam said. 'Nobody's got any flowers in their
front gardens.'

Paddy grunted.

Liam got out of the van as soon as Paddy stopped. 'I won't be long,' he said.

'I'm coming with you,' Paddy said. He's not pulling that shite, he told himself. Liam started to argue, but Paddy was already out of the van. Thought I'd fall for that, did you, you bastard. Not my fault, Mr Flynn, it's the calibre of the old men you give me. One of them in the van out there now, last century's model Paddy Kiernan. The patsy. 'Patsy' Kiernan, that'd be it. They would be looking for one. Flynn was a nasty piece of work, more intimidation than idealism.

Paddy looked about; there was little sign of the gangster's profits here. Probably keeps the riches under wraps, he thought.

Liam knocked on the old-fashioned door-knocker. They could hear a vacuum cleaner at work inside the house. A young woman opened the door. She seemed in a bad temper.

'He's expecting you,' she said, pointing towards an open door off the narrow hallway. She hadn't turned off the vacuum cleaner to answer their knock. She let out a deep sigh when she shut the front door loudly behind them.

The famous Flynn did not get up as Liam and Paddy came into the room. He was sitting in a large armchair by the empty fireplace, his feet resting on the edge of a low glass-topped table.

You wouldn't look twice at him in the street, Paddy thought. Paddy was disappointed. The man looked like a school teacher or someone who worked in a bank, with his neat reddish greying beard and the long strands of hair smoothed carefully across the balding top of his skull. Must have been a bit of a weakling at school, Paddy thought. Flynn also looked as though he had suffered severely from acne as a kid. That's why the beard, Paddy thought. The great man's teeth were badly stained, and the fingers of both hands were dark yellow with nicotine. He was smoking a cigarette now, and Paddy noticed that the ashtray which was built into the arm of his chair was brimming over. Flynn stubbed out the cigarette and reached absent-mindedly for the pack on the glass table. It was an awkward movement and he had to take his legs off the table to reach it. Paddy and Liam stood and watched him take his legs from the table and reach for the packet of cigarettes as if they were seeing a magic trick being performed.

'Tea?' Flynn shouted, looking over his shoulder to the door of the sitting-room. There was no answer. 'She's in a mood,' Flynn said. 'Round slamming doors and breathing heavy all morning. And the vacuum on full blast. Whoever said a daughter brings comfort to a man in his old age? Well,' Flynn said, 'What's all this, then?'

He let Liam tell the story about Kitty O'Shea. Liam didn't tell it very well, Paddy thought. Flynn asked what Liam had done to make sure she was safe. When Liam mentioned Brendan, Flynn cut him short. He said he didn't need Liam to tell him about Brendan Walsh. That stopped Liam. Paddy thought he could hear the rasping sound of the asthma coming back.

'Tea, then,' Flynn said. He shouted for tea, but the daughter never answered. They heard the vacuum going. Then it stopped.

'Ah,' Flynn said, but then there was the sound of the door slamming. 'No tea then,' Flynn said. 'Poor Brendan,' he said. 'He was a hero of the Congo. Did you know that? But that, of course, was long ago. Us old fellows, we should step out of the way, make room for the young men, am I right, Paddy Kiernan? You'll take a whiskey, Mr Kiernan?' he said. 'You're no Pioneer, I take it?' Paddy smiled. A couple of old comrades together, Paddy thought.

Paddy needed the drink.

'Go on, drink it down,' Flynn said. 'To Brendan Walsh.' Then he said, 'He should never have been on his own. You should have gone, O'Tomas. There should have been two of you.'

Suddenly Paddy knew that the Englishman had already been tried and condemned by Flynn. Flynn stood up and went to turn on the television set. 'There's a race I want to see,' he said, sitting down again. 'We lost a packet at the Curragh on Saturday,' he said. Then he laughed. 'You can stop fretting,' Flynn said. 'I can set your minds at rest.' He put on a pair of metal-rimmed spectacles. He was concentrating on the television. 'We know where the woman is,' he said.

Paddy had a second whiskey and he sat there wishing he had a third.

'Our young American friend,' Flynn said, 'is not far from Limavady. It won't be long before we have the exact spot. I've good men working on it.' He seemed more interested in the racing but he looked away from the horses. 'You'll get your chance, O'Tomas,' he said. He turned to Paddy. 'You'll be fit to drive back to Dublin, then?'

116

Paddy was careful not to slam the front door behind him as he left the house, thinking all the time: what a turn-up for the books if what he had to tell Doyle would save Liam's life. If Doyle didn't get to this lot first, Liam was a dead man. That was the way it was. Liam should have known that. He could have made a run for it when the American woman got taken; gone back to England and called himself Lionel Thompson again, sitting round Croydon somewhere calling the Irish a pack of ignorant Micks. Perhaps he was a braver man than Paddy gave him credit for. Or even more of a fool. That was more likely, the way he had been just sitting there not knowing when Paddy knew right off and could feel it there in the room all around them.

Paddy drove down the hill. In his jacket pocket, he could feel the strip of card on which Doyle had written the telephone number which would always reach him, day or night. That was a bit of stupidity, bringing that, he thought. He should have memorised the number. But he'd probably have disremembered it by now. But he wasn't going to run straight to a telephone box. Flynn's men might be watching. There'd be a telephone along the way. First, Paddy had to deal with a much more urgent priority, which had become ever more pressing in that close little sitting-room in Flynn's house; and, he thought, he might as well have a drink to settle the nerves. Then, if they were watching, they'd report back that he was just the drunken old has-been Flynn had known all the time he was. She was in an old cabin outside Limavady. Doyle would have the RUC and the British Army there and Flynn would be there, and the Orangemen inside. It would be the hell of a bust-up.

14

Blood poisoning makes people rave in delirium, they'd be disappointed what they'd get, load of stuff about Brooksie, or perhaps Grandad O'Shea's French-Canuck girl he kept for years across the bridge in Willimansett, when all the family thought he was working for charity. The fuss they made about that when it came out. An early memory. Hypnotism, you go back to early childhood. More likely the night with MacBride, the last pleasant night to remember, but it wouldn't take much, the atmosphere in here is absolutely tense, the German's the worst, right on the edge, they get at him all the time, talking as though he weren't here, making him do all the dirty work. On the last trip to that lavatory, he seemed close to tears. He must have known already that they'd like to be shot of him. It makes him pathetic, though, his knowing what they think of him. He tied the ropes even tighter afterwards, really twisted them, afraid for his eyes again. Not that the pain in the finger isn't enough to drive a person mad. Beating, like a pulse. Does that face of his hurt? He knows about the eye, he can see it watching, caught that look standing there in the beautiful light with the purple hill, and wild marjoram, just growing, and he put his hand to his cheek where it was really gashed. Then he looked as if he was going to cry or hit out. But he only tied them really tight and said something in German. There was something then, youth calling to youth; and the same class.

Can all that stuff he said be true, about what they've done? He must have been shooting a line to frighten me into telling them about all that money. No one could do that to little kids, could they? God, it was horrible, that story of the people blown to pieces and the blood dripping from the branches of the trees in the orchard. Do those bullets they use really explode inside the soldiers? He enjoyed telling it, anyway. That stiff English 'the velocity of the bullet is three thousand, eight hundred feet per second'. As if a woman would be interested in that.

He got the painkillers, though. Why should he do that? He wasn't supposed to do that. The pain makes it impossible to think of anything else except the pain. He got a Grateful Beauty smile as though he'd brought roses, like that boy from the Williston Northampton School who had the thalidomide arms and hands and brought that big bunch of autumn damasks when he had a crush on the Holyoke Colleen Queen. How did he carry them, a great big bunch of roses? Of course painkillers make a person drowsy. He's scared he'll get his eyes scratched out again. Better doped up, that's all it is and not kindness.

Just one little finger of the right hand missing, will it be like a cripple, people turning away? 'I kiss your hand, Madame,' a funny old song, 'Your dainty finger tips run up and down my lips.' Next time they'll cut off another. Then another. Be like that poor Williston boy with a crush, hitch-hiking over to Miss Davenport's with that big bunch of old-fashioned yellow roses. It's enough to make anyone cry, thinking of him. And Mimi Vallard, so cruel and heartless, said, 'How ever did he ever thumb a ride?' They jest at scars who never felt. Try to pray to Jesus now for all of us together. Please God, no more of it. That's the worst, waiting for the next time. Squat a woman down on broken glass. 'In Algeria,' Karl said, 'the French did that thing, got a lot of nice information doing that,' he said in that flat German accent.

The wind was getting up in the trees outside. There must be trees, she thought, out of sight somewhere. The wind was stirring the dust on the floor, and there was the smell of herbs carried in on the breeze. Oh God, she thought, how beautiful it was. But the whole of her right hand was throbbing, and she felt a dreadful chill all over. Everyone's held together by pain, she thought, but each alone. When it comes to it. Brooks, Sidney, even MacBride, had loved her. The man went through a most bizarre, singular act of worship, all curious ritual gyrations and salaams before the Temple of the Female, offering up the phallus as if it were a religious act. 'With my body I thee worship.' When she wasn't being carried away by lust she used to find it all ridiculous, and disgusting, sometimes, too. How simple and beautiful that all seems now. Not like Karl's Asian girls, with dildoes, pieces of meat. Crazy men, chop off a woman's finger like a butcher chopping chops. Nasty boys cutting off a poor little grass snake's head – Conrad Wayland it was, from Morgan Street – then chased the girls with the red stump where the head had been. 'Boys will be boys,' mother said, as though boys were another form of life altogether. Why should men be different?

They're going out again. If they leave Karl here alone, he'll start his torture stories. He was talking before about wiring up a person for electric shocks. Said they'd got electrodes, recourse to electricity, he said, with the car batteries. Common practice in Latin America, Karl said. They pour water on a person to boost the charge, Karl said. The German talks if the others go out.

What time is it? Still light outside, anyway, or the birds wouldn't be making that racket. Fighting, some of them, making the hell of a din. Even birds! Violence just makes them forget everything else while they fight it out. Any predator could just pick them off. Isn't that odd? It's more powerful than the instinct to survive. Don't suppose there are many cats round here, though. But foxes, and the birds of prey get them while they're squabbling.

Must think. Listen to that blackbird. Is there anywhere in the world where the blackbird doesn't sing like that? How to escape? That's the thing. And then, where is this place? What are they going to do? Who are they? Think it out, make a list. Sidney's a great man for lists, and he spends his life with loonies. Not like these, though. Sidney's loonies know there's something wrong. Full circle, back to Ireland where it all began. Poor mother'll be upset. And Sidney? Sidney'll be heartbroken because the beastly world has singled him out for another painful blow to make him suffer all the more on top of the kids' orthodontist bills and the alimony to Miss B.U. And then he'll laugh at himself for thinking such a thing.

That German boy is really young. Probably he thinks this is idealistic stuff. God, the way he stares, knowing he's being watched. How long has he been watching? The thought of him.

'I know you can see,' Karl said to Kitty. 'If I thought you wouldn't start screaming I'd take out that gag out your mouth. But I think you'd bite.' He undid the gag. Her hands and feet were still tied.

'A drink,' she said. 'I need water.' The German boy brought a cup. 'Thanks,' Kitty said. He had to hold it to her lips and the water ran down her chin and neck. When he went to kiss her she showed him she wouldn't bite. 'I can't with my legs tied,' she said. She smiled as if it were a joke, her being tied up like that. Let him do it, she thought. He'll do it anyway. Open them for him. Be willing. His horrible soft mouth at the tit. This is their weak link. Tell him he's the greatest fuck. No worse than those Asian girls in the magazine, they all pretend. He's wriggling about, no more thrusting than a girl. He can't do it and all of a sudden squirting like a kid. That look in their eyes afterwards, cowed, even MacBride was like that, all of them like that, and then all strutting about.

A sudden quick gust of fresh air. The door opening and closing in the wind. Someone was out there. Was probably there all the time. The crowman Falk. Had to be. Karl whingeing, says he's put upon. He says he is a student of urban warfare and guerrilla tactics, but his skills are not appreciated by Tyler and the primitive Irishman.

Are they the IRA? No, can't be. The woman they wanted was bringing money from back home for the IRA. An American woman. But not to them. These are the others, whatever they call themselves. The followers of that big preacher who sounds like an Old Testament prophet when he's on the TV news. Karl wants to get away from here. Listen to him – how bad they are to him, how they hold him back and stifle his imagination. Money's the key. It exists. Not here. What kind of a courier would walk round with the stuff on her? Bank drafts, a signature. Tell him that. Sounds convincing, anyway. He doesn't know about that stuff. They're gone. Poor Karl, left with the woman.

'Sezy?'

What's sezy? Oh, sexy. My Paris drawers. Tell him, together, afterwards, we'll be with the money. Get to Belfast, get the money, get out. Together. Black silk lace cami-knickers. God, what kind of woman was going to Paris?

How to get away? There must be a farm. Sheep belong to someone. Ah, anything, anything, once. Now smile. Hot for him, like he's hot for it, gazing at that stuff. Hot whore stuff, all tricked out for Paris, France.

A drink, a drink! Her voice was muffled. He understood. Ah, that's good, Karl, don't put it back on. Not till they come back. And the arms, Karl. The pain is terrible.

No, no scratching. Not anymore. He smiles and says he wouldn't like to be scratched again, even without shit.

She smiled at him. The bandage where her little finger used to be was full of blood. The hand was puffed up twice its normal size.

'When we hear the car,' Karl said, 'they must go back.'

Treat him like some prep school kid or boy from Amherst who's come over the Notch on a winter Sunday afternoon to sit around in North Mandelle, and then take you out in his car to make out when it gets dark.

'Like at home,' Karl said. 'In Hamburg. The girls in the windows wear these costumes.'

Any moment, Kitty thought, he could lash out and kill like a rattlesnake. Think of him as Brooksie as a boy, then he'll realise there's no danger to him. Just treat him like Brooksie at the very beginning when he didn't know anything at all and had to be shown.

15

Doyle lay on his bed, fully dressed except for his shoes. The telephone sat silent on the bedside table. Next to it was an English paperback edition of an American book about computers, much thumbed. It had been lent to him by Detective Sergeant Byrne who was a whizz-kid on the computers. Byrne had at one time wanted to be a priest, and the book, which Byrne said was a 'big bestseller' in America, 'proved' that the very top computer scientists kept 'running into God' every day as they 'investigated the universe'.

In the everyday earth-bound world, Doyle kept running into the devil. It was obviously more grand and altogether more wonderful exploring the realms of potential intelligence from some snug university. Doyle had been to Clongowes and Belvedere, where he played rugby. He had survived only one year at University College, Dublin. He was not academic. In the bedroom Doyle had an old black and white television set. The colour TV was in the sitting-room. What Doyle liked to watch at night was movies about old-time cops, and they were mostly in black and white. The programme he had on now was the RTE late-night religious programme. A Jesuit was talking about the Pope going to Paraguay. The Jesuit had been a long time in Latin America. Doyle thought the priest talked like a terrorist. Doyle could see the Jesuit, in dog collar and soutane (which he was not wearing now) sitting behind a machine gun under a palm tree somewhere. The priest wasn't all that progressive. He was with the Pope against birth control, and was actually talking about 'populating Heaven'. The priest didn't seem able to make the connection between over-population here on earth and Latin America's wretched slums. Each big city in Latin America, the priest was saying, had hundreds of thousands of homeless urchins, who turned to prostitution and crime. The

Pope was creating souls for the devil, Doyle thought. Populating Hell for him.

Doyle was waiting for Paddy Kiernan to telephone. He had been waiting through a film with some suave but now dead English actor playing a Wall Street stockbroker turned detective. The English actor wore a series of very expensive overcoats. Doyle, lying on his bed, thought that his one respectable weddings-and-funerals suit coat would be getting wrinkled. He got up and turned off the Jesuit. He took off his coat and hung it up.

He listened to the traffic, still heavy a block away on Ballsbridge. Someone in one of the converted mews houses, that had once been the stables for the Georgian terrace where Doyle had the top flat in the corner house, was playing a Sidney Bechet record. Doyle could just hear the higher notes, oddly punctuated by the inaudible lows. Doyle recognised that it was Sidney Bechet, which must make Sidney Bechet very unfashionable among the smart people now, he thought. He picked up the paperback from the bedside table beside the telephone, but let it drop unopened on to the duvet cover.

He knew he could not altogether blame Paddy for his own nervousness. Doyle thought he should have alerted the people in the North when he first heard about the other Kitty O'Shea. But what had he really had to tell them? It might all have been a false alarm, and it would have done across-the-Border relationships no good at all to waste their time on something he couldn't even substantiate. Once he had Kiernan's confirmation of where she was, and perhaps even who held her, he could put the wheels in motion. And keep some of the credit, at least, he thought. His side had been having a bad press recently with crazy judges freeing villains and wild goose chases over the Border. But he'd get the credit now.

At least, he would so long as Kiernan didn't let him down. It was nearly midnight.

Doyle wondered if Paddy Kiernan was really stupid enough to believe that clap-trap about going to the South Seas – Hawaii or Australia or wherever it was. Kiernan was kidding himself if he believed that. Doyle pictured the man's scarecrow figure in his shiny old First Communion suit walking along the golden sands under the green palm trees. Maybe he could go to Paraguay, Doyle thought, and help the Marxist priest with the machine gun. Paddy

Kiernan was informing because, like a lot of people, he was sick of living. Most people weren't so lucky. They didn't have such friends to betray. Friends who would waste them in a hurry. Most people had to do it the hard way, step under a bus, or go on living some more. Of course, Doyle would do his best to protect him. It was good business to protect him. But would Paddy protect himself? He wouldn't. Doyle could tell, the first or second time he met the man, that he was tired of living. Doyle knew the signs. He had them himself. Old men went on living to eighty or ninety. Fifty seemed to Doyle to be an awful lot of years to live. If you had a good memory, as Doyle had, then it seemed too long a time.

Doyle got off the bed and walked slowly into his front room. The two casement windows overlooked the street, and a similar terrace opposite. Doyle never drew his curtains. He liked to sit beside the window with the lights off, staring down at the doings of the street. The traffic warning light at the intersection gave out its winking beam, virtually lost against the street lamps. The cars still raced up the road, even at this time of night, scarcely slowing for the crossing. There would be a terrible accident there one day. A car door slammed in the street. A group of students, who lived in a flat in the house next door, got out and walked up the path to their front door, singing and laughing as though most of the residents would not have been in bed and trying to sleep by now. How did so many grown people get into one car at the same time? Doyle felt old and sour watching the students and hearing them laugh. He poured himself a whiskey, and took it back to the bedroom.

The telephone rang. It was Paddy Kiernan. He was drunk. He knew Paddy Kiernan didn't know what day it was, but he thought he should have some idea of the time. Doyle regretted giving him the money on account.

He was full of excuses. All the telephone boxes in Derry were vandalised. And, of course, he couldn't have rung from the telephone in any of the public houses where he had been trying all night to find an instrument with any kind of privacy for there wasn't a man there who didn't look like an old spy, was there now? Why even now, he was speaking from . . . well, the number had been rubbed off, so he couldn't really say for sure.

Doyle said he didn't care where he was speaking from, what had he got? It was his kidneys, Paddy said. That's what he'd got, but a few weeks in the sun would put that right. The man ran round and round in circles, as though he were deliberately teasing his paymaster. All sorts of nonsense about not involving anyone in Dublin, and how his friend would reject him utterly when he knew what he had done. Sean, he said, Sean was his best friend left now Brendan was dead. Doyle thought Paddy might start weeping or singing.

In the end, Doyle got some sense out of him. Some Loyalist paramilitaries were holding an American woman called Kitty O'Shea. She was the same one who had been snatched at the Curragh racecourse right from under Liam O'Tomas' 'long English nose', Paddy said, which was an odd thing to say, Doyle thought. She was now somewhere in the hills not far from Limavady. Flynn did not know exactly where the place was. But – and Doyle could understand that this was a big mouthful for a drunk who was as drunk as Paddy Kiernan was drunk – 'they have set in train a rescue operation which would restore her to her own kind.'

But how long had he known this? And how far off were the Derry group from finding the place? Doyle could practically hear Kiernan's brain working to avoid answering.

'Oh, just an hour or so.'

Doyle looked at his watch. After midnight now, for God's sake, and Kiernan must have been in the pub for hours.

Doyle cursed himself again for giving the shiftless bastard money. Without that, he'd have known all this hours before.

He sat on the edge of the bed when Paddy had rung off, holding the receiver in his lap.

These gangsters had an innocent woman. At least, they had the wrong woman.

Doyle still thought it possible she was a decoy for the one with the money. But either way, there was going to be the hell of a stink about it if he wasn't careful.

The Kitty O'Shea they had under lock and key, that little hell-cat, was certainly the real terrorist. A clear case of mistaken identity.

This wretched woman held near Limavady – and Doyle knew well how bleak and deserted that country was – could certainly complicate things.

It had been a successful operation so far, but now the Ulster authorities would have to be brought into it, and because the woman had got herself snatched in the Republic, it was going to be impossible to cover up a botched job. That would take the gilt off the gingerbread as far as the red-haired vixen who called herself Kitty O'Shea was concerned. Doyle now knew the real name of the woman they had arrested at Shannon Airport. They had a long computer print-out on her. A Mrs Roberta Lobello, aged 26, maiden name Byrne. Born in Tuskaloosa, Florida, March 23rd, 1962. Mother Jacqui Choquette Skinner, cocktail bar waitress, born Willimansett, Massachusetts. No data on Bruce Skinner, the mother's first husband. The father of Mrs Roberta Byrne Lobello was a Bernard Byrne, now a naturalised US citizen, but at the time of the suspect's birth, an illegal immigrant born Skibbereen Co.Cork, Republic of Ireland, and working as a bartender at Roberto's Havana Hideaway Dine 'n' Dance. Jacqui Choquette Skinner and Bernard Byrne married by Justice of the Peace in Tuskaloosa, Florida, February 14, 1962. Never lived as husband and wife. Bernard Byrne received Green Card from US Immigration, March 25, 1962. Jacqui Choquette Skinner divorced Byrne April 1, 1963, married Roberto Dann, proprietor of Roberto's Havana Hideaway Dine 'n' Dance (renamed Roberto's Cuba Libra Dine 'n' Disco in the 1970s) June 6, 1963. Roberto Dann charged child molestation November 25, 1974, bound over on own recognisance, two years' probation. Found guilty July 8, 1976, transportation of female minor over state line for immoral purposes. Sentenced three years, sentence suspended. Minor female, Roberta, aged 14, placed on probation, juvenile court. Reported missing from home December 28, 1977, age 15. No further data until September 28, 1979, aged 17, married Lamont Labello, an 18-year-old parking lot attendant in San Bernadino, California. No issue. No divorce. Roberta Lobello left the matrimonial home on or about August 6, 1980. Whereabouts unknown. No data. Husband Lamont Lobello now working as telephone repair lineman in Wichita, Kansas, seeking estranged wife's whereabouts for purpose of divorce.

'Jesus,' Doyle said aloud, 'I wonder if those computer analysts have got this much on God?' Probably, Doyle thought, there's a touch of the Bruce Skinner factor about God. No data. And, of course, the real gen was missing in all this. How did Mrs Lobello get involved with the IRA? Who were her contacts here and in the US? But, Christ, he thought, did she know that she was Roberto Dann's daughter, half-Cuban on her father's side and French on her mother's, and not Irish at all? Would it really matter to her? Not when you saw all that desperate rootlessness. Still, she bit Detective Sergeant Pat Byrne's finger. Byrne was a Corkman. I wonder, Doyle thought, if that could have been an uncle she was trying to chew.

The computer print-out on the other Kitty O'Shea showed a solid, stable background. It made for boring reading. Born Holford Park, Massachusetts. Miss Davenport's School in Northampton, Mass., Phi Beta Kappa from Mount Holyoke College, South Hadley Center, Massachusetts. Majored English Literature; minored Plant Science. Kitty O'Shea Lawrence was so boring the computer had made weight by supplying data on her parents: father born Holford Park, died Holford Park; grandfather born Holford Park, died Willimansett. And there, Doyle saw, was the only connection. That oddly named town was where the mother of the other Kitty O'Shea was born. This Kitty O'Shea was no decoy. She had married a Protestant, Brooks Acton Lawrence, in Enfield, Connecticut in June 1981 in a civil ceremony. She was divorced, no issue. It would be no marriage in her eyes. Father a judge. Grandfather a judge, the most exciting thing he ever did was die in this Willimansett where Jacqui Choquette was born. Willimansett, it looked to Doyle like a misprint.

For a second Doyle was tempted. An unidentified female body. If there were questions, she was Mrs Brooks Lawrence, American divorcee. But then there was MacBride, who was in love, at least every time he took a drink he was; he might not let the matter rest. And the poor woman was innocent, in extreme danger. This was a story which would do nothing to make the task of attracting American tourists any easier for Bord Failte. Defending the innocent was also what Doyle was supposed to do.

Doyle began to dial. At this time of night, it was difficult to raise anyone who could issue the necessary instructions and set things in motion. He enjoyed these moments of sudden activity in the middle of relentless routine, but God damn Kiernan, it was going to be too close a race against time. And if the IRA got her, God knows where they would hide her out. It could be days. And if the IRA discover she's the wrong woman, he thought, then Heaven help her. Men would be out, he was told, but not till first light. The RUC knew the area. She had a chance now at least.

Then, when it was all over, and Doyle was unwinding, like an actor after a show, he pulled the contents of his coat pocket out on to the bed and sorted through the pile until he found MacBride's telephone number.

The phone rang and rang in Belfast. Another five times, and he'd have to assume MacBride was dead drunk, or elsewhere. Finally a mumbling voice said, 'Hallo?'

'MacBride?'

'Who is this?'

'Doyle. From the Shelbourne Bar.'

Doyle could tell this seemed to cheer him.

'I think this is he,' MacBride said.

He wasn't all that drunk, Doyle thought. Probably one of those drunks who crashes out at 9 p.m. and, if you can wake them, is sober and raring to go an hour or so later. He'd had a night's worth of sleep by now, Doyle thought.

'Is it news of Kitty?' MacBride said.

Doyle thought he should say, yes, news about Kitty O'Shea. Your girlfriend is a perfectly innocent tourist who has been kidnapped by some Loyalist paramilitaries, and if she's not dead already, she soon might be, for even as we speak the Provisional Irish Republican Army and the Royal Ulster Constabulary, with the tougher elements of the British Army, are about to attempt to rescue her in what will possibly be a most God Almighty shoot-out. But he said: 'I'm not sure. Is there anything you can remember, anything at all, about where she'd planned on going? Did she know anyone here?'

MacBride thought for a moment. 'No,' he said. 'She was some kind of James Joyce freak, I think. But I rang every hotel in Dublin when I was there, the day after I saw you, and she wasn't staying there.' He paused. Doyle said nothing. MacBride went on, 'Look, I've been thinking. I probably overreacted. I'd only just met her. She broke our date. She probably found something better to do, and didn't bother letting me know because she didn't think I'd be silly enough to turn up. She's American, after all. They're much more casual than we are.'

129

'If that's how you feel,' Doyle said. The poor fool, Doyle thought. He thinks she got bored with him.

'You've got my number,' Doyle said. 'I'll let you know if we get anything.'

'Tell me one thing,' MacBride said.

'What's that?'

'What do you want her for?'

'I thought you were the one that wanted her,' Doyle said, and put the phone down. The poor bastard, Doyle thought, thinks he's just another middle-aged man found wanting by a young girl. And the poor bitch, he thought, she's out there all on her own, a girl like that, probably no one's ever said boo to, and now she's in the middle of a war.

Liam had never imagined darkness like this, out on the open hillside without a sign of a star in the sky. It had never been like this before, when he had sat out on an abandoned dockside, or in the doorways of broken-down warehouses waiting for a dawn. In the city, it was never really dark. Here it was like the lights in a room had suddenly gone out. Once Paddy Kiernan had tried to tell him about the blackness of the night in the open air, far from human habitation, and Liam had dismissed it as more romantic Irish nonsense.

Crouched against a boulder, his shoes soaked in dew-sodden grass, Liam felt a slight breeze very cold against the hair at the back of his neck. The back of his neck was wet with sweat. But he was still shivering in the cold.

A pick-up truck had brought him here. He had sat bumping along in the back with six or seven of Flynn's men. They wore hoods with slits for their mouths and eyes. They gave Liam a hood. They didn't speak.

Now, on the side of the hill, he couldn't see them, but he listened to the sound of his invisible companions breathing and shifting position as they waited. He couldn't see the truck either. When he deliberately held up his hand in front of his face, he could see nothing. He felt light-headed; it was nearly twenty-four hours since he had slept, and almost as long since he had eaten. He reached out a hand, and touched another man's boot.

He pulled off the woollen balaclava. The wool was scratchy against the stubble on his cheeks and chin, and the wool sodden round his mouth and nose where his breath had evaporated in the cold night air.

All the others were armed. Liam didn't have a gun. He thought he should have a gun. They must have known how brave he had been in England, even though Flynn looked at him oddly when Liam said he was afraid to go on the raid because of his asthma, he might give the game away with a fit of coughing. Night air was the worst possible thing for asthma. He had told Flynn that, but the man just shrugged and said it was an emergency. Some emergency, Liam thought. Flynn wasn't here. He was safe at home being terrorised by his sour-faced daughter. Flynn was a filthy capitalist, in fact. They'd deal with men like Flynn when the time came.

Finally succumbing to the cramp in his legs, Liam stood up, feeling the chill damp penetrate the seat of his thick trousers. It was unfortunate, he thought, that they had to make use of men like Flynn until then.

'Sit down,' a voice said in the dark close by him. Liam had expected to be treated with more respect. He could see that in an operation like this, the man in charge had to know the territory and he did not. But he had great theoretical knowledge of tactics and man management. He would have thought they would have been eager to draw upon that knowledge. The man in command hadn't even spoken to Liam. That was stupid. These men – he could hear them shifting round him on the rock-strewn grass – were cannon fodder. Training and study had created in him, Liam O'Tomas, a leader of men. That could not be denied. It was there for anyone to see. It was bound to be recognised sooner or later. The trouble was, he thought, they're Irish.

Something stirred close to his head; some small night animal, or perhaps a reptile. Liam raised his hand and picked up a rock to strike it or frighten it away, whatever wild creature it might be. It was very different in a city at night. Even on a very dangerous job he had felt, if not exactly secure, at least not next door to panic as he was now. And it had been extremely dangerous in the city, putting the bomb inside a building. You could be discovered any time, and the explosion could go off early. Before its time. While you had it in your hands. That had been known to happen. It was all very well for these masked men, armed to the teeth on the hillside, but how would they be in an English city? Surrounded by the enemy? And with the police after them. When a bomb went off in an English city, blowing dozens of people apart, why, the police stopped at nothing to get their man. Each policeman you saw. Every ring at the bell. You had to have a special sort of courage for that. Liam wondered how many here on the hillside could operate like that.

Liam could not understand how other men did not share what amounted almost to a phobia about the animals in the country at night. He felt as if he could be reduced to humiliating tears. He was sensitive. Well, yes, a sensitive Englishman. There was no denying your antecedents. He had simply risen above that, he had trained himself. And it was true, he could wish he shared the lack of imagination of the Irishmen around him in the dark. But he didn't. He was different. Who would have thought the empty darkness could be so loud?

Then, soon as light came, they would attack. In the light. The Orangemen were armed. There was sure to be shooting. He could feel himself trembling. Then his leg inside his trousers became warm. Oh, mother, he thought, this is not for me. I'm yellow, he thought. He could see his father looking at him, his father seated in his favourite chair in the lounge in the Croydon house, about to say something stern before Liam's mother stepped in to protect her boy. Then Liam thought how brave it would all be if he suddenly leapt to his feet and said, 'Forward, we'll attack now!' Then they would follow him. Or he'd go alone, shooting down whoever it was wherever. Then they would crowd round him, their hoods off, slapping him on the back, smiling broadly at him. But Flynn had made it impossible, by depriving him of a weapon. It wasn't his fault. But he knew he was yellow. It was cold now inside his trousers where it had been warm.

All of a sudden the animal sounds ceased. Then the silence was uncanny. Liam could feel the men around him on the wet grass become alert. He felt in his pocket for his respirator. If he had a terrible asthma attack they could not say anything. He wouldn't be fit. He couldn't be blamed for that. A physical weakness. Suddenly Liam realised that it was not really the dark open country that scared him. He would stay back with the frightening animal sounds on the moors, he would do anything rather than advance with these silent hooded men upon an armed enemy, an enemy who, unlike civilians dancing in a disco pub, would be most likely waiting for them well-prepared. He could hear footsteps now, brushing through the dead bracken. There was an electric torch, its light jerky and feeble as someone approached from among the rocks. Then Liam saw, in the beam of light, right near him a pale heap which could have been stones, but which suddenly moved. Liam cried out. Then the heap leaped up and ran away with a scattering of stones and a loud baa. God, Liam thought, it was just a stupid sheep. And the others heard. So what, he thought, what did he care about them?

The hooded men were whispering in the dark. Liam strained to hear what they were saying. Were they talking about him? They would be furious at his crying out like that. But no, they seemed not to have heard. They had sent a man ahead and he had returned to report that the old byre where the men they were after had holed up with the American woman was less than half a mile ahead. Their scout had seen the men in the cottage as they came out of the door with the light behind them to relieve themselves. There were three, the man said, and the woman. He had seen her inside, when they opened the door. She was tied up. The scout said he had watched until they put the light out, and then waited. It was all quiet now.

'It's black as pitch,' someone said in the darkness. 'Not even a star.'

'It'll be the new moon tomorrow,' the other man said.

Their voices came out of the void, like echoes, muffled by the balaclavas partially covering their mouths with wet wool.

So they had not noticed him crying out like that in fright like a girl. He had been given a second chance. He would be brave now. After all, there were only three of them in the hut. The old byre, the man said. They could be expecting nothing if they strolled out like that, with the light behind them, to relieve themselves. And there were seven men with Liam. Eight, counting Liam himself. But he was unarmed. They would hardly expect . . . Still, they might give him a rifle. He had asked. Liam thought he'd better ask again for a weapon. Otherwise it would look as if he didn't want to fight. But he didn't ask and he was glad when no one seemed to pay any attention to him. After all, he thought, he was an observer. Merely along to see how this end of the operation works.

'Tyler's there,' the man who had done the scouting said.

'That means Falk's there, too,' another one said.

Liam wondered if Paddy Kiernan and Sean Cafferty spoke of him in that particular tone of reverence and fear with which these men spoke of this Falk, whoever he was. These men, he thought, were local men. It was incredible, but they knew one another. That only went to prove Liam had no part in it. He was out of a business like this. He'd refuse to go if they gave him a weapon. He'd hand it back. Everyone had his own speciality. This wasn't his. They'd see that, if he was firm enough. Even Flynn would see it.

One of the men said: 'Tyler's a tough man. He's the manager of a soldiers' bar near Lurgan. Or he was.'

'He did the Strabane bombings.'

Liam remembered that. Four women and an old man killed, and a passing priest, caught in the blast, blinded for life. The priest may have lost an arm or a leg too. Liam smiled to himself. If that was the best they could do. It didn't start to compare with his bombing in England in the centre of a great city, right under the noses of the finest police force in the world. He felt new heart. He looked and could see the hooded men. They had lifted their hoods up over their mouths and were drinking, passing a bottle of whiskey about.

'Well,' he said. 'Are we going to get on with the job, or sit around boozing all night?'

He could tell they were a bit taken aback. Not used to the voice of command. The man Flynn had appointed leader, a big man with long arms like a monkey, said gently: 'We'd better wait for the dawn, to see where we're going. They're not showing any lights.'

Liam nodded. 'Good thinking,' he said, but he wished he hadn't spoken up like that. It had slipped out.

Only a short time later the sky to the left had begun to lighten, a strip of pale opal turning to faint rose. The birds were terribly loud, and gradually Liam could hear something else.

The hunched dark men heard it, too. They looked up from where they sat on the grass.

'Jesus,' one of them said. 'Helicopters.'

'It's time to go,' the leader said. He jumped to his feet. The men gathered their rifles. Those who had raised them pulled down the sodden balaclavas over their mouths, zipping up their anoraks, and stamping their feet to bring back the circulation. Some moved round the far side of the truck to take a piss. They were nervous, too, Liam saw. It didn't make him feel better. They couldn't go now, surely, with the security forces' helicopters out. They had sharpshooters who could pick them off from the air. The other men were moving out. Liam did not follow them although he knew he should. Better to stay aloof, he thought. They should be aware that he was not one of them but an observer.

'Come on,' the leader called to Liam.

The man, who had spoken so gently before, had such a commanding voice that Liam got to his feet, but still, Liam thought, were they making fun of him? Why should he die for Ireland?

In the very faint light they set off across the rocky hillside. Against the strip of lightening sky they could see the helicopters hovering in the distance. Liam struggled to keep up, his chest painful as they climbed, his breathing fast and too shallow. His hands were trembling as he reached into a pocket and got out the respirator. He used it quickly. Some of the others looked round for the source of the strange noise. Liam waved the respirator, started coughing. He stopped walking and clutched his chest.

'Don't do that,' a man said.

'I can't help it,' Liam said. 'Asthma.'

The man said something but it was drowned in the sound of the helicopters as they turned and started another systematic sweep of the hillside.

16

The earth floor made a hard bed. Kitty, in a sleep that was not like sleep, but more a mysterious state of disembodiment in which she looked down from a high place at her waking predicament, dreamed that insects crawled across her face. In her sleep she put up her right hand to brush them away, and the intense pain in her hand awoke her.

Nothing was visible, and there was no sound. The awful stabbing pain in her hand eased once more to a grinding ache, and she felt sick to her stomach again. Close to her ear, she felt his breath. His mouth was at her ear.

'Noon,' Karl said in a very low voice. She thought for a moment that the German boy might be saying 'moon'. There was no sign of moonlight through the cracks in the boarded windows, or through the crevices in the dry stone walls of the cabin where sometimes she had been able to see chinks of daylight. It was still night, no chorus of birds had heralded the dawn.

'At noon,' the German said. His lips were against her ear as if he were kissing. 'They go off to visit a meeting at noon. We make our escape at that time.'

Kitty turned towards where the German boy's voice was coming from. Just as if, she thought, she could look into his eyes to tell if he were lying. He misunderstood this turning of her blindfolded face to him. Kitty felt his mouth pressing on hers. She felt his hand reaching between her legs. She tried to open them as much as she could with her ankles tied. He was all fingers unbuttoning her trousers.

He wouldn't dare, Kitty thought, not with them. He's making enough noise already. They'll hear him. How do they not hear him? They're so close. One of them snuffling in his sleep. They were going to kill her. But there's only so much anyone can do to a person, and they can't do anything more once they've killed a person.

Karl slipped one of her legs out of the rope. But he still couldn't get her pants far enough down over her hips. He was cursing under his breath.

There's an owl, Kitty thought. And again. And there's something rustling in the dried litter by the wall. Please, not rats. When Grandad O'Shea was living, when she was a little girl, he took her down to a county fair outside Chicopee. He met some woman he knew there. She had a funny accent, French-Canuck. She remembered it as though it was yesterday. Even her name, what was it? Babette, he called her. Grandad and Babette took her into one of the showmen's tents where they had this huge rat with long red teeth. He said it was a giant rat imported from some awful foreign place, and had got that big eating dead people, and its teeth were red from human blood. It was a coypu, of course, not a rat at all, but Grandfather O'Shea's friend, Babette, she screamed and screamed, clutching on to Grandad's arm. Then Babette laughed until the tears ran down her face and she had to take out her compact and 're-do,' she said, 'this ugly mug of mine'. She'd never been able to tell anyone, because it was Grandad O'Shea's secret with her, and she'd promised. Naturally, a few years later she knew all about it. Yet, even though it had been Grandad's French-Canuck mistress screaming, she'd been the one terrified of rats ever since. Funny to remember that now. Sidney would say it was fear reproducing the trauma of childhood. The unconscious trying to colonise terror by relating it to past fear which didn't lead to disaster. Some mumbo jumbo like that. Even with Brooksie doing his most cold-blooded fucking, Kitty thought, she had never felt as absent as she did with this German psycho rubbing himself off against her thigh. Maybe she was the cold-blooded one. Poor Brooks. Did he ever know about Brewster? Brooksie's own wife fucking his brother that time, wanting to get even. How could a person ever begin to apologise? God, they'll hear him, grunting so, and clutching like that. Ah, at last, it's over with. Spunk all over the place, like the lady in the graffiti sucking cock on the women's room wall at Shannon Airport.

Watchful Falk was aware of the sound and stench of animals in rut. There, he saw them across the room, filth squirming in the dirt of lust. The German boy must go, whatever Tyler said in his defence. What was the likes of Karl doing there anyway? And her, Falk watched her, with her buttocks gripped from behind, moving in the dark.

Falk gazed at the German boy with something approaching pity. A poor specimen, a frail lustful body. He was whispering secret German words into the bitch's ear, kissing her white breasts. Bound and gagged she was more than a match for the German half-wit, frigging himself off in the night, thinking no one can hear his hot breath hoarse with lust.

Falk suddenly sat up, quivering with rage. In the dark he could hear Tyler sleeping still. There's innocence for you, Falk thought. Tyler snorting like a pig in his pit while the bitch inveigles her way into the mind of the dimwit and gets us all killed.

Falk stood up. He had slept in his clothes, and he stood there patting the pockets of his trousers looking for matches. He'd seen whores all his life, going up the alley with the foreign sailors, Chinks, Lascars, Maltese and Greeks. His mother lifting her skirt. His own mother, one of them. She thought he didn't know. He knew. Where were the matches?

Kitty O'Shea, with her eyes blindfolded, could not see Falk standing with the oil lamp held high, looking down on her like something out of a judgemental Victorian painting. She heard movement, scuffling, and she could smell him. And then Tyler said, 'What time of day do you call this?' as if it were a domestic scene of peace and quiet in the night suddenly disturbed. She did not hear Falk speak, but he must have said something to Tyler about wasting too much time already because Karl said, 'Hamstring the bitch.' What's that? Kitty thought. Hamstring the bitch?

'Yes, young woman,' Tyler said – and in the blind darkness Kitty did not at once realise that this formal address referred to her – 'then you'll never walk again. You'll spend the rest of your life on your knees.'

'Like a good Papist,' Karl said.

Kitty knew. Hamstring meant cutting something in the back of the knees. Oh, Jesus, she thought, I wish I had the money. But they would never say thanks and apologise for the inconvenience. She was going to be dead. Mutilated and dead. The knife would hurt horribly, and something would give, the strings at the back of the knees would snap.

There was a great beating about outside but Kitty was unaware of it.

'What the hell's that?' Tyler asked. 'It's helicopters,' he said, answering himself.

'The military,' Karl said. 'Practising.'

'Christ,' Tyler said, 'That's all we need. You and your frigging fire of green wood.'

'That was two days ago, the fire,' Karl said in a hurt voice.

'Even so,' Tyler said. Then he said, 'There. They've gone off. They get up in those hills sometimes and have a good nose round for themselves.'

'Listen,' Karl said. 'I'd like to tell you something.'

'And what's that, I wonder?' Tyler said. 'You want to fuck some more with the American? I'm not deaf or blind, you know. And if I was, I'd still have my sense of smell.'

'No, no. It's important,' Karl said. 'Come outside for a moment.'

Sweet Jesus, Mary and Joseph, Kitty thought, he was going to tell Tyler about her plan to escape, and the money she had waiting for her in a Belfast bank. She was a fool to think she had seduced him. He would think her admission that she could get the money would be a feather in his cap with these killers. At least, she thought, they could hardly limp her into a Belfast bank with her hamstrings cut to sign them over the money. They'd have enough trouble explaining away her signature with a mutilated hand twice its normal size. She didn't know the name of a single Belfast bank. She'd have to play brain-damaged with shock, unable to remember. Must be a Lloyds, Lloyds of London, insurance everywhere, and there's a bank, too. They may suggest names it could be. Then inside the bank she would scream the place down, don't care if we all get shot as long as they get theirs. She listened to the sound of the helicopter. The British Army, he said, Tyler. That'd be too good to be true.

The door was open. She could tell by the breeze. It must be daylight. Tyler and the German boy were still outside whispering. Karl must think he's outsmarted them all, Kitty thought. Good

God! What's that? Some sort of terrible explosions like the air's being blown apart. She heard Falk move somewhere behind her. The noise had set her ears ringing and she could smell something acrid up her nose. It was gunshots going off. She tried to sit upright, but she was thudded flat on her back and could feel a large man lying on top of her breathing heavily.

'It's all right now,' he was saying in her ear, in a voice which was somehow not right.

PART THREE

THE HUNTER AND THE HUNTED

17

When the girl came out, he could see that her right hand was wrapped round with a cloth and that there was blood on it. Something flashed metallic in her good hand. Then he looked again and saw it was a kitchen knife and that the girl was concealing it up the right-hand sleeve of the big woollen pullover she was wearing.

It seemed to Liam like an odd thing for the girl to do, but then she had been through a terrible experience. She was very dirty and unkempt and hurt-looking with that bundle of stained cloth around one hand. Niamh in the morning, Liam thought. But the American woman was like a film star in comparison with thin Irish Niamh.

After the excitement of the shooting Liam felt drawn to the tall American. He could see the outline of her beautifully curved legs and thighs, and especially where they curved up behind and disappeared under the bulky pullover. He was exhausted but at the same time exhilarated. He thought how lovely it would be to be in bed in his childhood room at home with the woman in the early morning, with the smell of the suburban garden drifting in through the open window. Here, in the pale morning on this barren Border moorland, patches of mist still lay like spilled milk on the black hillside as it gradually took shape in the encroaching light of day. One of the men brought out a suitcase to the girl. A girl like that, Liam could see, was a class apart. He felt the old resentment. The American woman was arguing with the man, who had his hood pushed back off his face and looked like a skier after a race.

'I really cannot go back in there,' the girl said, surprising Liam with the sound of her American voice, and with the firm way she spoke. The man said something to her that Liam couldn't hear, and then she walked round the wall of the stone building, carrying a suitcase and a bundle of clothes in her arms, and moving, with those long curving legs that disappeared under the big sweater in a way that made Liam feel weak and inferior.

A man, still wearing his hood pulled down over his face, called to Liam, motioning that they should go out of earshot of the others and have a private talk.

The actual attack had been ridiculously easy. Two of the men had been talking to one another outside the building. Their bodies were lying where they had been standing. As Liam walked over to talk to the hooded leader of the attack, he saw one of the others turn one of the bodies over. The corpse, Liam saw, was young and blond and obviously foreign. The pale blue eyes were open, the tongue lolling from the mouth. Liam could see one of the wounds. It looked like pink and white icing on a cake. The man who had turned him over with his foot was now bent over, going through the blond corpse's pockets.

'God Almighty,' Liam heard the man say, 'he's actually carrying ID!' The man laughed. Then he read out a name. 'German,' he said. 'Another terror groupie.'

The man turned to the other corpse. 'Carson Tyler himself,' he called to the others who were standing a bit off.

Liam moved away from the group with the leader, who had his head bent as though deep in thought.

I did well, Liam told himself. They didn't notice anything, and he'd kept right up with them. He hadn't been afraid. The man was going to tell him how good he did and ask him to put in a word for him with Flynn about the one that got away. They had had two men round the back, but the man had leaped from the window firing and killed them both. They said the man who leapt from the window firing was Falk. Those dead men were the reason, Liam thought, that they were all so subdued. If they had given him a rifle, Liam could have been round the back with the other two and the man coming through the window shooting couldn't have got all three of them. That's what he'd tell Flynn, anyway, Liam thought, no matter how much this man begged Liam to put in a good word to excuse his own incompetence.

'Who'd have thought,' Liam said, 'he'd be able to shoot like that leaping from a window.'

'What?' the man said. He seemed far away, lost in thought.

'Of course,' said Liam, 'It was a lucky shot. At least the second must have been lucky.'

'Yes,' the man said. 'Yes, it would be.'

Liam heard the apologetic tone in the man's voice. Perhaps Liam would put in a good word for him with Flynn after all. These men were now his comrades in arms. He felt good about that. It would be a shame if he was forced to complain about the man's lack of basic military strategy. Liam breathed deeply. His asthma had disappeared as soon as the long wait on the damp hillside was over.

It was light now, a watery sun barred with dark bands of cloud rising above the brow of the hill.

Someone was shouting from outside the cottage, asking the American woman to hurry, saying there was no more time for her to change her clothes. When Liam turned to look down to see the beautiful American girl, the hooded man shot him once in the back of the head.

'Was that a shot?' Kitty asked. She came round the side wall to the front of the stone cabin wearing jeans and a crumpled cotton shirt, pulling the big sweater on over her head.

'Just an accident,' the man said.

Kitty looked down at the two corpses, now face-up and staring.

'We've got to hurry,' the man said.

It was the same voice, the voice of the man who had suddenly thrown himself across her in the cottage, to protect her from the line of fire. It was an Irish accent, not the English voice of a British soldier which she had been expecting her rescuers to have. It had taken her some time to realise what had been wrong with the voice. Falk had got away. Before Kitty even thought of her clothes, still in the filthy white trousers covered with the dead man's spunk, she had gone to the table where the storm lantern still cast its flickering light. No one was looking. Without a moment's thought, she scooped up the kitchen knife and put it inside her shirt. The cold touch of the blade against her bare stomach felt good. Later, coming from the hovel, she switched the knife up inside the sleeve of her right arm. She wondered how good her left arm would be for stabbing a man. You had to get them in the stomach. That way you didn't hit bone.

They were all rushing away from the cottage now, running across a stretch of grass cropped as close as any lawn by the sheep. Behind them she could see a plume of white smoke rising. The smoke was black where it was close to the ground and then rose dead white. It looked like a platinum blonde with dark roots. They must have knocked over the lamp, in their hurry.

Kitty felt despair. This, she knew, was another gang of Irish murderers. They were different, but the same. She must escape, she thought.

Hunched like a black rock against the damp hillside, Falk watched unblinking. Black shadows moved in a strange exaggerated ritual dance against the faint light of the storm lantern through the broken windows and the open door. He had heard the voice of the American whore saying something. Falk now saw two of them walk off from the others. They came towards him, where he crouched among the boulders. He considered shooting one of them. He had only the one shot left. Then he'd have got the other with his knife, and have the dead men's guns to get rid of the rest when they came running to see what had happened. But then the hooded man shot the one with the hood pushed up off his face. The dead one was young. Falk could see him lying dead not ten yards away. Hair showing through the black knitted hood. He looked like an Englishman. Probably a British soldier. Hardly wet behind the ears for an undercover job on his own. Lucky for him they didn't torture him to death. His dead face, with the forehead blown out at the bullet exit wound, reminded Falk of an English officer in Korea with the Ulster Rifles.

Falk ran his finger inside his collar where, wet with sweat, it stuck to his unshaven neck. No one else would kill her now. No one in Belfast need ever know the details. He would manage better alone, without Tyler or any degenerate Germans. Lot of use a boy like that was when it came to the real thing.

If he had had a rifle, he would have got a classic hunter's shot at the whore when she had been in full sight of him, behind the wall, where her rescuers couldn't see her, pulling off the rags, standing naked, breasts exposed, with her arms raised over her head, and those trousers that had been pure white fallen from her white hips. Hanging off her, those once white trousers were, stained with blood and the marks of unspeakable depravity. Now he saw those great pale breasts open to the air. She stood naked on the grass, with the wind blowing her hair. Whore, temptress and corrupter, putting on the trappings of innocence.

The girl had dressed herself and gone from view. Falk lay still. He could wait there all day if he had to, then cut across the hills at night. But he must not lose the whore. He turned his head slightly so he could see the murdered man. He was the same sort as that young English officer in Korea. As though the clock had been turned back. Falk thought of the Chinese Laundrymen.

There was something reflecting the weak sun in the dead man's coat pocket. Something glass. Just a cheap ballpoint pen. Young officers keep notebooks. Write things down in them. Falk crawled across the sharp heather stalks to the dead man's side. No notebook. There was a letter in the shirt pocket. Lionel Thompson. There were some good Englishmen left. But to be so stupid, keeping a letter like that (a woman's hand) on yourself. Not even opened. Falk would not let this murder go unrecorded. He took the ballpoint pen from the dead man's coat pocket and wrote on the envelope: 'MORDEREN SCUM SENT BRAVE ENGLISH SOLJER TO ERLY GRAVE KITTY O'SHEA.'

Falk smelled smoke. They had set the shack on fire. That would bring the helicopters back. There would be no place to hide waiting till dark.

Falk moved diagonally down the dark hillside towards the patch of grass where Tyler's car was parked. The keys were in the burning cottage, but he could cross the wires. Crawling in the bracken and heath that scratched his arms and legs, and made his hands bleed, Falk approached the grey car.

The sound of boots, scattering loose stones alerted him. Falk lay flat among the sharp stalks. There was no cover. There were still four or five of them, not counting the woman. And he'd only one shot in his revolver. As long as he got the girl. Let the rest torture him to death, but she must die. They were coming closer. Thank God, he thought, for all those roadblocks, Tyler had got out of the habit of locking the boot. Falk climbed inside, holding the arm of the catch with his left hand to hold it closed, and clutching his .38 ready to fire into the face of anyone who tried to pull it open.

They were making a lot of noise now. Running. But not all of them. Two males and the woman. The others must have gone on to whatever vehicle they came in.

Close to his face, Falk could hear a man breathing hard. He was going to open the boot. Then, from the front of the car, a voice said: 'Hurry up, for Christ's sake. There's no time.'

Then the same voice said: 'In the back, quickly, Miss O'Shea.'

Falk heard the two front doors of the car closing, then the back. He could smell her, inches away. The sweet stench of polluted female flesh. They were laughing in the front seat, grumbling about the springs being worn out. The car bucked and twisted down a rutted track. Some of the men, still on foot, were following the car, but soon he could hear the sound of their feet fade as they were left behind.

Later on, the car stopped as they reached an asphalt road. There were voices, and then another, bigger, engine running. The driver got out of the car. Falk could feel him leaning against the boot. They were laughing and joking. It was impossible to make out what they were saying. They chatted as if they had no sense of urgency.

The driver got back in his seat and they moved off. Fresh air began to blow through the boot. Very carefully, Falk pushed the boot lid slightly upwards, at the same time holding the catch to make sure it did not start to rattle. He could see a truck moving off the verge and setting out to follow them along the narrow road. There was another engine though. Much louder. They were a good distance ahead of the truck. Falk saw two helicopters, very low, hovering above the road close to the truck. Falk could still hear them beating the air very loudly as a turn in the road took them out of sight. They got some of the bastards anyway, he said to himself.

Powell, Falk thought. In Korea, the name of the English officer who had called the Chinese Laundrymen. The dead Brit on the hillside looked like Captain Powell. Captain Powell had been a proper Englishman, a sporting man who was a dead shot at five hundred yards or more. Falk thought how he would get a rifle and pot Kitty O'Shea at a long distance, like Captain Powell potted the Laundrymen.

18

It had been a long time since the Shamrock Hotel in Derry had seen an American tourist. The grey slab hotel dominated an area close to the old city wall. The main shopping street wound up the hill in the rain behind it.

When Flynn's men brought Kitty into the foyer of the Shamrock Hotel, Joe, a teenage boy of all work, who was at the Shamrock studying to be a head waiter, thought Kitty was an American film star, travelling under an assumed name. He was of a romantic turn of mind, and Kitty did wear dark glasses, to conceal the bruises she had received from Tyler, and this served to confirm Joe's impression. He told Emer, the maid, he was sure he had seen her in a film on the television only a short time before.

Mr Flynn had given Joe a tenner to keep an eye on the American woman. 'See she makes no outside calls, Joseph,' he said. Mr Flynn made it sound most mysterious. 'If she does try to phone out,' Mr Flynn said, 'you just tell her the switchboard is temporarily off.' Mr Flynn made it sound as if the American woman would be calling out for drink or drugs, or men or worse. It was powerful stuff, Joe told Emer.

Emer was only a year older than Joe but she knew that whatever Kitty was, she wasn't a film star. Emer had seen the bandage on the American woman's hand. She had also scooped up Kitty's soiled clothes to wash them. She had seen the bloodstains, and the rest of it. But Emer was silent. She got on with her life as best she could, and jobs were hard to come by. When she was trained up enough she would go to a hotel in Dublin. Like Mrs Mooney, who ran the hotel since Mr Mooney her husband was bed-ridden, she often spoke with pride about how she managed to lead a normal life in the midst of the Troubles. And, in fact, Emer was once on

German TV, with subtitles, telling viewers how she managed to lead a normal life. The German viewers were apparently very moved. One woman in Hamburg even wrote her a fan letter – one of the TV men staying in the hotel translated it for her. The German woman said Emer reminded her of her young self, for she also managed to live a normal life, in the middle of the Hitler times. That was a wonderful thing, Emer thought. She showed Mrs Mooney the German woman's letter, and Mrs Mooney thought the same as Emer. Everyone thought the same – except Mr Mooney, who was ill and had become cynical.

Emer knew Kitty was some sort of prisoner. The American woman had a bandaged hand and her face was cut and bruised behind the dark glasses, and she was not checked in to the hotel. She was not staying overnight, just using the room for a few hours. Emer knew people didn't rent rooms by the hour in a hotel like The Shamrock. She was with the Provos, Emer could tell that right off, even if Joe was too stupid to see it. The American woman was also not happy. Emer had seen the way she was gazing out of the hotel bedroom window when she brought her breakfast. She was not looking at the rain, she was standing there as if she wanted to jump out, Emer thought.

'I've had an accident,' the American woman said, holding up her right hand. It was covered in nothing but old rag. 'Do you think you could get a proper dressing?'

Emer said, yes, she'd get the First Aid box. When Emer came back the woman was still standing by the window looking out across the bridge and the river. She hadn't touched her breakfast. She had the dark glasses in her hand and Emer could see she had been hit across the face. Emer stood next to her by the window and looked down at the wet empty pavement two storeys below. There was a stack of sandbags against the front of the building, and rolls of barbed wire around that. She wouldn't have a prayer if she jumped down on all that, Emer thought. When she helped put a proper dressing on the woman's hand she saw the finger had been chopped off but she didn't ask. Then Emer saw the woman slide a knife out of her sleeve and into her handbag.

When Emer went to get the breakfast tray from Mr Mooney's room the sick man said, 'What's this Joseph says about a film star?'

150

'She's one of Eammon Flynn's,' Emer said.

'Lord save us,' Mr Mooney said. 'I keep telling Mrs Mooney, but she says anything for a peaceful life.'

'The American woman, she's injured,' Emer said. She wasn't looking at the sick man sitting in the big bed. She was at the door, balancing the tray on one raised knee and one hand as she reached towards the door handle with the other.

'Wounded?' Mr Mooney asked.

'One of her fingers has been cut off.'

'Oh, Jesus,' Mr Mooney said. 'Somebody ought to tell that to the policemen, if this were a civilised place. I'd even tip the bastards off myself. I ought to do that. I will do it. I'll call them.'

'You stay in bed,' Emer said, opening the door. 'Mrs Mooney said the doctor said you're to stay in bed. Mrs Mooney knows all about Mr Flynn's guest.' Then she went out. She knew Mr Mooney wouldn't make any calls.

Somebody important called Flynn was coming to the Shamrock Hotel to see her. He would have a car to take her to Belfast. Kitty sat in the empty lounge that smelled of lavender polish, drinking milky coffee which was served in a quasi-silver pot from a china cup.

The first thing she had done, when she had been left alone in the bedroom, was pick up the telephone by the bed to ring the police. It was one of those phones you still got out in the backwoods in the United States, where you have to ask the operator for an outside line before you can make a call, and at first she hadn't thought much of the delay before someone on the switchboard picked up her call. It was the voice of the boy on the desk. He told her he was very sorry but the switchboard was out of order, and it was not possible to make an outside call. The boy was very apologetic, and said he'd be delighted to run any errand if it was something she needed from the shops, which would be open at nine, he said, quite soon. Kitty put the phone down on him. A little while later, when she had washed and changed, the boy Joe came to her room to say Mr Flynn would be coming to fetch her. Kitty was waiting for this Mr Flynn.

The hotel was quiet. All around her, she thought, people were living ordinary lives, going about their everyday business, getting up and eating breakfast before going out to work. Yet none of them seemed to use the public rooms. There were staff everywhere, but no sign of the guests. There was only one other person in the lounge, and she knew what sort of guest he was. To prove it, she got up in an impatient sort of way and walked briskly into the foyer. The man stood up, watching her. Kitty caught him out of the corner of her eye. In the foyer was another one who rose politely when Kitty walked towards the door leading out into the street.

'I thought I'd get a breath of fresh air,' she said.

'Mr Flynn will be here any minute,' the man said. 'Besides, it's raining.'

Kitty could see women outside the hotel, hurrying to work in the rain. They wore neat black skirts and coloured tights, or jeans and anoraks and were seeing children off to school from the bus stop by the old city wall. There was a brisk wind, and she watched a young girl struggling with a striped umbrella turning inside out as she tried to open it. How marvellous that would be, Kitty thought, to be that woman struggling with that umbrella in the rain.

Kitty put on a show of being irritated that Flynn was keeping her waiting. She wanted to have time to think. Her instincts pushed her to keep moving, to be doing something. That was the only way to keep her terror at bay, she thought. Perhaps she should have jumped from the bedroom window. The stupid servant girl had come in while she had been standing there thinking of doing it. There was another thing. Falk might be out there. It was silly to think he had fled in terror for his life. But Falk had been there when she arrived at Shannon. He had followed her. And then he had got her.

She must put him out of her mind. She was a prisoner. These people might think they were her friends. They did obviously believe she was one of them. But once they knew she was not the woman they thought she was, they would certainly kill her. Kitty poured more coffee, the spout of the silvery pot clicking against the china cup as her hand shook. She felt her handbag on the chair beside her, where she had hidden the kitchen knife. But she could never really use it, she thought, not really.

Her only hope was to convince this Flynn that she was indeed the woman he expected and then steal away.

Kitty wondered again exactly what kind of woman that was. How would she have reacted to captivity and rape, and having bits of herself cut off for refusing to tell what she didn't know? Except this other woman did know. How long would she have held out?

This morning she could tell the others, the sinister men with the hoods, thought she was terribly brave. Flynn would think the same. But how did a brave woman, a woman who had held out against torture, how did such a woman act?

When Flynn finally did come into the Shamrock Hotel lounge, Kitty thought he was an old fellow delivering a message. He was an inoffensive-looking man of about fifty. He looked like a high school shop teacher, the man who taught metal work and carpentry, and not at all something important in a terrorist system which was actually an issue discussed from time to time in the Congress of the United States. When Kitty saw the state of his fingernails she thought he looked even more like the woodwork teacher. His teeth were awful, too. If, she thought, Flynn were really all he was cracked up to be, he'd have his dentist shot to encourage the others.

Flynn apologised a great deal for being late. He seemed ill at ease with a woman. There had been, he said, a minor disaster. Nothing to trouble her, but the Security Forces had picked up some of his men on their way back from rescuing her.

Kitty wondered if he wanted to make her feel guilty, the way he told her about the capture. She tried to look sad about his men. Flynn said 'rescuing' her in a coy way that annoyed her, as though it were a euphemism. She wondered if she should feel anything for the men who had attacked the cabin in the hills and killed the people who had abducted her. Maybe she should, she thought, but she didn't feel a thing. They'd missed Falk, after all. He was out there still.

Flynn was sitting there in a deep chair saying something about how fortunate it was that she had got well away by the time the Security Forces' helicopters landed. That would, he said, have been the last straw, wouldn't it? He laughed and then she laughed. They both laughed, like, she thought, people who were always dicing with death might laugh, but she had no idea what they were supposed to be laughing at.

Sitting there, she got a sudden creepy feeling of danger. Flynn saw her shudder, and he talked of shock and needing rest.

Then Flynn said something that really gave her the creeps. He said the boot of the car they'd come away in had been opened.

153

'We believe,' he said, 'the one who got away made his escape in the boot. Who would have thought he'd be so daring? Or foolhardy?' Flynn asked. He seemed to think that was also a great joke, but this time Kitty didn't even smile. Falk had been there, right behind her in the car. She felt as if she might faint.

'Are you all right, Kitty?' Flynn asked, using her first name for the first time. 'I think you'd best have a whiskey, despite the time of day. Or a brandy. Joseph,' he called, 'Joe, for God's sake, however are you going to become a head waiter?'

The boy came.

'Two large ones, Joseph,' Flynn said.

Flynn turned to Kitty.

'It's Falk, isn't it? One or two of our men thought they recognised him.'

'Yes,' Kitty said. 'Falk.'

'Oh,' Flynn said. 'You knew his name?'

'I heard it.'

'That was careless of them.'

'I'd an idea they didn't care,' Kitty said.

'Where's the money, Kitty?' Flynn said. 'Let's get this over with, and you can be on your way.'

'Falk asked me that same question.'

'I'll bet he did,' Flynn said.

The boy Joe came with the large whiskeys.

Kitty thought maybe she should simply say Falk got the money. But they had seen him leaping from the window. They would know he hadn't been carrying a satchel full of dollars. They were suspicious of her anyway. Of course, Kitty thought, Flynn thinks I might run off with the money. He certainly looks like he would. Whatever she told Flynn, he must believe her, and go along with her until she got to Belfast and could contact MacBride for help.

'The money's in Belfast,' she said. 'I'm to contact a man called MacBride.' It was the first name that came to her mind.

'Ah, well,' Flynn said, 'that's wonderful. I'll take you there.'

Flynn sat back smiling. He was in a good mood, Kitty could see.

'Tell me, Kitty,' he said, 'were you ever tempted to take the money for yourself? Just between ourselves. The temptation must have been great. It's an awful lot of money.'

154

'I was spared that temptation,' Kitty said. 'I only know enough to get me to MacBride in Belfast.'

'And you never mentioned MacBride to Falk and Tyler?'

'I never thought of it,' Kitty said.

'You're a very brave young woman,' Flynn said, but she could see he was thinking how smart someone had been to fix it so she couldn't grab the money and run. She caught Flynn's eye and for a moment she could see that he thought anyone who had a million dollars and didn't keep it for herself but gave it for a hopeless cause was insane.

The maid Emer, was taking a break. She stood watching the American woman and Flynn from the half opened pantry door. So there you are, you see, she said to herself, she'd been wrong. The American woman and old Flynn were the best of friends. So what if Old Man Mooney had called the RUC? What fools they'd have looked, the pair of them, herself and Mr Mooney. Plus all Derry'd know she was an informer and a snitch. It's best, she told herself, to keep right out of these things and try to lead a normal life.

19

It probably wasn't much after seven o'clock in the morning. Falk's watch had stopped. He wanted a smoke, but his last pack of cigarettes had been left on the table of that hovel with the German psychopath. What a close shave that had been. All Tyler's fault, so sure of himself.

Falk was standing in the doorway of a pub. He gazed at the dull residential street full of cramped redbrick houses. At one time he thought he knew the lives that were led behind the blue, black or grey painted doors of those rows of terraced houses, but now he wasn't so sure. Not too many family motors around nowadays, he thought, on account of the car bombs. Kids joyriding too. Little bastards, brought up living for thrills. A nice cooked breakfast, though, Falk thought, that was a decent thing. But someone had told him the women didn't do them anymore. They were the ones went out to work now, and the men stopped at home.

Falk felt dirty. He looked at his hands. They were black. He tried to remember the last time he'd had a proper wash. He never got into a tub. There was something disgusting about people in bathtubs full of hot water, lying there for hours, some of them, soaping themselves. In the army in the field he'd washed every day out of the helmet. There in the field, he kept himself clean where others didn't. It wasn't the same, standing at a basin to wash. Not like being in the field. He would like to go out to the woods somewhere. In Canada they had great forests still that a man could live in.

He wouldn't have long to wait now. The wives and mothers had started to leave the houses, going to work. The one he was waiting for would be out soon, and then he could go in to see her husband. The man was a cop. Falk had been watching the house for some time. He had seen the policeman come home at least an hour ago at the end of the overnight shift, wheeling a bicycle up the hill. He could have put out a hand and touched the thick blue stuff of the policeman's uniform. As he passed close by pushing his bike, Falk could hear the man breathing, a faint whistle after the climb. He'd had a few, too. The smell blew back in Falk's face as the man passed. He hadn't known Falk was there. Falk could have stopped him then but there was no point in alerting him yet. There was no way of telling how they might react caught in the street. It was better to corner them in the house. They would agree to almost anything to get you out. Falk would wait until the wife was out taking the children to school before he went in. He wanted a rifle that broke down and could be packed away in one of those smart little cases like the executives have. He might get a clean shirt off him, too.

In the shelter of the doorway, Falk settled to wait, his neck sunk into the collar of his black coat. It was uncomfortable with the weight favouring his good leg. A woman in a dressing gown came out of a nearby house to pick up cartons of milk on the doorstep. Falk wondered if the old-time glass bottles had all gone for petrol bombs. The woman looked out on the morning and seemed to take fright at the sudden sight of Falk standing there looking at her. He watched her turn quickly and re-enter the house. But she reappeared, looking across the way at him.

What's going on now? he thought. Hatchet-faced bitch. The woman had a maroon cloth coat over her dressing gown and she carried something under her arm like you sometimes see a man with a newspaper. She walked towards Falk. He edged back into the doorway of the public house. Once a woman had come at him like that in the street somewhere and said 'You're Sheilagh Falk's big brother. I forget your name.' 'Falk,' he'd said, and the woman had laughed. They were always finding things to laugh at. That was the sort of thing they did behind those closed doors. His sister was like that. She'd left home as soon as she could. She lived in California, L.A. they called it. The woman in the maroon coat was standing looking at Falk, one hand clutching the coat to her neck. She reached across for what was under her arm. Falk had his right hand in his pocket gripping the handle of the .38. He'd give her a quick crack across the head if she tried anything, but he couldn't figure out who the hell she was.

157

'Here,' the woman said.

It was a brown purse she had been carrying under her arm like a newspaper. She was holding out a fifty-pence piece to Falk. She paused and added a tenpenny piece. Falk still had his hand on the gun in his pocket. He held out his left hand, it was dirty, and took the coins from the woman. Dirty bitch, Falk thought, she thinks that'll take her to Heaven.

It was a time for women and children coming into the street.

'You'd think he was dead,' one woman, with pictures of cats on the headscarf tied tightly over her hair, said to another as they passed Falk. He knew they thought he was a wino waiting for the pub to open.

The policeman's wife came out of the house. She had two girls with her, old-fashioned and respectable-looking, with plaits and knobbly knees. Falk could see there was something wrong with the clothes the girls wore. They were too big for them. He remembered that was what they used to do. A kid grew into them. The women coming by had shopping bags on their arms. The pillars of society, Falk thought. Shopping and nagging. Thank God he had never. Imagine being married to them. Faces like a mousetrap, including the cheese. Falk laughed aloud. A woman shied away, tugging a child. That was the trouble these days, he said to himself, nobody saw the funny side. Falk tried to see the lighter side. Except about religion. There was nothing funny about God. God was very serious, and had had everything written down for men to read in His book, but they refused to read His words. Falk smote the enemies of the Lord, hip and thigh.

When the parade of women and children ended, Falk went to the policeman's house. He knew the front door would be locked and the man himself already snoring in bed. Falk went down the side entry of the house, thinking he would break in at the back, but she had left the back door open, and he strolled into the kitchen. They would have no fear of burglars with a policeman in the house, but what about the Republicans? Gunmen could stroll in.

In the kitchen there was a smell of toast. He could hear the man snoring upstairs. The snoring, Falk thought, was probably much more effective than a dog. Falk ate some toast left over on the breakfast table. He was hungry. Then he went upstairs. The double bed was big and looked as though it might overflow the bedroom. The big policeman was lying on his back with his mouth open. Even in his sleep, the man seemed to know there was someone in the doorway. Falk hadn't made a sound, but the policeman knew. The snoring stopped and Falk watched the man reaching under the pillow for a handgun even before he had opened his eyes.

'It's me, Billy,' Falk said. 'Don't shoot, not this early in the morning.'

From the bed, Billy recognised the black figure in the doorway. I can smell him from here, the policeman thought. Falk looked at the expression on the man's face. He knew that expression of old.

Billy kept watching Falk. His policeman's trousers were hung over the end of the bed. There was some money in the pocket. He can have it, Billy thought, just so long as he buggers off quick. Falk could go through the pockets himself. If Falk wanted more money than that the man would have to get out of bed. Billy hoped Falk wouldn't make him get out of bed. Then Falk told him what he wanted.

'Christ,' Billy said.

He blasphemes, Falk thought. Tyler blasphemed like that as well. They didn't think they were, but they were.

'For the love of God, Lucas,' the man said. He would have to get out of bed now. He wore only his underwear and he felt embarrassed.

'In one of those black cases,' Falk said. 'And I'll need something for this.' He pulled the .38 halfway out of his pocket so the man could see it. 'And some cleaning stuff. I don't trust those soldiers to clean anything these days.'

'You can't clean it here, Lucas,' Billy said after he showed Falk the rifle, broken up and neatly packed in its case.

'I'll go downstairs,' Falk said.

'Have a bit of sense, if Wendy comes back.'

'I don't trust them,' Falk said.

'Who?'

'To keep them clean. The soldiers.'

'Look at it,' Billy said. 'It's perfect. Like something in a jeweller's shop.' That's all he needed, he thought, the wife coming in to find Lucas Falk cleaning a fucking rifle on the kitchen table.

'A suit,' Falk said. 'Lend me a suit.'

159

'Oh, Christ,' Billy said.

'And a clean shirt,' Falk said. 'And a tie.'

'Christ Almighty,' Billy said.

When Falk left the house, he went to the railway station.

Falk walked slowly. There was no hurry. He had heard enough in the boot of the car to know that the American whore was being taken to Belfast. He would telephone from the station, to make sure someone from the Shankhill group picked up on her and found where they would be putting her up. Falk felt good. At the railway station he bought a ticket and went to telephone Belfast. Afterwards there was plenty of time for a coffee from the machine. Falk saw other men with small flat cases and dark coats like his. They were gathering like starlings on the platform, but none of them spoke to him. Falk leaned against the wall drinking from the thick polystyrene cup.

Someone was speaking to Falk. He was a fat man in a dark blue coat too small for him. Falk knew the coat he was wearing didn't fit either. He was smiling now, Falk thought, but soon he would start telling him about losing his job and mortgages.

'Well,' the man said, 'here we are.'

Falk did not speak.

Surprised to get no response, the man looked into Falk's face, then hurried up the platform looking hurt and puzzled. Falk, leaning against the wall with his weight on his good leg, seemed to be studying the drips from the guttering on the roof of the platform opposite. He was thinking of Kitty O'Shea. What a brazen whore she was. A good woman would have died first.

On the train, Falk in the dark blue suit seemed to merge with all the others. The man in the badly fitting clothes was not in Falk's carriage. Maybe I should have spoken, Falk thought. The man might remember him for not speaking. But perhaps he gets treated like that all the time. Probably he does. He would. A failure like that. The others smell it. Still, if I'd spoken, he might remember me all the more, Falk thought. He recalled that it was just five days since he had first caught sight of Kitty O'Shea at the Shannon Airport.

Doyle left the radio on in the bedroom. He listened with half an ear as he shaved before the bathroom mirror. The appeal of the Irish Bombers had been turned down. It had been a foregone conclusion, but was there anyone in England who really believed those men were guilty? Still, Doyle was a policeman. It was hard to reverse the assumption of guilt. No one dedicated to upholding law and order could easily face the implications of showing the law to be an ass. Poor bastards though. They must have had real hopes this time, with all the publicity pointing up the absurdity of the evidence. At the same time, the English court wasn't really setting a precedent. That had been set long ago and everywhere. Men were guilty because the public interest demanded that someone be punished. Even Jesus Christ Himself wasn't the first poor bastard to get done on that one.

Doyle was late. He had overslept. It was ten o'clock. When the telephone rang now, he thought it must be Detective Sergeant Byrne wondering where the hell he was. He turned off the radio and answered the phone.

Detective Sergeant Byrne sounded pleased.

'There's been a call from Belfast,' he said.

'What have they got?'

'There was a woman,' Byrne said. 'They're pretty sure she's the real Kitty O'Shea. They're in no doubt of that, in fact. The RUC are working on it now, with the Provos they got coming from the scene in a truck – hoods, guns, everything but the girl.'

Doyle didn't say anything. The girl certainly had bad luck. She'd had the good luck all her life, he could see all the good luck she'd had just reading her print-out, but now the poor bitch was having a lifetime's bad luck all in a few days, ever since she first took that step off the Paris-bound plane.

'The Provos killed two Loyalist volunteers,' Byrne said.

'There was shooting, then?'

'Oh, yes.'

'Anyone we know?' Doyle asked.

'One we know. Tyler.'

'I've heard of him.'

'And a German.'

'A German! That's amazing.'

'Not so, according to the RUC. They get these terror freaks,' Byrne said. 'They get hooked on violence. Beirut's full of them.'

'What's more amazing,' Byrne said, 'was a third body. An

Englishman, with an IRA hood. And a note pinned on, written on the back of an unopened letter addressed to Lionel Thompson at an address on the North Side of Dublin, saying the murdering scum sent this brave English soldier to an early grave. And it was signed, Kitty O'Shea.'

'What? That's incredible,' Doyle said.

'Not half as incredible as the spelling,' Byrne said.

'You've got the note?'

'We've got a copy. We checked with London. There is a Lionel Thompson. Whereabouts unknown.'

'Undercover?'

'They won't say. Could be.'

'Poor bastard,' Doyle said.

Doyle went back to the bathroom to finish shaving. The soap had dried on his cheeks, and cracked as he smiled at his reflection. They'd fucked up the rescue. Poor American bitch, he thought. Where the soap had dried, his face looked like a jigsaw puzzle. He rubbed it off and started all over again, pouring himself a morning whiskey while he did so, but the telephone rang again. What a nag Byrne was, Doyle thought.

The call was from a pay phone. He recognised Paddy Kiernan's voice.

'What do you want?' he asked.

Paddy cleared his throat. 'I was wondering,' he said.

Doyle had known this was coming.

'Money?' Doyle asked. 'You've had money.'

'Money for the payment in consideration of the tip-off about the wanted woman,' Paddy said. When Doyle said nothing, he added, 'Of an American type'. He was drunk still from the night before, and was trying to sound official.

'The deal,' Doyle said, 'was that you'd be paid when we got something worthwhile.' He could feel the soap drying on his face again. He was irritated with himself. He had acted on a whim in the pub, feeling sorry for Kiernan, giving him all that money, enough to get drunk and leave passing on his information till it was too late. It was Paddy's fault that the American woman was still in danger. Doyle could tell Paddy Kiernan didn't know what had happened near Limavady. He's not so important as he thinks, Doyle said to himself.

Paddy was under the impression that the RUC had captured Kitty O'Shea.

'Well, you got the woman,' he said, 'I gave you Kitty O'Shea.'

'That's not Kitty O'Shea,' Doyle said. 'Not the Kitty O'Shea you think she is. She's the wrong woman.'

'She can't be. It's not possible.'

'I'm telling you she is, Paddy. You owe us for wasting our time. Plus,' Doyle said, 'you got yourself so drunk you called too late. We didn't get the girl. Your lot got her. Now we want her back. If we don't get her, I'm going to get you for murder.'

'Murder of who?'

'Of the American girl.'

'Is she killed?'

'She'd better not be,' Doyle said.

'But if it's the wrong girl?'

'Yes,' Doyle said, 'She's the wrong girl, but she's a perfectly innocent American. That's why we've got to rescue her.'

'Again?'

'Jesus H. Christ, yes, again.'

'That's twice the money,' Paddy said.

Jesus, Doyle thought when he went back to finish shaving, what makes me think I can trust someone like Paddy Kiernan to keep his mouth shut. He was reluctant enough about informing for the first time. He wants the money though.

Doyle was surprised he didn't cut himself shaving. He sat down and poured a second whiskey. He was starting to feel bad about the American woman all over again. There'd be trouble about the note. That would get in the papers. They'd go for that in the States, too, and be up in arms in Dublin, going ape-shit about the fucking tourist trade. A judge's daughter, too. Must have some influential friends of the family still and the husband sounds like two different US Senators with that name of his. Doyle thought he should put out a description. Except, if they don't know she's wanted, she might be able to give them the slip. It all depended on what kind of woman she was. She didn't sound like the type who could take care of herself.

Doyle checked MacBride's number in his pocket book. He rang Belfast and MacBride answered at once.

'It's about your Kitty O'Shea.'

'Hardly my Kitty O'Shea, would you say?'

'We know where she is.'

'Is this a guessing game?'

'She may try to contact you, that's all. If she does, ring me.'

'Look here, Doyle, you can't just leave it at that. Where is she? Why do you want her? If she'd wanted to speak to me, she'd have done so by now.'

'She couldn't.'

'Look, Doyle, you seem to know something about her I don't. If she's some sort of undercover agent I don't want to know. I don't want to be involved.'

'Nothing like that. Tell me,' Doyle said, 'would you say she's resourceful?'

'How would I know? Our relationship was,' MacBride stopped. 'She's very bright,' he said.

'Bright?' Doyle repeated.

'Yes, very bright.'

'Resourceful?'

'You asked that before. Yes, she probably is resourceful. Now what's this about?'

'If she phones you, or gets in touch with you in any way,' Doyle said, 'let me know immediately.'

He put down the phone. Time to go to work, he told himself. Then he wondered what 'very bright' covered in MacBride's book.

20

There was something odd about the streets, but Kitty could not quite see just what it was. She took off her dark glasses the better to see this famous city.

Everything seemed in despair. The street she stared out at from the car window was scattered with refuse. There was the remains of a high, old-fashioned baby's pram, a grimy grey mattress, an abandoned car, charred by fire and full of rust. People walked with quick scurrying movements, their heads bowed in the rain. If she leapt out now and ran, where would she run to down these unfamiliar streets? If she could get out – there was a man in the back-seat behind her and Flynn at the wheel. She would be lost. These terrible streets were full of Flynn's people. They would see her running. They would hold her captive until Flynn came to reclaim her. And Flynn would know then that she was not what she seemed. He'd take her behind one of those boarded-up derelict houses and kill her, leaving her body like more refuse.

The road climbed uphill from the city centre. At the corners of the streets, each identical with the one they had passed, were small shops still functioning behind boarded windows. It was raining and Kitty thought how even more hideous it would look in the bright light of a fine day. Many of the houses were empty. Their windows were without glass. They looked sightless. Front doors, here and there, were broken open. And all over the rest was daubed the most crazy writing. Slogans, they were, in bright green and orange paint in the irregular lettering of poison-pen letters. It wasn't aimless assertion like the subway graffiti of New York. The messages here were clear and direct. The writing on the walls of Belfast was easy to decipher. And they were repeated over and over again. The Belfast walls called for action. They wanted someone killed.

The road had not been mended. It was full of potholes. The car jolted and went slowly, Flynn cursing. There were few people about and they did not linger. They darted in and out of the dark interiors of the shops. They moved before the slogan-painted walls and boarded windows like actors in a theatre doing a small scene in front of the fire curtain while unseen behind them the set for the really important act to come was being prepared by the stage hands. A British Army patrol, in an oddly shaped high-sided armoured vehicle with an intricate system of fenders, like metal skirting that almost trailed on the ground, drove towards them. It looked like something operated by remote control, as if it contained no real human beings she could run to arms outstretched, calling for help. Kitty bit her lip, and looked anxiously about. There were nervous furtive eyes in the street as well. They were the eyes of men coming out of porn shops. There was a telephone kiosk on a corner. But it was burned out. A British Army foot patrol was moving down a sidestreet by the burned-out phone box. She could go to them. But the soldiers had their rifles raised and looked about with the same anxious darting eyes. The same eyes as the people, as Kitty herself.

Of course she had seen some of this on television at home. And it did look familiar but confused in her mind with Beirut. But in the Lebanon there was sun, and the buildings that were left standing were white and tall.

Here everything was squat, raw red brick, grey in a drizzling rain that carried its own sound effects in the hiss of the car tyres on the rain-slicked road. Kitty could see this was a war zone, but somehow it was domesticated. Belfast looked too much like a New England milltown to be a real war zone. Wars were something that happened far away among palm trees and brown-skinned people. These streets might be at home, in the old poor neighbourhood where the spinning mills used to be. There were no wars at home, home wasn't exotic. Belfast was from the same culture Kitty came from. All she could think was that there must have been a flood or hurricane, some terrible fire or storm, a natural disaster. When she was ten she had memorised the chief products of the major cities of the world. Belfast was cloth. And something else. She could not remember. Yes, ships. The neighbourhoods round the mills at home were also disused. She recognised the empty terraces of houses awaiting demolition crews.

But here the Irish were squabbling, picking over the rubbish among the ruins. They could not pack up and go to California. Where could they go? Oh, God, she thought, why did she get off the plane to Paris? She could be in Madrid, in a church full of gold and silver and neon lights round the Virgin's head. She'd be laughing, thinking what Sidney would have to say about such a religion – 'Where do they kill the goats?' he'd ask.

'That's the Divis Flats,' Flynn said. He might have been proud of that hideous apartment block the way he said it, slowing the car so she could get a good look. Kitty had seen it on TV. 'It's a famous building,' Flynn said, as though it were Notre Dame Cathedral or Buckingham Palace. The ugly stained thing had the romance of the fortress in El Cid, the way Flynn spoke its name. But the building could be anywhere, anywhere at all. It was faceless and miserable, and it could be anywhere. The world was an ugly horrible place, all falling apart in the drizzle.

Flynn was telling her about the world-famous Royal Victoria Hospital. Perhaps she could run from him now, Kitty thought, go through the entrance of the famous hospital and into those clean corridors full of people trained to soothe distress.

She actually recognised the imposing face of the hospital. Just three weeks ago she had been bored by a television documentary about it. Sidney, the medical practitioner, had insisted on seeing it. Irish nurses trained there could get a job anywhere in the world without an interview. They were uniquely qualified in dealing with wounds, and with heart attacks, too, because of the Troubles. There were more died, Sidney said, from heart attacks than wounds, but the heart attacks were also because of the Troubles. Just three weeks ago it had been when she had watched that documentary, being very bored by Sidney being medical; she thought he was showing off about knowing the human body as well as the mind.

How stupid she'd been.

Kitty saw herself as she was then, getting on the plane in Hartford, with her mother and Sidney there to see her off – Sidney putting on his best bedside manner, absolutely charming her mother, who was wearing her mink coat and pearls to go to the airport. Kitty saw herself looking perfectly ridiculous, all dressed up with Paris to go to. Going to see some art and look

167

romantic with a broken heart; the young college widow, the beautiful young woman with the very clean hair, carrying her broken heart round Paris and Madrid and Rome and Florence. How disgusting and stupid she had been, so full of herself. She had been lucky to win someone like Brooks – he was a fine young man – and it was unbelievable a man as wise as Sidney could care for her. MacBride, the poet, too, though he was a drunk and a foreigner, and only knew her for the one night – still, he should have been able to see through her thin disguise, it was so transparent. She was such a sham. The German, she'd given herself to him – offered herself up to him – you could only use the old cheap cliches – on a plate. There was, she thought, no difference whatsoever between herself and those two monkey-grinning Filipino girls in the magazine. She deserved what was happening to her. It was her fault.

Gazing across the gravel through the iron railings of the famous hospital, Kitty felt the building like a magnet drawing her towards peace and calm. Inside they could see to her hand, which still throbbed with pain. She should, she knew, jump now. The traffic had stopped. Flynn tapped the driving wheel with his fingers, just like any suburban motorist.

'Traffic gets worse all the time,' he said. 'I'd hoped we'd miss the rush hour.'

The man in the back-seat made a back-seat-driver noise. He'd heard Flynn complain like this before.

'They'll have to do something,' Flynn said, 'about the traffic.'

Kitty clutched her handbag. She could feel the hard length of the knife inside. She tensed herself, preparing to open the car door and run. Then the man in the back leaned forward, joining in Flynn's conversation.

'Stopping people parking in the streets,' the man said, 'should have helped. But it's only made it worse,' he added in a sad, defeated voice.

Kitty now saw what had been odd about the streets. Imagine, she thought, an American missing that. There were no cars parked at the kerb.

'You're not allowed,' Flynn said, 'to leave a car or any other vehicle stopped without someone in it.' He sounded like the President of the Board of Aldermen, as if he was about to start bragging about how many miles of paved road they had.

'The Army will blow it up in case it's a car bomb,' the man in the back said. She didn't turn to look at him. His breath was close to Kitty's ear. The man laughed at some memory of exploding cars or congested traffic.

The traffic eased, and Flynn began to curse the potholes in the road again as they moved on.

More ragged slums stood seemingly awaiting demolition.

'The Falls Road,' Flynn said, his voice filled with civic pride. 'We'll stay at Siobhan's for the night,' he said, turning his face to her and smiling. 'You can get down to your man MacBride first thing in the morning. Is that OK?'

Kitty said it was fine.

'Siobhan's a wonderful woman, very quiet,' Flynn said. 'You'll like her. She's got a very cozy place. I stay there myself in Belfast in preference to a hotel. Yes,' he said, going on as he had gone on about Belfast's famous landmarks, 'Siobhan's a fine woman. What you call a home-maker.'

Kitty heard the man behind her in the back-seat grunt.

'She is,' Flynn said, glancing up in the rear-view mirror at the scoffing man. 'Don't you be putting Miss O'Shea off now.' Flynn was being jocular. He turned and smiled at Kitty. 'Siobhan's a big woman. Well,' he said, smiling at his understatement, 'a large woman. Strong as a horse though.'

'Two horses,' the man said.

'These young fellas here, like Fancy Dan in the back-seat,' Flynn said in a good humoured way, 'think I don't know they call Siobhan Fat Siobhan behind my back. Fat Siobhan. Well, Fat Siobhan's all right with me, big as she is.'

'Big,' the man in the back said, 'she was after becoming a nun, but she couldn't get into the habit.'

'That's enough of that now,' Flynn said smiling. 'Don't be putting Kitty off. We know what the American ladies are like with their slimming.'

There was something horribly prissy and fussy about Flynn, in that fussy prissy pursed-lipped middle-class way Kitty hated. She had an aunt in Framingham just like that. After the suburban cursing of the traffic, after the pride of our civic heritage, and the romantic notions of the living monuments to our heroes, he's now on about the little woman. The big woman, Kitty corrected herself. Then she heard herself laugh aloud.

'That's the spirit,' Flynn said. 'Nil desperandum. Don't let the bastards grind you down. That's what I always say.'

When Flynn stopped the car, he said, 'If there's anyone after you, you'll be safer staying with Siobhan than in a hotel.'

Kitty looked about her.

They were in a sidestreet of terraced houses, like dolls' houses they seemed so small. The end of the street was blocked off by a monstrous brick wall, daubed with more mad slogans. Most of the street's paving stones had been ripped up and not replaced. It was still raining and so dark that lights had gone on in the front room windows of the tiny backstreet homes. This was a slum. Kitty had never been in a slum before. She shivered. And there was no way of being sure that Falk was not lurking in the shadows. If she ran now from Flynn, what if she fell into Falk's arms?

'OK,' Flynn said. He must have noticed something in her face. 'It'll be all right, Kitty,' he said. 'I know it's not what you're used to, but it's only the one night.'

So he's seen even that, Kitty thought. The snobbish look upon the lady terrorist's face. I must watch it.

Flynn got out of the car.

Kitty couldn't open her door. She had been locked in. She couldn't have run. They didn't trust her. Thought she might run off to the South of France with the million dollars. Flynn knew he'd run off with the money, she thought, so why should he trust anyone else?

Flynn came round the front of the car and opened the door for Kitty to get out. 'Door sometimes sticks,' he said. The other man had got out of the back.

'You know where to find me,' he said to Flynn. 'I'll be at my brother's.'

The man was younger than she had imagined. Unlike Flynn he looked very poor. He had a belly showing over the top of his cheap tan trousers but he didn't look fat in a healthy way, only in the modern way that poor people everywhere in the West now had. He looked puffy and ill. Kitty saw that he was several years younger than herself. He gave her one of those looks, like the young fellows in the market did just before they carried your shopping bags out to the car. The Stop 'n' Shop Swineherd and the Beachwagon Princess, Sidney called it. If the boy comes back, Kitty thought, she could get to him, the way he looked at her. What did a young man like that want with blowing people up?

'You've made a conquest there, with Fancy Dan,' Flynn said to her. 'We'll have to get you away before you break all our hearts. Like Joseph at the Shamrock.'

Got to be cold now, Kitty thought.

Flynn led Kitty to the front door of the house. It opened directly on to the street. He bent over and shouted through the letter box, 'We're here.' Then he opened the door with a key, saying to Kitty: 'Don't want to take her by surprise.'

The big woman was standing there, smiling and blushing in a shy manner. She filled up the narrow hall. She was standing there drying her big red forearms with a teatowel. She had been in the kitchen. There was the smell of bread baking. They had caught her baking, she said.

'You're welcome,' she said to Kitty, and smiled at Flynn. 'Eammon Flynn, you're late,' she added to him, in a different voice, quite soft and with something of the little girl in it.

Oh Christ, Kitty thought, it's his sweetie. Or at least, she's stuck on him. Kitty wondered what Siobhan must weigh. She was enormous, with a great round face in which her features looked very small, the mouth thin, and the eyes narrow. Her greying hair was pulled back tightly and twisted into a mean little knot at the nape of her mountainous neck. She's a Sumo wrestler, Kitty thought. How had she got like that? Kitty felt weak and thin, like a small child, standing beside a grownup. The knife in her purse was too small and fragile. It would break in two in all that massive flesh.

She followed Flynn into the front room. She was fussy and prissy like Flynn. Siobhan invited her to sit down. The room was stifling, as if the windows were never opened. There was a fierce coal fire in an open grate, and an electric heater on full beside the over-stuffed sofa. Heavy curtains masked the window. The curtains were in the same stiff, glistening, turquoise brocade that covered the sofa and two matching armchairs. There was little open floor space with

171

all this furniture. The fireplace was surrounded by a row of mock marble tiles in pale pink. Above it was a mirror framed with gilt leaves. Kitty looked for a telephone. There must be one telephone, Kitty thought. There had to be a phone.

'I put on the fire,' Siobhan said, 'because I know American people feel the cold.' There was no warmth in her voice. She looked down at Flynn, who was sitting in one of the glistening turquoise chairs, and gave him a sweet smile. The smile came like a surprise out of that big face. 'And you're a chilly mortal yourself, Eammon Flynn, isn't that right?' she asked.

She's absolutely besotted with him, Kitty thought. The little-girl sound in the voice coming from such a giant creature was grotesque, more frightening than comic. She's a monster, Kitty thought, with some weird sort of monster love. The way she said Eammon Flynn, run in together as though it were one word. There was a self-conscious cuteness about that. Jesus, Kitty thought, she's flirting with him.

There was a sound of subdued voices coming from somewhere. Kitty turned and saw an enormous television set muttering to itself in the corner, and there, beside a drooping pot plant on top of the TV set, was the telephone. How many MacBrides would there be in the book? And what if MacBride were unlisted. A man like MacBride would be just the type to have an unlisted phone. She had told Flynn she had a name, but how could she give the number? The number was something she would have had coming to Ireland like this. If she had nothing else she would have had that number.

'You'll want to see your room,' Siobhan said.

The giantess picked up Kitty's suitcase, and led the way up the steep narrow staircase.

Kitty watched the big woman's nimble tread. Fat Siobhan had that dainty way of placing her feet that Kitty had seen some fat men possess. Siobhan's feet were small, and the shoes she wore were as out of place as her walk and the flirtatious little-girl's voice. The shoes were the sort of thing you only wore going out in the evening, or perhaps some women might wear them in the afternoon at parties or in town. They had three-inch heels and a diamante clasp over the open-toed front of the shoe. There was a band of tiny rhinestones on the heel. They were actually expensive shoes, Kitty thought, and dangerous. The high narrow heel could easily snap off, if Fat Siobhan were to mistime one of her quick, dainty, dancer's steps, and land at the wrong angle.

At the top of the narrow stairs was a cramped landing with coarse beige carpet. Through an open door off the landing, Kitty could see into a room with a big bed covered in dazzling virginal white. Did they? Kitty could not help wondering, and was it even possible? There was a gaudy crucifix on the wall over the bed, with a cute-looking Christ gazing down in a prim manner. There was another telephone on the bedside table by a gooseneck lamp which was very businesslike and was exactly the same as the one Kitty had had at home when she used to read herself to sleep every single night of the week until she discovered boys.

Siobhan followed Kitty's gaze. 'I read a lot at night,' she said, 'when Eammon Flynn's away. You'll be here just the one night?' she added.

'I'm afraid so.' Siobhan looked at her coldly and smiled.

She knew, of course, Kitty thought, that she was a terrorist. 'Only the one night,' Kitty said. 'Then I'm off.'

'Of course,' Siobhan said. 'I'm a great reader myself,' she said. 'Are you a reader?'

'Oh, yes,' Kitty said.

'I am as well,' Siobhan said. 'A great reader.'

She took Kitty into a back bedroom. The room was so small that Siobhan seemed always about to brush the walls on either side. Kitty saw there was only the one window. It looked down on the yards at the rear of an identical row of terraced houses opposite.

When she put down Kitty's case, she turned with her amazing light step and left the room. She was back in a moment, smiling, carrying two books. They were fat paperback novels. One had a picture of a slender girl in a long Edwardian dress gazing out of a tall window at a night sky. *The Idle Time of Love*, it was called. The other cover was filled with the face of a beautiful Botticelli sort of woman. *Dreams Are Not Shadows*, it was called. They were written by women with three names each. Siobhan stood still for a moment looking at Kitty. 'You might want to read one of these,' she said.

'Oh, thank you,' Kitty said.

'Do you have someone?' Siobhan asked.

Kitty did not know what she meant. 'Someone?' she asked.

'Don't you have someone?' Fat Siobhan said, 'someone of your own? A husband? Of course maybe you're too young to be wed?'

'I was married,' Kitty said, 'but now . . .' Her voice trailed off. She couldn't start telling this murderous monster about Brooksie.

'Oh, that's too bad,' Fat Siobhan said. Kitty could tell the fat woman thought she was a widow.

Siobhan shifted with a dainty step.

'I was never a bride,' she said. 'I might've been, but I wasn't. I was going to be a Bride of Christ. A sister in the Order of St Joseph. I loved the singing. But I never took to the nursing. It is a nursing order. Then I met Eammon Flynn. You should have seen him then. Slim. Like a rake. "Don't you feel embarrassed, Eammon Flynn," I often said to him, "being seen with a girl of such a full figure, and you yourself so slim." "Not at all, Siobhan," he always said back to me, "I like a girl with a full figure." A full figure, he called it. When I heard he was married with a child I thought I'd die.'

Kitty sat down on the bed. Her right hand was throbbing with pain. The room was even more airless than the one downstairs. She could feel the tears welling up in her eyes. The fat woman must have noticed and misinterpreted them because she said: 'I know it's a sad story. But his wife died. Eammon Flynn's wife. It was a blessing.'

'Was she terribly ill?' Kitty asked, but the big woman appeared not to have heard her. She said: 'Before that, you see, Eammon Flynn was committing the sin of a double life with me at home with him in Belfast and the other one in Derry. I told the priest but the priest said it was I who was the sinner, but I never saw it that way and now she's dead.'

Jesus Christ, Kitty thought. But then Siobhan suddenly left the little room and it seemed a lot bigger.

Kitty tried to open the window. The frame was nailed shut. Burglars? she thought, and then she realised Flynn had enemies who would break in and shoot him down.

She sat on the edge of the bed and the dreamy Edwardian lady gazed at the night sky on the cover of *The Idle Time of Love* and the Botticelli woman, who she saw was wearing modern earrings, looked full of secret sorrows on the front of *Dreams Are Not Shadows*. There was another cheap crucifix on the wall over the bed. On the other wall was one of those grotesque Sacred Hearts of Jesus, with Jesus standing holding His shirt front open, showing off a ghastly Valentine's Day Heart wreathed in thorns. What kind of religion had so much bad taste? And the sort of people who worshipped at such things? Poor cringeing people without hope. They're the same as me, Kitty thought. This is my religion too. All the bad art and everything. She even liked the art because it was bad, and loved the people because they were poor and liked bad art. Sidney said it was a form of inverted snobbery, but he knew it wasn't. He understood the reason because he was religious, unlike Brooks who only saw it as something social.

On the wall by the chest of drawers there was Our Lady in her same old blue, but with a tear in her eye, for the sins of Mankind. Kitty's middle name was Mary. She usually made a joke of praying to some of the other Marys. When she was a girl it seemed like more fun praying to someone like the Venerable Mary of Madrid, who miraculously grew a beard to keep lustful men away, or the Blessed Mary of the Incarnation, who seemed terribly sweet because she compiled a dictionary for the Algonquin and Iroquois Indian languages. But now Kitty prayed to Mary the Mother of God, saying, oh, please, Mary, get me out of here and I'll never do anything at all ever again, you know what I mean.

Kitty opened her suitcase and took out *Spring Harvest* by G. A. MacBride. She read a poem about a car bomb going off during a Saturday morning shopping rush. She threw the book back down on the bed. The face of MacBride watched her.

A blackbird started to sing outside. Kitty got up from the bed and drew back the curtain. A misty red sun turned the roofs of the houses opposite bright crimson. It was the colour, she thought, of the raw red nerve ends of her finger. The bloody light glinted on corrugated iron nailed across windows. To the left, at the end of the street, a great brick wall about twenty feet high marked the end of this small world. It was covered with slogans, like a billboard advertising hatred. She was filled with hatred against Flynn and Fat Siobhan. But the blackbird still sat on the top of the wall singing. Its golden beak gaped as it poured out the notes, almost unbearably sweet, it seemed to Kitty, in that ugly, forbidding place. A woman, wearing a headscarf with red roses printed on it, with her hair curlers underneath showing dull pink, hurried along the street, pulling a sulky child by one arm. But she, too, stopped to look round at the bird. She pointed it out to the child. The child flapped his arms and screeched. The bird flew off. The woman jerked the boy's arm, then smacked him hard across the face. The boy's wailing almost drowned the startled shrilling of the blackbird's warning call as it flew away.

Kitty turned her face from the window. The dark sad countenance of the poet G.A. MacBride was staring up at her. *Spring Harvest*. Kitty picked up the book again, opening it this time at the frontispiece where MacBride had signed his name for her. She hadn't even bothered to see what he had written in the bookshop in Limerick. How long ago it seemed. But it was not even a week. He had very flamboyant writing, but childish, with big loopy letters. 'In memory of our meeting in Limerick' he had written. Well, she thought, he didn't know her then. And then, after his signature, a telephone number. With a scrawled message: 'I live in hope!'

Kitty closed the book and stared at MacBride's face on the back. There, she thought, the prayer is answered. She had MacBride's telephone number. It was a number that could prove her story if Flynn doubted her.

Siobhan called to her. It was time to eat. Don't take the book, Kitty told herself. Hide it away. She picked up her bag, feeling the knife reassuring through the soft leather. She slipped the slim volume of verse in beside it.

Downstairs she sat by Flynn on the shining green sofa. The fat woman brought Flynn and Kitty food on trays, and they sat side by side watching television. Someone was singing a cheerful country and western song. Kitty hated country and western music but she was afraid she would cry listening to this. She was overwhelmed with homesickness. She glanced down at the fry-up of bacon and eggs and boiled potatoes bursting their skins because no one bothered to peel them. She was so hungry she didn't look at what she was eating.

Afterwards she moved to one of the glistening armchairs. Fat Siobhan sat next to Flynn on the sofa. The fat woman had her hand on Flynn's knee. She kept asking him, in that arch and breathless manner, if everything with the food was all right for him. Flynn ignored her, staring at the television as though absorbed. Siobhan seemed to blame Kitty for Flynn's lack of response.

'We mustn't miss this,' Flynn said. He was peering at the folded page of a newspaper. 'It's the finals of the song contest.'

The TV screen was full of people singing songs Kitty had never heard before. Kitty felt herself dropping off.

'They're new songs from all over Europe,' Siobhan explained.

'Ireland won it the other year,' Flynn said.

Kitty felt bored. How remarkable, she thought, to be bored. The song competition seemed to be going on all night. 'Do you mind?' she said, half-rising. 'Will you think it awfully rude of me?' She was standing.

'Not at all,' Flynn said. Fat Siobhan smiled warmly.

They can, Kitty thought, what is it, canoodle now. She went upstairs, but she couldn't sleep. She read MacBride's poems.

Through his poems, he emerged as a man who did not want to be involved. He praised the people who managed to lead normal lives. That's all wrong, Sidney had told Kitty when they went to see Anne Frank. There's nothing heroic there, Sidney said. Why didn't old man Frank think to have a back door? Why didn't he arm them all to take one of the bastards with them? Kitty saw what Sidney meant about Anne Frank. There was nothing noble about living an ordinary life in a situation like that.

From downstairs she heard the raised voice of Flynn complaining.

'How could they give it to that song?' Flynn said. He seemed quite enraged. 'Sung in a language no one speaks. Even the English song was better than that one,' she heard him say.

'Time to lock up, Eammon Flynn,' Siobhan said.

Kitty could hear him turning, locking the doors.

There was a light tap on her door. The head of Flynn entered smiling. 'Tomorrow's the big day then?' he said to Kitty. 'We'll go to see MacBride first thing in the morning. Goodnight.'

In the darkness, Lucas Falk sat for a moment resting on a low wall outside a block of offices. The office block was empty, and Falk saw that it had been standing empty so long that even the For Sale sign was falling to pieces. He had all night to wait. He looked about at

177

the miserable street lined with what had once been small factories, now long deserted. Then he idly pulled a cotton handkerchief from his right-hand trouser pocket. Falk stared at the thing in the pale light of a single street lamp.

Dirty American slut, he thought, not scarlet, but the tiny nail was covered with something that glistened. The skin of the finger was already green-tinged, puckered, with the bone looking dry and brittle. There was some fluff sticking to it. And it smelled. Tyler had thrown it out. Falk had gone and picked it up. He would keep it for her, for when he got her back. He folded the handkerchief over the severed finger and put it back in his pocket.

Falk knew where she was. Tyler's contact in Belfast had found her easily enough. The city was full of busybodies and spies, all pretending that they saw and said nothing. But there were eyes everywhere. Falk could feel them on him now. They knew he was here all right. Like a strange animal wandered into the grazing land of another herd.

He was still the hunter, though. Where he sat he could see the street to his right, where Flynn, the Papist profiteer, had taken her.

There was fear all around him, but he did not feel afraid, even alone in this mean and dirty street. In the daylight he had stood out in this part of the city. In the borrowed suit, and with a clean shirt and tie, as well as the shiny leatherette case, he looked a typical Protestant. But he needed a shave and his hair was unevenly cut and filthy. He might pass for a Pape in the dark, he was dirty enough for it. He looked round in disgust at the state of this Catholic street. There were poor Protestants, of course, but they were tidy. Falk admired tidiness but somehow he had never got the hang of it.

He got to his feet. Two pigeons which had been huddled sleeping on a window ledge awoke, startled as he moved, and flew off to the safety of the rooftop gutter of a nearby empty shop. Falk was all at once filled with hatred of the Catholics' poverty. All the Protestants might not be rich but they had rich Protestants behind the Loyalist cause. That was why his side was going to win. They had the forces of money on their side. And history as well. He knew about the history. But mainly it was not money or history but God's own Protestant truth that was on Falk's side. Suddenly in this mean alien street, Falk was filled with a great love of God. How beautiful it was, this love of God and His plain simple straightforward gospel with no chanting priests or humbug. He saw the unadorned Protestant churches of his childhood. The light came through windows unstained by idolatry. The voices of the people raised in joyful hymns of praise. The Bible stories. Samson smiting the Philistines with the jawbone of an ass. And the Psalms. They were comforting. Falk had been many times in the valley of the shadow of death. He was in such a valley now. And yea though I walk through the valley of the shadow of death, I shall fear no evil, for Thou art with me, my rod and my staff.

A thin watery beam of moonlight fell across his knees. It was getting late. Falk bent his head away, pulling up the collar of his coat. He leaned over and picked up the flat case, then with one final glance at the entrance to the street on his right, he turned and melted away among the buildings, the case in his left hand and his right hand inside the coat pocket holding the snub-nosed .38 calibre revolver.

21

In the overly bright early morning that had about it the promise of later rain, Paddy Kiernan walked out of the Back Gate of Trinity College with the sun warm on his shoulders. The chestnut trees on the far side of the College playing fields, already mown for the start of the cricket season, were coming into flower. They almost hid the grim grey wall which fortified the University against the din and bustle of Dublin outside.

Paddy had returned Liam's van to the car park near the maintenance depot. It was a beautiful April morning and Paddy was full of hope. He passed Greene's Bookshop on his way into Merrion Square. There were travel books in the window. Paddy stopped and looked at the bright exotic covers. There were far too many of them featuring snowy mountain tops for him. He didn't want any more cold. On the cover of another one a dashing fellow, stripped to the waist, stood in an old rowing boat affair in the middle of a jungle river, holding a pistol in his hand. He didn't want any more guns either. 'That isn't what Paddy Kiernan's got in mind,' Paddy muttered in the empty street.

His eye took in the now out-of-date poster for the Russian play Liam O'Tomas had been doing the electrics for, and alongside it in the window, Paddy saw the photograph of a happy but serious-looking man peering at him quizzically from a display. 'A TCD Poet, G.A. MacBride,' it said. That was the man Kitty O'Shea picked up for the night at the country hotel, Brendan had said. MacBride it was. Paddy thought Doyle might be prepared to pay for that name.

Paddy disliked Irishmen who looked like that fellow in the photo in the bookshop window. The sight of the self-satisfied face filled Paddy with a sense of failure. 'They got the brains,'

180

he said aloud again in the street. And they get the women, too, he thought.

He turned and walked back towards Kildare Street, to head up past the Dail towards St Stephen's Green.

Yes, he thought, MacBride, a TCD poet, was the kind of man the American gals took to. And she took him to her bedroom and spent the entire night with him. If he had the money, he thought, he'd take a room in a posh hotel and invite Niamh along. He wondered if she'd come. His mind was full of dreams of escape to beaches and far-off bedrooms full of beautiful foreign women ever since he'd taken Doyle's money.

Still, he knew Doyle was going to cheat him. Paddy could see the irony of the situation. He was only Paddy Kiernan, 'Patsy' Paddy, and he was always being cheated, so he could expect to be cheated again. Paddy laughed at himself and the rest of the poor. He smiled, too, about all his agonising over betraying his friends, and then Doyle had told him the woman he was shopping to the authorities was already safely behind bars. And the money with her, Paddy presumed. That meant there'd be no more payment for that job, particularly with Liam done for, unless he found out from Flynn where he was keeping Kitty O'Shea. Doyle'd pay for that.

But he had already decided what he would do. It was not out of revenge, or not altogether. He had sold his soul, and he hadn't been properly paid for it. At the same time he felt guilty. With the money, sunning himself in Spain or Australia, of course he would have found a way to quiet his conscience, but now he felt there was only one way to cancel out his previous disloyalty and keep his kneecaps intact.

He walked deep in thought. When he looked up, he was in Baggot Street. He crossed the road, and went into a bar, where a cleaning woman was polishing the brass fittings on the outer door.

'We're closed,' she said.

Paddy ignored her. Inside it was cool and dim, with a strong smell of polish and wet wood where the floor had been scrubbed. It would be like that in Spain, only with sun. The barman, who knew Paddy well, was sitting on the customers' side of the bar reading a newspaper. He looked up and greeted Paddy.

'Need the Jakes?' he said.

'No,' Paddy said, 'not this time. Want to use the phone.'

'Help yourself, but don't put any of my money on your horses,' the barman said, and turned a page of the newspaper. Paddy dialled a number he kept on a scrap of paper in the top pocket of his jacket. When she answered the phone, he recognised the gruff voice of Flynn's daughter, the one Flynn had been so frightened of he wouldn't ask her to make a cup of tea. Christ, Paddy thought, she was still hoovering. The sound of the vacuum cleaner droned in the background. Lots of women like that, he thought.

He tried to make her see how urgent his message was. She sounded very bored. Her father, she said, was in Belfast. She said she had a number for him, but she seemed very reluctant to give it away. Can't blame her, Paddy thought. She said she would give Flynn a message if he called. Paddy took a deep breath and tried to sound very calm. 'Mr Flynn,' he said, 'needs this information at once.'

Grudgingly, she gave him the telephone number of the 'person' who would know where Mr Flynn was. Paddy was going to repeat it back to her, to be sure, but she had already put the phone down.

The woman who answered when he rang Belfast sounded defensive. Eammon Flynn was not there, she said. He had to go out early. He had business to attend to. She expected him. She would give him a message. Who was this? She repeated his name slowly, as though she was writing it down.

Paddy could see the barman growing restless at the length of the call. He knows it's more than betting on the horses, Paddy thought.

Finally Paddy lost his patience listening to Flynn's Belfast woman.

'Just tell him,' he said. 'We got the wrong woman. The genuine article was picked up by the Gardai at Shannon days ago.'

'What?'

'Just tell him,' Paddy said. 'And tell him it was Paddy Kiernan told him, he's got the wrong woman. She's not the Kitty O'Shea.' He put the phone down.

'Them phone calls cost,' the barman said.

'You'll get your money, Jimmy,' Paddy said.

'Horses,' the barman said.

Hedging my bets, Paddy thought. A man had to live as best he could.

* * *

She must have slept because she woke with a start at the sound of the telephone ringing. She looked at her watch. It was after seven-thirty already and she felt as if she had only just closed her eyes. Kitty got out of bed. She checked the knife in her bag. She put the copy of *Spring Harvest* in with it. She felt guilty that she had wasted time when there was so little left. As she was dressing she felt full of energy and had the idea she might simply walk out of this horrible little house and rush across Belfast to MacBride. She put on the same jeans and white blouse as yesterday but she tied up her hair in a chiffon scarf. Then she packed her suitcase, leaving out the big sweater for when she got outside, away from the stifling heat inside the house. Downstairs, Siobhan was alone in the stuffy sitting-room. She did not look up as Kitty came in.

Kitty stood gazing at the heavily curtained window. She felt the fat creature's eyes on her. Kitty turned and saw a curious expression in Siobhan's narrow eyes. She's jealous, Kitty thought. That was ridiculous. Kitty, who was not used to being disliked, would have smiled at the woman once, but now she merely looked back at her with blank eyes. That's what's happened to me, she thought.

'Where's Mr Flynn?' Kitty asked. 'We've got business.'

For some reason, Fat Siobhan made no attempt to hide her dislike.

'Eammon Flynn is out for half an hour,' she said. 'He went out just this moment ago, which is a shame. He missed an important call.'

Something more to it than that, Kitty thought. You'd think from the way she's acting Flynn came into my bed last night.

In the morning light filtering through the net curtain at the front window, Fat Siobhan looked white as a full moon. She looked ill, she had a bad colour, and her neck was mottled with dark red.

Love in bloom and high blood pressure, Kitty thought. Carrying all that weight. She couldn't put up much of a pursuit.

'Where's he gone?' Kitty said.

'You're quite safe,' Siobhan said. 'He told me to look after you.'

There was, Kitty thought, a definite edge to her voice. Presumably, the night before, she didn't dare show her feelings about another woman in her house in front of Flynn.

'I have to use the bathroom,' Kitty told her and went up the stairs to the bathroom next door to Siobhan's bedroom.

Kitty went in, making a loud noise closing the door, flushing the lavatory and running both taps in the basin. Then she opened the door and hurried across the beige shag pile carpet to the big woman's room. Kitty dropped her bag on the white bed, and with her left hand pulled out MacBride's book. The number was right there but she kept repeating it to herself, as though it might vanish on her. She picked up the telephone receiver, raising her right arm to hold it against her ear, noticing without surprise that her hands were shaking. This was a lot worse than attacking the German boy Karl in hot blood. Then with her left hand she dialled the number MacBride had written, on that jokey afternoon which might have been a hundred years ago instead of only last Friday.

Kitty waited, the ringing tone in her ear, her eyes anxiously moving over the room. There was an unemptied ashtray on the bedside table, and Jesus, Mary and Joseph all over the walls. Outside the window, little puffs of white cloud cruised across a blue sky. Outside, in the real world, the sun was shining. Would MacBride never answer? If he didn't, what was the police emergency number? Back home it was 911. She'd have to try 911. It could be the same as back home, but she just knew it wouldn't be. She hung on listening to the heartbreaking sound of an unanswered telephone. She was going to put it down. She could hear the water running in the basin. She was going to put it down and then sit down and weep. She supposed she could call the police, but if she called them what would she say to them? She didn't know where she was. The nearest road she knew the name of was the Falls Road. And she did not know the fat woman's last name. She'd be in a hell of a state trying to tell the police that, with an American accent, with Fat Siobhan throttling her with those female wrestler's arms of hers.

Jesus fucking Christ, she said in desperation to His bleeding heart picture on the wall, put your shirt back on and go and make him answer the goddam phone. She looked at her watch. It was three minutes past eight o'clock in the morning. MacBride had to be home.

'Hallo?'

At the sound of his voice, there was a horrible moment when she thought she was going to start laughing and crying all at the same time, and not be able to speak a word.

'It's Kitty,' she said, switching the receiver to her left hand and holding it as close to her mouth as she could. There was a smell of antiseptic mouthwash on the mouthpiece. She spoke in a whisper.

'Kitty?' he said.

'Kitty O'Shea,' she said. 'I can't talk,' she said. 'I've got to get away. I must see you.'

'Kitty,' MacBride said, 'What are you talking about? What are all these phone calls from the police about?'

'Tell me your address,' she said.

'My address?'

'Yes, for Christ's sake, your address. Where do you live?'

'Oh,' he said, 'it's twenty-four Jubilee Drive.'

She repeated it aloud as he said it, to fix it in her mind. MacBride sounded puzzled. 'Twenty-four Jubilee Drive,' he said. 'It's near the University. But, listen, where have you been? The Dublin –'

Kitty had her back turned to the door of the room, hoping that would muffle the sound of her voice. She didn't hear Siobhan come in, and first realised the big woman was there when Siobhan's great fist suddenly descended on the telephone rest, cutting MacBride off.

The fat woman grabbed the receiver, throwing it down. Her face, leaning over Kitty, was bloated, almost purple with fury. She was panting from climbing the stairs, and there was spittle at the corner of her mouth; she was foaming at the mouth with rage.

'Imposter,' she said.

'What?' Kitty asked, backing away. The woman had used an odd word, she said something unusual. Kitty had not got it.

'Imposter,' the woman said again.

'Oh,' Kitty said. She couldn't think what was wrong. After all, even if Siobhan had been listening downstairs, she knew Kitty was going that day to see a man called MacBride.

'Paddy Kiernan,' Siobhan said, 'Paddy Kiernan told me about you.'

'Paddy Kiernan?' Kitty said. 'Who's Paddy Kiernan?'

'He knows,' she said.

Fat Siobhan's face shook with rage. She was a horrible sight, and powerful-looking. The muscles stood out on her arms, and in her neck. She did not look like a funny fat woman anymore. Kitty put

185

the white bed between herself and Siobhan, but the woman was blocking the door and the windows were nailed shut.

Kitty looked round for a way of escape. She could see her handbag lying open on the white coverlet beside MacBride's book. She reached down and took out the knife, jabbing it forwards where Siobhan leaned across the bed to grab her. She cut the woman's forearm and there was very bright red blood already spurting all over the white bedspread. Siobhan pulled her arm back, like someone who'd touched a hot stove.

She stood looking down, surprised at the blood coming out of it.

The fat woman straightened and moved back. She was a tall woman, taller than Flynn and almost as tall as Kitty. Kitty followed her, holding the knife pointed at the great bulk behind the kitchen apron that she wore tied round her waist. The woman turned, blocking the doorway.

'Get out of my way,' Kitty said.

Siobhan was incoherent, jabbering abuse. She turned and ran down the stairs. She moved much faster than might be expected of someone her size. Kitty ran after her, watching Fat Siobhan's dainty feet in the ridiculous studded high-heeled shoes.

I'll just keep going straight out the door, Kitty thought.

But in the hall Siobhan turned and came towards her again, her huge arms raised, one of them all red.

She's going to throttle me, Kitty thought.

'You'll never get out of here, imposter,' Siobhan said, laying heavy emphasis on the word 'imposter' which had seemed so ridiculous to Kitty when she first used it.

Kitty, backed against the bannister, jabbed forward with the knife. With her left hand, her thrust was not powerful, but she cut at the woman's hands and fingers. Siobhan pulled her hands back and stood examining them as though she had been stung by a bee. They were bleeding and her dress and apron were red with blood.

'Oh,' the fat woman said, in her little-girl's voice, 'you are wicked.'

She made to come at Kitty from Kitty's right side and Kitty slapped out at her with something that smacked hard on the woman's hand. Only then did Kitty realise she had MacBride's book in her right hand. Siobhan backed away, then saw it was only a book and leaped forward at Kitty, who brought her left hand with the knife round to warn her off, but the woman came fast and the blade was inside her before Kitty knew what had happened.

'Oh, my God,' Siobhan said. She moved backwards, with Kitty still holding the knife in her.

Will she die now? Kitty thought. She went to draw the knife out and it snapped. Half of it was still inside the fat woman. There was blood all over Siobhan and on the floor. Siobhan was limping. Kitty saw that one of her three-inch heels had snapped when the fat woman lunged at her. That was what had thrown Siobhan on the knife.

If Flynn came in now, Kitty thought, she was done for. She chased after the retreating woman. Siobhan was limping where the high heel had snapped and she couldn't move fast enough. She was trying to lock the door so Kitty couldn't get out. Kitty stabbed her three or four times with the snapped end of the broken knife before she realised she was holding it in her right hand. The knife was very sharp where it had broken off but it was an irregular shape and it gouged out pieces of the woman's flesh. She stabbed at her neck and face, once driving the blade into her cheek, laying bare a great chunk of meat like beef on a butcher's slab. The woman was making the most terrible noises, but all Kitty could think of was that Flynn would come back and shoot her there and then on the spot. Fat Siobhan slumped to the floor, sitting upright, breathing heavily for a moment, before falling backwards.

Kitty stood over her. Her own hands were covered in blood. She looked down and saw that the front of her blouse was all stained. She couldn't go out like that. Besides, she didn't know where she was.

She looked at the door. If Flynn came in she would say Falk had broken in. Falk was a madman. Flynn would believe it.

Kitty went to the front door and put the catch on. At least she'd hear him before he could get in. She could flee. Out the back, over the wall, through a window, smashing the glass. Kitty looked about wildly for a weapon. There was an umbrella with a steel shaft. She took it in her right hand. She looked at her watch. It was seven minutes past. All this had taken just four minutes.

She knew she couldn't go out covered in blood. And where did one get a taxi in Belfast? She would have to run the risk of Flynn coming back early and catching her.

There was a telephone book in the fat woman's bedroom. Kitty went upstairs. Entering the room she was surprised at the amount of blood all over the white bedspread and across the floor. The phone book had several taxi numbers printed in ballpoint on the cover.

Christ, she thought, I don't know the address. There was a drawer in the bedside table and there were letters in it, bills with the address.

When she dialled the number, the man had a lot of trouble understanding what Kitty was saying. 'Mr Eammon Flynn gave me your name,' she said.

'Oh,' the man said, 'any friend of Mr Flynn's.'

Kitty gave him the address.

'Oh, we know Mr Flynn's address. And how's his good lady?'

'Siobhan's resting,' Kitty said. 'I'll meet you at the corner of the Falls,' she said. 'By the shop.'

'We'll be there in two minutes,' the man said.

When she put down the receiver, Kitty thought she could hear someone moving downstairs and she could feel the hair on the back of her neck rising, just as it had when the fat woman first screamed 'imposter' at her. Kitty's hands were trembling and she could not feel pain or any sensation in the right hand where her little finger had been.

In the stuffy little back bedroom, she put on the big sweater. There was no time to change out of the bloody blouse and the jeans which had blood on the legs. She took the suitcase and made for the stairs, the umbrella hooked over her right arm, handbag under the right elbow against her body, carrying the case in her left hand.

Any minute now, she'd hear Flynn's key at the door. She reached the hall. Something was wrong. Fat Siobhan was not there. There was a trail of blood leading into the sitting-room. 'Siobhan!' Kitty called out.

She heard a moaning. The woman was calling to her to come and help her.

'Oh, Jesus,' Kitty said, 'I can't leave her to bleed to death.'

Or could she? After all, they would kill her if Flynn came back with Siobhan alive to tell the story. The fat woman was calling out. She sounded in great pain.

When Kitty got to Siobhan lying on the sitting-room floor, she could see that it was the first slashing cut, the quick jab she had made in the bedroom, which had severed an artery. The woman's eyes followed her but she seemed barely conscious. 'Oh, you big fat bitch,' Kitty said aloud, 'You're going to get me caught.' She tore a piece of Siobhan's skirt and made a tourniquet for the arm, winding it tight with a ballpoint pen. All the time Kitty kept listening for the sound of Flynn at the door. Once she started, the hair on her neck rising. But it was nothing. Fat Siobhan's eyes never left Kitty, but she did not speak. Her face was a mess. Kitty looked at the gash in the big woman's cheek. She took the scarf from her neck and tied it round Siobhan's face. Afterwards the fat woman looked like a cute picture of a boy with toothache.

When Kitty had finished, she looked at her watch. It had only taken forty-five seconds to apply the tourniquet. When she went to stand up she felt something tugging at her leg and looking down saw that Fat Siobhan was clutching the cuff of Kitty's Levis. The fat woman was hanging on to her for Flynn. Siobhan's hand was cut and covered in blood and there was no real strength in it. When Kitty stepped back, Siobhan's grip loosened.

Kitty went into the hallway. She picked up her suitcase, and the blood-smeared copy of *Spring Harvest* which she put under her right arm with the handbag. The carpet was smeared with blood. It looked like a butcher's block. The three-inch heel of Siobhan's fancy shoe was lying in a corner. When Kitty went to the door she found that it was unlocked.

Outside she took a deep breath of the still early morning air and walked towards the taxi she could see waiting at the corner. She was weeping so much she could scarcely make out the shape of it.

'Are you all right?' the taxi driver said, when she had got into the back of the cab and pulled the case in after her.

'Just an emotional parting,' she said.

'Are you American?'

'Yes,' Kitty said, 'over seeking my roots.'

'Well,' the driver said, 'and did you find them?'

'I rather think I did,' Kitty said. She was full of confidence.

'All right now?' the taxi driver asked.

'Oh, yes, everything's wonderful now.'

'Where to?' the man asked.

'Twenty-four Jubilee Drive,' Kitty said.

'By the University?'

'That's right,' Kitty said. 'The name on the door's MacBride. That's G.A. MacBride.'

'MacBride,' the driver said, 'twenty-four Jubilee Drive.'

It was the fourth Army patrol to pass him, Falk thought. Possibly the fifth. He could not afford to let them see him, pull him in for questioning. They'd have done that the first time they passed, if they'd seen him waiting. A man just standing watching the world go by was loitering with intent, as far as the Security Forces were concerned. And those Tommies couldn't tell the difference between the Papes and a loyal Brit. Each time he heard the distinctive sound of the Landrover engines labouring up the hill, Falk had to get out of sight. Nor could he dodge down the same shadowy sidestreet more than once, or some busybody Papist bitch, who couldn't keep her own children off the streets, would be yelling for help from the local unofficial vigilantes, and in this part of the city, they were a greater threat to him than the soldiers. But at least there weren't many about. Just the one old biddy in the house opposite the fat bitch's hovel, where the Colleen Queen was hiding out. Even now, Falk could see the old biddy in the house opposite was twitching her curtains looking out at him.

It was still early. The sun was too bright to last. He could see the thick black clouds already massing in the sky to the west. But an unnatural glaring sun caught the upper stories of the terrace opposite and turned the dull brick to fiery red. Where there was glass in the windows, the reflections looked like flames.

On the other side of the road, in contrast, the houses were in darkness, casting weird angular shadows across the destroyed pavements and the potholed roadway. Another Army patrol had just passed. Falk had heard them coming and had gone walking briskly up the hill away from the street where the fat woman's house was.

He watched the patrol go out of sight, with the lookouts in the rear of the vehicle with their rifles raised ready to deal with trouble.

Falk did a quick turn and hurried back, but he knew it was getting very dangerous being there. He thought he should perhaps break into the house and shoot her down. There was no one but the fat woman with her. Not much chance of him getting out of that alive, though. But the Papist bastards would get him anyhow if he stood where he was much longer.

He saw her then, getting into the back of a black taxicab. One of that vile gangster's fronts, probably. But how was she alone? Surely they would not have sent her out alone? She was going for the money. That must be it. She could not have handed it over. He was sure of that. She was going to collect it. But why alone? Stupid bastards, he thought, she's stealing it. Large as life with that big Yank smile she was walking off with their money to live the life of Reilly. She was smiling at the taxi driver, and shouting out an address in that big American voice. MacBride, the name of the bookshop fancyman. Falk wondered if she had the money with her.

He glanced behind him up the street. He had to follow her. There was not much traffic about yet. One car passed, with two passengers. A small Peugeot driven by a middle-aged woman. Falk stepped out into the car's path, his hand raised like a traffic policeman. The woman stepped hard on her brakes. Her mouth was open with fear. She knew what was happening. He had the muzzle of the snub-nosed .38 pointed at her. Falk kept it trained on her as he moved round and opened the door. She got out. He threw the flat black case with the rifle across to the passenger seat and got in. The engine was still running. Falk drove off after the taxi. The car smelled of the foul perfumed flesh of the painted hag. The stench of feminine corruption. The American would not escape again. She planned it all along, he thought, stealing the money.

22

Moving in a world of deceit and danger made Eammon Flynn a cautious man. Before he even reached Fat Siobhan's front door, he knew something was wrong. Upon closer examination he saw the door was unlocked. He stood for some time debating whether to go in. Across the street, he saw that the bent old biddy, the street's amateur spy, was out washing her front window. All the better to peer through, Flynn thought. He knew her well. Nothing escaped her watching eyes. Flynn crossed the street to her, an ingratiating grin on his face. The crone looked at him with a mixture of envy and moral outrage. She had been a widow many years, Flynn knew, and thought of Siobhan as living in sin.

'Have you seen anything, Mrs O'Dowd?' he asked her. 'Only the tall dark girl – is she a foreigner? – leave the house with a suitcase, looking as if she'd stolen the family silver. She rushed off in one of your own taxis. And then a Proddy-looking mad man, who'd been loitering all morning, commandeered a woman's car in the Falls and went after her.'

Flynn entered Fat Siobhan's house with his gun in his hand, gaping at the state of the blood-stained carpet. There should have been a body to go with all that mess, he thought, but there wasn't. Flynn turned and went into the front room. There was Siobhan, hacked to bits. She looked dead, but he couldn't tell for sure from a distance. Flynn was wary of touching her. He was used to death, or, at least, to hearing that people he knew were dead, he ordered it without a qualm, but he was not used to handling it at close quarters.

Flynn bent over Siobhan. There was a bandage on one of her arms and she had a colourful bandanna wrapped round her face. Flynn spoke to her and saw that she made some attempt to answer. Thinking it was the bandanna that hindered her speech he put down the Browning automatic – a weapon he'd never fired anyway, not even in practice – and undid the cloth. The poor woman's face was disgusting to see. He felt quite ill. He thought he might be sick. There was also a terrible smell. Flynn did not at first recognise it as blood.

He couldn't look at her face, but he heard her trying to speak.

'Eammon Flynn. Help me,' she said. He could barely make out what she said. She had been stabbed in the mouth. It was horrible to look at. He placed a handkerchief over his mouth.

Flynn tried to pull her upright, but she was too heavy. He saw the snapped-off blade of a knife in her side, and a shaft of sunlight creeping gradually along the hallway from the front door caught the edge of a great pool of blood Siobhan had been lying in. It had soaked the carpet. The sun brought out beautiful iridescent lights in the dark red where the blood was already drying. The television was on in the room. He could hear a scientist talking about the Chelsea Flower Show in London and making a red delphinium in a laboratory.

'Where's the girl?' he asked, shaking Siobhan's arm to bring her round.

'A priest, Eammon Flynn. Bring me the priest.'

'Where is she, goddammit?' Why, Flynn wondered, was the girl not dead or lying here wounded? He could not imagine a woman, especially one like the American Kitty O'Shea, stabbing Siobhan like this.

Siobhan coughed. There was a bubbling sound in her throat.

'Oh, Jesus,' Flynn said. Look at that mouth, he thought, and her face.

'Who did this?' he asked.

'Kitty O'Shea,' the fat woman said. Her voice was weak. Flynn could see she was going.

'Where is she?' he asked.

'Twenty-four Jubilee Drive,' she said, and her voice was feeble and sounded as though she was gargling.

Flynn held the handkerchief tightly over his mouth. Some maniac had obviously broken in. It couldn't have been done by Kitty O'Shea. Siobhan was hacked apart. She was like some of the bomb victims he had seen.

'What happened?' Flynn grabbed her shoulders, but his hands

slipped hopelessly on the wet blood. He looked at his hand. He went to wipe off the blood with the handkerchief and smelled the stink of it and realised that the awful stench had been Siobhan's blood.

'Eammon Flynn,' she said with great effort, 'I'm going. Get me a priest.'

Flynn stood up.

'Eammon Flynn,' Siobhan said, 'please. A priest.'

Flynn went up the stairs. His shoes were slippery, and when he looked down, he saw they were leaving bloody footprints on the beige carpet. The door to Siobhan's bedroom was open. There was blood all over the bed and on the walls. The telephone was off the hook. Whoever stabbed her, he thought, did that so Siobhan couldn't call for help on the telephone downstairs. He rang the taxi number. They had come for an American woman and brought her to twenty-four Jubilee Drive. Flynn realised that Kitty O'Shea had stabbed Siobhan. It was obvious, she was stealing the money. He'd expected it all along. Only a fool would have thought she'd do anything else. He would have to stop her. Perhaps the money would be with MacBride at twenty-four Jubilee Drive. Now, he thought, that would be a wonderful thing.

Flynn went down the blood-soaked stairs. He was nervous and kept checking the handgun in the holster under his left arm. He heard Fat Siobhan's voice, feeble and pleading.

'Stay with me,' she was saying, 'I'm dying.' Flynn looked in on her. Anyone could see she was going fast. What good, he thought, would a priest do her? No priest could get there in time, and Flynn would be held up. Kitty O'Shea would be off with the money while Flynn was talking to the police. There would be police. He couldn't simply have Siobhan's great lump of a corpse rolled out of a car in a field somewhere.

'Eammon Flynn,' she said, 'hold my hand, stay with me.' She tried to say something else, but Flynn couldn't make it out, her mouth was full of red bubbles.

He looked down at her for a second and then ran out of the house, leaving the front door swinging wide open. Pray God, he thought, he wasn't going to be too late, but he didn't reckon Kitty O'Shea had that much of a head start, and she'd find it hard to get away with the money.

Kitty O'Shea was nervous, moving quickly in her tight jeans up the path to number twenty-four. She rang the bell, jigging from one foot to the other with impatience, glancing back and forth, looking round. She pushed the doorbell twice before anyone could have answered the first time.

She was there ringing the bell as Falk pulled the Peugeot into the kerb under the shadow of a dark ornamental tree. The tree drooped over the railings of what looked to Falk like a cemetery. Falk knew he was lucky; he might have missed seeing which of the tall Victorian villas she'd gone into. But that was as far as his luck went. He had no time to assemble the rifle before the bookshop man was answering the door and they were in each other's arms. Now that, Falk thought, would have been a wonderful shot, both of them; perhaps even with a head shot, but, no, the human skull was too thick. It would have been something for the drunken lover to have her head explode, disintegrating while his lips were kissing. Then a fast second shot to the drunken pen-pusher's heart. Falk could shoot that quick. He knew he could. But he didn't have time to get the rifle put together properly. Then she had gone inside.

Falk thought he would creep round the back and enter the house but he didn't know which floor she'd be on. He could see number twenty-four was divided into flats. But now she became clearly visible through a big sash window on the ground floor. Falk, with a clear view through the open car window, raised the rifle. But the man, the drunken pen-pusher, the ageing Romeo from the Limerick bookshop, kept walking in front of her, blocking the shot. That was bad luck. But if he'd really wanted to, he could have got her then. Falk had a little day-dream of shooting her up close. He saw her dying a few feet from him, the front of her body blown away. He saw himself bending over her whore's corpse, opening its clenched hand, and placing the missing finger in it. That had some significance, although he did not know what it was. It would bring things full circle. He would have to write something, too. At least make some mark. He saw her forehead marked in some significant way with her own blood. That would demonstrate that it was not just another murder. The body of the drunken pen-pusher would be in another room altogether.

The two figures disappeared from view. Fallen upon each other, Falk thought, like ravening beasts. Copulating on the floor. They were animals in rut. There would be all sorts of bestial sounds. He had often heard the beast sounds of love. He waited, watching the window where he had last seen them. From time to time he looked at the dark clouds that discoloured the sky in the west. When that storm came, he thought, it would grow dark. He would go round the back and move in on her then. They would be lying naked, exhausted and unwary.

23

When Kitty came through the door MacBride could see that everything was all different now, without any jokes, or what she had called college banter when they were in the bar of the hotel down South. Her hand was wrapped in a bandage and there were bloodstains on her jeans and shoes.

'What the hell's happened to you?' he said.

Kitty told him some of it. 'Good God,' he said. Then he said: 'And you used my name?'

'Just the MacBride part, MacBride,' she said, trying to sound like her jokey old self, 'but not the initials.'

They were there in the big room, with books all over the floor, in the front part of the flat. MacBride sat down. 'Sit down, sit down,' he said, 'before you fall down. You look awful.'

'It's my hand. It doesn't hurt all the time anymore and I think that might be a bad sign. Like when a tooth never hurts, and the dentist says it's dead.'

'You said they chopped off your finger?' He couldn't believe it. It was all too much for him to take in.

'Yes, yes,' she said. 'I don't want to talk about it.'

'Better let me look at it,' he said. He knew he should have said that first, before he got cross about her using his name, but he hadn't. Now he could tell she was looking at him and seeing, as others had seen, that he didn't want to get involved. 'Come into the kitchen and I'll look at it. That bandage is filthy.'

'You know,' Kitty said, rising, 'when we met I'd never've guessed you'd have such a clean home. Even the windows are sparkling.'

'Well, the floor's rather cluttered,' he said.

'Oh,' she said, 'that's a classy sort of clutter.'

In the kitchen, which she saw was neater still, Kitty took the old bandage off and held her hand up for him to put a new dressing on.

'Good God,' he said, 'your finger's missing.'

'Yes,' she said, 'that's what happens when they chop your finger off. I didn't tell you I was raped along with it, but I was.'

'You were? Where?'

'In the usual place,' she said, but she could see MacBride thought that was in bad taste.

'I read your poems,' Kitty said. 'All of them, last night. They're all about how wonderful people are trying to lead normal lives in the middle of all this.'

'Well, isn't it wonderful of them?'

'Maybe it is. But, no, I don't think it's so, not at all. I think it's dreadful. I read them last night, up in the room of that terrible house. Did I tell you I killed a woman?'

'Yes, yes, you did.' He could hear an edge of hysteria in her voice. 'This finger'll have to be seen to,' MacBride said. 'By a doctor. You could lose your hand. I had an uncle with a foot once –'

Kitty laughed.

'It's serious,' MacBride said. 'Gangrene.'

'She was a big fat woman,' Kitty said.

Oh, God, MacBride thought, she's going to start to cry.

'I feel incredibly exhausted, MacBride. Like I was watching the world from inside a goldfish bowl.'

'You need whiskey.'

'Protestant or Catholic?'

'Protestant.'

'I wish they had some Jewish whiskey. Or Buddhist, that's what they need in Ireland. Buddhist whiskey.'

MacBride gave her a drink. He didn't pour one for himself. Better keep a clear head, he thought.

Kitty sat down in a chair by the kitchen table. 'I wonder if I really did get raped,' she said. 'I led him on. Does it count then? If you lead them on? He did have an erection, though, right from the start. Before he put it in my mouth. An erection! God! what a word!'

Good God, MacBride thought. He'd never heard a woman say a thing like that, not about another man at least.

'You're suffering from shock,' he said. 'Delayed reaction. You'd better not speak.'

'Remote control,' Kitty said, 'no warning given. You see, I have read your poems: "Remote control, no warning given/As a bomb and also sudden love". You're sweet, MacBride, but your head's in the sand. What do you think a rapist does to a woman? Of course he wants to see his prick in her mouth.' She seemed calm but she switched topics in the same breath. 'If I were in charge in Ireland,' she said, 'I'd make all the women go on strike, like thingy did, you know?'

'Lysistrata?'

'Exactly. But I say it differently. Lisa-strata, makes her seem more like a gal back home in Holford Park. But no matter how you slice it, there'd be no cunt till the boys came home from war. Not any of your "Lie still, my love," and how does it go?'

'I can't remember now.'

'Sure you can, you old ostrich. Something something and cover your ears against the something something. "Be still, my love, for it's not our something something war."'

MacBride stood watching her. He was extremely nervous. He was waiting for her to start shrieking and weeping. He thought he should put his arms round her, but he knew he wouldn't.

'Well, you certainly give it something,' he said.

'That's better, MacBride. Now we're the nice old divorced couple being pals. I'd have, if I were Queen of Ireland, MacBride, everyone go on strike.'

'We tried that.'

'Not hard enough. Do you think I'm a whore, MacBride? I felt like the most terrible whore. Do you suppose all the little rape victims feel like that?'

'You'll always be virgin territory,' MacBride said.

'That's a typical European remark, MacBride. Henry James stuff. The virgin territory of American womanhood. Well –' Kitty got the bottle and poured herself another whiskey. 'Well,' she said, 'Me getting fucked by strange men is not front page news back home. Killing fat ladies is another thing.'

MacBride watched Kitty shudder, her entire body flinching two or three times and her mouth twisting as though she were a refined American lady being offered a plate of something grisly in a foreign restaurant.

'I can't have the police,' she said. 'I've got to get out.'

He would have to get out as well, MacBride thought. He looked round his modern kitchen. He'd had it done the spring before. Already he could see it standing empty. She's put the mark on me, he thought. They'll be looking for me. They'll think the two of them skipped with the Provos' money. And she had led them to him. He started to hate her, looking at her sitting there, with her face bruised and a cut in her lip, speaking in that high, clear voice that did not come through the nose, the way people always imitated Americans speaking, but was projected at you with the jaw pushed slightly forward and the head tilted slightly back. She sounded like someone doing a Katherine Hepburn. That, at least, was the only time he'd heard that voice before and he thought it must be a ritzy New England voice and this knowledge made him dislike her all the more for being seated here in his kitchen.

He thought he should say something so he said: 'Do you still have my book of poems?'

Kitty laughed. 'I didn't leave it behind to connect you.'

So, MacBride thought, she sees through me. Well, that's the way it is. She doesn't understand.

He watched her pour herself another drink. She's still like an American college girl on a spree, he thought. Except her face now, it's drawn.

'Do you think you should have so much?' MacBride asked. 'You're in a state of shock.'

'"Cover your ears against the thud in the night", MacBride,' she said, quoting a line of his verse. It was about lovers in Belfast hearing a bomb going off while they lay in bed at night. 'Truth is, MacBride,' Kitty said, 'I'll bet half of the men can't get it up anymore except in bullshit verse.'

'Make no mistake,' he said, 'they'll kill me too.' He was angry now and it had come out without thinking.

'I'm sorry, MacBride. I really am. But you see, the motherfuckers have been trying to kill me too.'

It was strange hearing that elegant, educated voice say 'mother-fuckers'. 'I know,' he said. 'It's not your fault, but you don't understand. I've never been involved in anything like this.'

'Well,' Kitty said, 'I have. And this is what my brother Tim of the US Marine Corps would call a haul-ass situation.' She could see MacBride's face and the expression on it. 'God, MacBride, there's something I absolutely love about you donnish Europeans. No, really, I'm not being sarcastic. There's Princeton, MacBride. You said they wanted you as the petrol bomb poet. They'll think you're cute at Princeton. The poet on the lam.'

'I'd better pack.'

'No, you don't, MacBride. You'll start selecting books. We'll be sitting here arguing whether Eliot or Joyce is essential reading.'

'Joyce.'

'And the police, or worse, will be breaking down the door.' Kitty stood up. She crossed the room to the kitchen cabinet.

'Mind that whiskey,' MacBride said.

'This is gin. The whiskey's gone. You just come in that bummy tweed suit of yours. They got shirts, and even books, in New Jersey.'

'New Jersey?' MacBride said.

'That's where the fools put Princeton. Don't worry, it's near Philadelphia. You can always pop over to spend two weeks there any weekend.'

'Have you got any money? I don't have any money,' MacBride said.

'I've got plastic. Don't worry, no one expects a poet on the lam to have any money.'

MacBride went into the other room to get his cheque book out of his desk in the big front room. He didn't know how drunk she was, he thought, coming out with all that college banter. Probably best, after all. Better to put up with that than have her falling down weeping. A little pissed and loud and even abusive was better than weeping. She's cool, too, after a business like that with her hand. She could lose it, the whole hand. They have plastic hands, fibre and aluminium, fingers working on the nerve endings, the brain going through the old motions sending messages to the plastic and metal. Good as new, or better.

MacBride groaned. Looking out of the window he saw a man outside in the street. The man was looking at the numbers on the houses. He was next door.

MacBride put the cheque book in his inside right coat pocket and picked up Kitty's handbag and suitcase from the floor. The handbag was opened, and when he picked it up *Spring Harvest* fell out. MacBride bent over to pick it up, but when he had it in his hand he saw all the blood on it. He dropped the book on the edge of the desk. When he got to the kitchen door he was going to go back, thinking the book was evidence. But he could hear someone trying the front door.

Kitty was sitting in the kitchen. She wasn't drinking. She was staring at her bandaged hand.

'There's a man coming to the house,' MacBride said. He spoke in a whisper.

'What's he like?' She didn't keep her voice down. 'Does he look like a corpse?'

What in the name of God did she mean by that, MacBride thought.

'He looks like a shabby civil servant,' he said. 'About fifty. Bald on top. Very bald on top, reddish hair growing over his ears. Not attractive.'

'It's Flynn,' Kitty said. It was hard to breathe, and her knees felt like rubber. She thought, how could it be Flynn? He didn't know where she was. Then she thought, Fat Siobhan's alive, she told him. Or the taxi driver. They were Flynn's people, the Catholic taxi drivers.

'He's at the door,' MacBride said. 'He's coming in now.'

They could hear the lock being broken on the outside door at the front of the house.

'My God, MacBride,' Kitty said, 'I've got to get away from here.' She was on her feet.

'Come along,' MacBride said. 'Out the back.'

Kitty was dithering. MacBride grabbed her arm.

'Quick,' he said, 'before he gets in. We can go through the garden.'

There was a French window in MacBride's bedroom which opened on to a small balcony only a few feet above a lilac bush.

They could hear the door to MacBride's flat being broken in.

'Come on,' MacBride said. He pushed Kitty on to the narrow balcony. The railing was less than a foot high, designed to hold window boxes. MacBride could hear the queer moaning sounds she was making. He thought she might faint or burst into tears. Oh Jesus, he thought, she's going to have hysterics on me.

'Where are we going?' Kitty asked. She had one foot on the balcony railing.

'To the airport. In my car,' he said. 'Hurry. Jump.'

'Lead on, MacDuff,' Kitty said.

MacBride didn't laugh but he thought, that's better than weeping. As he leaped over the lilac bush MacBride heard the sound of the glass panel in his front door breaking.

The last time Falk saw Eammon Flynn, the Fenian had a full head of red hair and he was clean-shaven. Falk didn't recognise Flynn coming up the street to number twenty-four. He lowered the barrel of the rifle a little as the man ran along the pavement across Jubilee Road towards MacBride's house. He looked like a school teacher to Falk, panting for breath as though unfit, with wispy hair and a great bald dome. Poor eyesight, too, Falk thought, by the looks of it. Just the sort to call on the pen-pusher and have a natter about books.

Some of the house numbers were clearly marked, but the number of twenty-four, like some of the others, was marked on the gate, and the quick hedge had bushed out and obscured the number. Falk watched the man move on to twenty-five, and then come back. Falk studied him some more. He looked like an official of some sort, but there was something wrong. Brown shoes, instead of black, and the jacket was a shade too bright. He was too old for a door-to-door salesman. Falk thought they probably still had such things as peddlars in a suburb like this, but the man had no samples. He watched Flynn ring the bell. He's left-handed, Falk thought. No, he decided, the right hand was holding something in the jacket pocket. A gun, of course, and then Falk thought: it's him, it's Eammon Flynn. He saw Flynn break the lock of the front door and go inside. He brought up his rifle. Flynn, the bastard, he thought, he wasn't going to have her. But it was too late. Flynn was inside.

Falk started getting out of the car. He'd go in now. He'd kill her and the profiteer Flynn together. As he was opening the car door, he heard another car coming up behind him. Falk quickly sat back in the driver's seat, pulling the car door shut. To get run over now, he thought, by something like that, one of those sit up and beg Citroens which looked like a couple of covered bicycles. As the car went on ahead, Falk saw the driver. Christ, he said, it's the Limerick agriculturalist. And her, the whore.

The Deux Chevaux was only just still in sight. Falk crashed the gears of the stolen car as he followed in pursuit.

Eammon Flynn moved carefully along the wall of the hallway to the door to MacBride's flat. The house was obviously divided into two flats, the stairs boxed off and a door marked with a large letter B marking the entrance to the upper. The ground floor had G.A. MacBride on a card on the door. Inside there was an old-fashioned bentwood coatstand in the hall. The glass panelled door to what was MacBride's sitting-room was locked. Flynn burst it in, breaking the catch with a single kick but the glass broke. He had the Browning automatic in his hand. The man might be armed, if he was working with her. She was no innocent. Flynn was fairly sure she had no handgun, but then he hadn't expected the knife either and he'd seen what she could do with that. There was no one in the big front room or the kitchen. He looked in the bathroom and then went in to the bedroom. The bed was made. Flynn opened the built-in wardrobe, and began pulling clothes out on to the floor. There was nothing there. Off the bedroom was an ornamental balcony; no stairs led away from it, but the French window was open and they had obviously escaped through it when they heard him coming in. If, that is, there had been anyone there. This was, Flynn knew, a respectable area, full of people from the University. They might forget and leave a window open like that in the bedroom.

Flynn was curious. He went back to the front room and began pulling books off the shelves. There must be some clue, but it was just books. In the kitchen there was only one glass and an empty bottle of whiskey. There was no lipstick on the glass. The woman didn't wear lipstick.

Flynn stood in the kitchen thinking. There was a plastic pedal bin by the kitchen sink. Flynn put his foot on it. Inside he saw a bloody bandage. Too much blood for an ordinary cut. He walked back into the sitting-room, with the bloody cloth in his hand. Could be woman's trouble, he thought. The idea disgusted him. He dropped the stained bandage on the floor and wiped the palm of his hand on his trouser leg.

He stood in the centre of the room thinking. She had come here. MacBride lived here and he was with her. There must be letters showing what kind of man MacBride was. They'd get to him and squeal it out of him. All Flynn had to do was get G.A. MacBride. He wondered who he was. Flynn saw *Spring Harvest* by G.A. MacBride on the desk. Prod face, he thought, picking up the book.

Flynn turned the book over. It was smeared with blood. It had already turned brown, but he knew what it was. Siobhan's blood. Flynn read the inscription. They'd met in Limerick. In a bookshop. It was all there, and he'd written the phone number for her to make contact in Belfast. They'd planned it together all along. She's the hard one, Flynn thought. She let them cut her up. Then she cut up Siobhan. And she'd acted as though butter wouldn't melt. He was writing poetry to her.

> Lie still, my love, under the soft sheet,
> Cover your ears against the thud in the night,
> Muffle the sound of screams and heavy feet,
> Be still, my love, for it is not our fight.

Lie still, my love, under the soft sheet; under the soft shite, Flynn thought. Woman's stuff. Lot of good those fellows had ever done, even when the Irish cause was riddled with poets.

Flynn threw the book down and went round to the other side of the desk, with his back to the tall window where the sun caught the slight distortion in the old glass with an odd iridescent effect of bottled rainbows. He tried to open the middle drawer. He put his revolver on the desk. The drawer was stuck. He jerked at the brass handles and it came out. There were a lot of sheets of paper covered in scrawl, typewritten but scribbled with notations. And there it was. Flynn smiled. The soft fool, the tough bitch had him wrapped round her one remaining little finger.

'To the American Kitty O'Shea,' Flynn read:

Child of the brash New World, untouched by our dying fall,
Search as you may, you cannot share our Irish pall.
Long, long ago, when first they left these shores,
Your forefathers divorced you then forever from our cause.

And that, I suppose, Flynn thought, gives her the right to run off with our million bucks.

They'd run off together with it. Flynn could see, it was as clear as day in the so-called poem. He heard someone laughing in the room; the sudden and totally unexpected sound of laughter froze him. When he turned he saw two police officers had entered. They were pointing guns at him. One of them came across the room and took Flynn's gun from the desk top.

'Not using a knife this time?' the policeman asked. It didn't mean anything to Flynn.

They looked at Flynn as though they were waiting for him to do something surprising. The first policeman had his gun pointed at Flynn's face and had a look on his own face as though he were hoping Flynn would do something and save them a lot of trouble.

'Mr Eammon Flynn?' the other policeman asked. He was holding a small black notebook in one hand. He still had his gun pointed at Flynn.

'What do you want?' Flynn asked, as if they were intruders. 'I'm waiting for a friend.' They couldn't get him on anything. G.A. MacBride wasn't going to prefer any charges.

'You always break down doors when you come calling?' the policeman with the notebook asked.

'It was like that,' Flynn said. 'I came in to check if Mr MacBride was all right. That's G.A. MacBride, the poet, you've heard of him?'

'Yes,' the other policeman said. 'We've heard of him.'

Flynn was cursing his luck. Getting done for breaking and entering. He'd be a laughing stock. Of course, later they'd have to let him go. But still, it was an inconvenience.

'Are you Eammon Flynn?' Flynn could tell the cops knew exactly

who he was, and how pleased they were nabbing him. The policemen were both young, both over six feet tall. They had short black
moustaches and looked like twins. All RUC men looked the same
to Flynn.

'What is it?' Flynn asked. 'I told you Mr MacBride asked me to
come. I'm worried about him, what with the door broken in.'

'Read him his rights, Malcolm,' one of the policemen said.

It didn't seem right to Flynn, using first names like that when they
were arresting a man.

'What the devil's going on here?' Flynn said.

'We're arresting you, sir,' Malcolm said to Flynn in a sarcastic
manner.

'You're making a mistake,' Flynn said. 'Do you know who I am?
This isn't what you think. I'm no burglar.'

'We know that, don't we, Alex?' Malcolm said.

'Yes,' said Alex, 'and we're very surprised and disappointed.'

The bastards, Flynn thought. They were having a wonderful time,
getting Eammon Flynn for housebreaking.

'I'm no housebreaker,' Flynn said.

'We're arresting you for murder, sir,' Malcolm said. 'For the
murder of Miss Siobhan Prendergast. Isn't that right, Alex?'

Flynn gaped. They couldn't be doing that. He was innocent.
'Siobhan?' he said. 'Me murder Siobhan? I didn't kill her. I wouldn't
murder Siobhan, for God's sake. She was still alive when I left her.'

'So you admit leaving the scene?' Alex said.

'I'll say nothing,' Flynn said.

'We got a witness. Plus a statement from the woman herself.'

'From who?'

'Miss Prendergast. She gave us a statement,' Malcolm said.

'Never. Siobhan would never.'

'Who do you think, Mr Flynn, sir, told us you'd be here?' the
policeman called Alex said. He sounded very polite and interested in
Flynn's answer. He remembered the state of the poor woman, nearly
gone, begging for a priest. 'Eammon Flynn,' she'd said, so piteously.
'Get Eammon Flynn.' It sounded almost as though she was crying
out an endearment, the young man thought, but then the subject had
been stabbed repeatedly about the mouth and face as well as the body,
thus causing a certain impediment to speech. Also the subject named

Flynn quite formally, using the full name of her assailant so there would be no confusion. A neighbour, a Mrs O'Dowd, who was the party who telephoned the police, also informed them that Eammon Flynn was the man last seen coming from the front door of the house 'as if it was on fire' and 'all covered in blood', and 'leaving the door wide open'. Mrs O'Dowd said she'd called the RUC because, she said, this wasn't a political but a cold-blooded domestic murder. Flynn and the subject co-habited openly in the house in which the subject was found dying from multiple stab wounds. It was a messy killing and Malcolm and Alex were used to domestics.

'This should put you away for life,' Malcolm said to Flynn. He smiled. Flynn watched both of them smiling.

'Can you imagine, Mr Flynn,' Malcolm said, 'a man like yourself with a finger in every racket and act of intimidation in Ulster, going down for life on a domestic. There won't be any of the privileges of the political prisoners there. That pleases me and Alex a lot, Mr Flynn.'

Flynn looked at them. They were like evil-minded schoolboys.

They handcuffed Flynn, and there were more heavy-footed police-men in the hall. Flynn could hear the sound of breaking glass from the back garden where the big clumsy RUC officers were investigating.

'I didn't kill Siobhan,' he said.

'Who did?' Malcolm said

'She was dying,' Flynn said. 'I found her dying.'

'Then why did you run away?' Alex asked. 'And who did do it, sir, if it wasn't you?'

And Flynn knew there was nothing he could say.

'I'd never kill Fat Siobhan,' he said, under his breath as though addressing himself.

'Well, we don't really care about that, sir. Do we, Alex?'

'Not very much, Malcolm,' Alex said.

They were walking Flynn out of the flat. Outside there were three police cars in the street.

'If you didn't kill this one,' Malcolm said, 'you did plenty of others. It doesn't really matter which one we've got you for, as long as we can prove it.'

'I think that's about it, Malcolm,' Alex said.

24

'Look at that sky,' Kitty said to MacBride. Like a person might say, she thought. An ordinary person.

There was a large, wide section of the sky in the west that was so dark it looked purple. Elsewhere the sky was a beautiful blue but in the west it seemed to be boiling and it was the colour of a plum that had gone off. They were driving to the airport in MacBride's little French motor. MacBride was looking glum. He wasn't saying anything and he was looking glum, like a man, she thought, who has got himself involved in trouble not of his own making and is going to have to run for his life and go into exile because of it. She could feel the vibrations coming off MacBride and the vibrations were none too good. She thought she'd better keep her mouth shut for a time and can the college girl banter. But she felt she must say something to let him know how sorry she was.

'Oh, MacBride,' Kitty said, 'I've really fucked you up.' MacBride didn't say anything.

The streets through which the little Citroen was passing were full of forsythia bushes, lilac trees and flowering almond about to bloom. There were daffodils, tulips and japonica already out in the gardens. It had been an early spring. The calm and solid middle-class suburban comfort around the university reminded Kitty of somewhere at home. Brown University, she thought, up on the hill full of suburban streets on the East side of Providence, Rhode Island.

'It won't be too long now,' she said, not knowing what she meant.

'No,' he said.

A police car came speeding up on the opposite side of the road, lights flashing. Probably only cops going to lunch, she thought.

They were leaving the city behind, coming to countryside which looked, Kitty thought, as though it had been built for miniature folk, all little peaks and hollows, with tiny green fields. Here and there she could see one of those small, white-washed cabins, centuries older than anything else in the Victorian city. She had come to see this sort of Ireland and she hadn't seen any of it. The dark massed cloud against the skyline gave the bright sunlight a curiously chemical quality, as though she was seeing through an orange filter.

The traffic was heavy. Huge trucks were going out of the city. She pulled her sweater off over her head.

When MacBride looked he saw her blouse was covered with blood. Good Christ, he thought, she really did kill someone, and that missing finger is no magic trick either. She unbuttoned the blouse and tossed it into the back of the car. She wasn't wearing a bra and he looked at her chubby little breasts with the closed-rosebud nipples. He leaned across and pulled an old t-shirt from the shelf under the dashboard. He dropped it in her lap. She held it up. It was stained with oil. Kitty pulled it over her head. She put the big blue pullover back on.

They didn't say anything for a time. MacBride spoke first.

'What'll we do?' he asked.

'How do you mean? We'll get the first plane out of here.'

'The Shuttle? To London?'

'Is that the first?'

'I imagine so.'

'That's what we'll get,' she said.

He felt as if she was in control, just as it had been at the hotel when she had led him upstairs to the room and taken off his clothes and pushed him back on the bed.

There was another pause. Then they both spoke at once. 'In London,' they started to say. They laughed, but the tension was still there.

'Sorry,' MacBride said.

'Well,' she said, 'Ireland has certainly been –' Then she stopped.

Kitty stared out of the car window, trying to think. The glass in the windscreens of the oncoming cars was reflecting the light like a person wearing glasses sometimes does, she thought. Just like when Sidney is standing talking out of doors and turns his head and his eyes are no longer there, only the bright silver shining of his glasses. Kitty thought of Sidney, seeing him, towering over her. He would have a tennis racquet in his hand and the mere fact of that tennis racquet would mean everything was all right and she was home, safe at home. Slid in to home plate safe. But that was baseball, not tennis. She would explain to Sidney about Fat Siobhan and then Sidney would explain it to her. It would take him weeks or maybe months or years to explain it, but he would do it. But now Kitty could see right in front of her that where the high heel of one shoe had come off Siobhan was walking up and down, up and down, coming at her with her hands all covered in red outstretched, blocking the way out of the front door shouting, 'Imposter! Imposter!'

'She was limping,' Kitty said aloud.

'Who?'

'I'm sorry,' Kitty said, 'I was thinking so much I thought you'd have heard me.'

'MacBride –' Kitty turned sideways in her seat to face him. She was going to say something embarrassing, he thought. She looked as though she was going to cry.

'Checkpoint coming up,' he said. 'Security. They'll want to search the car.' He didn't want her weeping at the checkpoint, although the soldier there would have seen a lot of it. You do at the best of airports, train stations, bus stops, everywhere where they say goodbye.

'What?' Kitty looked frightened. 'Checkpoint?' It sounded like the Iron Curtain. East Berlin, somebody shooting and a man running, then falling. What a fucking awful place the world is, she thought. Please God, let me get through this, I'll never complain again until later. God, it seemed so wrong praying just to get on a plane. Like the old woman coming over last week, Kitty thought, the woman who got on in Boston and said the Rosary halfway across the Atlantic Ocean until she fell asleep snoring. 'For that relief much thanks!' someone said and all the passengers laughed.

'The soldiers check everyone,' MacBride said. 'It's nothing.'

'But,' Kitty said, 'they – will they have my description?'

'Oh,' MacBride said, 'Whatever for? I mean, do you really think they might?' They wouldn't, he thought. He never rang Doyle, and there hadn't been any mention of her on the news. But once she said about that woman, it somehow made everything different. The cops might be after her for that. 'I don't suppose that woman's even dead,' he said. Still, he thought, you can't go round stabbing people. If they got her, they'd get him and

211

then the Provos would be waiting for him when the cops let him go.

'Right,' MacBride said, braking as the traffic slowed and then he stopped in line for the check. 'You know,' he said, 'I don't think I've ever in my life needed a drink as much as I do now.'

A Parachute Regiment sergeant, a very large young soldier came over to the car. His eyes were screwed up against the sunlight. The massed clouds behind him were blue indigo. The sky didn't look real, but like something done in a photographer's studio.

The soldier looked to Kitty like Red Skinner, who played tackle on the football team at Jeffrey when Brooksie was the quarter-back. He had been a large physical boy, too, with one of those grins. The soldier kept looking at her, but he didn't ask for any ID. It's all right, she thought, if he does I've got the passport saying I'm Mrs Katherine Lawrence, wife of Brooks Acton Lawrence.

They had made MacBride get out of the car and Kitty got out to be polite. The big soldier smiled at her.

'You're taking the good weather away with you,' he said, looking up at the purple part of the sky. The soldier had a curious accent, much more pleasant than the voices she'd been hearing for a week, Kitty thought. Yes, of course, she thought, he was English. That was an English accent she was hearing.

'Yes,' she said, 'you're going to have a storm.'

She could see that they had been checking the licence number of the car with some computer the soldiers had inside the command post, and now everything was all right.

They went into the airport and bought two single tickets on the London Shuttle. Kitty used her American Express card. It was a queer feeling, she thought, signing herself as Mrs Katherine Lawrence again, as though Kitty O'Shea did not exist. MacBride paid by cheque. Kitty thought of offering to pay for his ticket, but one look at his face warned her. And, she thought, she had all his year at Princeton to play Lady Bountiful. She wondered how Sidney would take to her having an Irish poet in tow, and it felt good to be thinking like a flirtatious bitch again. There'd be some men who wouldn't care at all for the missing finger, but, well, she could still give her friends a run for their money. Mimi Vallard had a scar just above her upper lip that made her look as though she was forever

212

sneering at you, but she'd had loads of lovers and married a richer man than any of them.

They went into the bar.

'How's your hand?'

'I can't feel anything. Do you think that's bad?'

'Does it hurt?'

'It doesn't anything.'

'We'll go to Harley Street in London.'

'Oh,' Kitty said, 'like in the old movies?'

'They'll fix it for you.'

They drank glasses of lager because their mouths were dry from being frightened.

'I'd rather have water,' Kitty said. '"You'll do your work on water, and lick the bloomin' boots of 'em who's got it". I'll be Gunga Din,' MacBride said. He got her a glass of water.

It's all normal now, she thought. It's like it was getting off the plane at Shannon before anything happened. It's exactly like that, except that she had left a little bit of herself, just the little finger, in the Old Country. Some part of a foreign field, she thought. When she got home, she wouldn't tell anyone, she'd just say she had an accident and no one would know; and then she'd tell Sidney and she'd go some weekends to Princeton to see MacBride and drag him along to New York to a really glamorous hotel where they'd fuck; and in the Fall she'd take him to a college football game at Princeton, it was nice there, and they'd get drunk and screw Saturday night away and first thing Sunday morning, except she'd get up and go to Mass on account of what she'd promised Our Lady when they had her in the hut. Everything would be just as it had always been, only a little bit different. And maybe MacBride would be a world-famous poet and literary gent and she'd marry him.

Whiskey patriots and women, look where it got you. Rushing off with the Provos' money. Lucas Falk had seen them laughing in the car. She must have the money on her, be running out on Flynn with the drunken lover. It was almost ridiculous. He wasn't much younger than Falk himself. Falk sang a song in his head: Oh Paddy is me darlin', me darlin', the only man for me. She won't be laughing long, though. Falk had gone over the fence, and was now limping along in the bright sunlight, his eyes burning in the glare. He reached a large maintenance shed. There was a man whistling down at the dark end out of the sunlight at the door.

'Yes?' the man said.

'Is this maintenance?' Falk asked.

'Yes,' the man said. Falk couldn't see him. He moved down the shed into the dark part where he could see the man standing by a forklift truck.

'Christ,' the man said, 'I thought for a moment you were a Catholic priest, in that dark suit with the little case. They often carry those for when someone dies. Have you come about the heating?'

'Yes,' Falk said.

'It's here the trouble is,' the man said. He had his back to Falk. 'In the old boiler here. It's chronic.'

Falk reached inside the jacket and took out the .38 revolver and struck the man on the back of the head. He pulled the man's body behind some packing cases and put on the man's brown overalls. As he went out of the shed another man in overalls said: 'Who are you? Where's John?'

'Eating,' Falk said.

'Eating?' the man said. 'This skiving off will have to frigging cease.'

'Some hope,' Falk said. The man laughed. Falk went back into the sun.

With his queer crooked gait, he moved carefully along the side of the airport buildings. Bad weather for it. People were hanging about, and gazing out of windows watching every little thing on a day like this. Falk held the black case with the rifle close against his body. Still, he thought, there's no wind if it has to be a long shot. It would be nice to try the rifle out on a good long range shot. There wasn't many in the Ulster Rifles could out-shoot Falk, and he'd kept his eye in.

Falk reached the apron. There was a plane on the tarmac, with a fuel tender parked next to it. Various uniformed men were running up and down the portable stairs to the forward cabin door, looking busy. If it was raining, Falk thought, there'd be no bugger about. Pressed back against the grey wall Falk watched as three men worked together on a fire tender engine. The bonnet was raised. Two had

214

their backs to him, but he could see the other, frowning, the tip of his tongue protruding between his teeth as he concentrated on fixing something in the engine. That's a good trade, Falk thought. If he'd gone in the RAF, he might have got a trade like that.

The man, however, must have felt he was being watched, for he looked up. He's suspicious, Falk thought. Falk didn't move. The man stopped work and started walking towards Falk.

'What is it, Bob?' Falk heard one of the others say.

'Won't be long,' the man said, still coming towards where Falk stood. Falk smiled at him. The man looked less certain. 'I'm going for a leak,' he shouted back at the other over his shoulder.

The man came towards where Falk was standing watching him. Falk didn't move. Then the man stopped and wiped his hands on his overall, not looking up at Falk anymore, and then he walked into the shed itself. Falk could see inside that it was the place where the passenger luggage got loaded on a conveyor belt. He felt conspicuous with the black case. He could picture himself getting caught now. There were two planes right out on the apron. It would be a hell of a thing, he thought, to assemble the rifle and then stand there and shoot her down. He wouldn't get away with a thing like that. If he were up above, well, with no wind at all, he could put one into the middle of the target at five hundred yards, if he were in the prone position. Falk looked up at the sky. There wasn't any wind. That's why the big storm away off in the western sky wasn't coming any closer. In a way, he thought, he was better off in the good weather because it meant there were a lot of men coming and going, skiving off, stretching their legs. They didn't notice one more lazy bastard doing no work. At the same time there was nothing secret about this place. Still Falk didn't feel any fear. Usually he could tell if there was fear around.

He looked up. There was a great commotion. Men were shouting and running in and out of the maintenance shed. Christ, Falk thought, if they have discovered him already, that'll be it. Should have killed her at Shannon. Or with that short fat one, the old fellow in the car. He couldn't have foreseen the way it would be and what a bitch she'd turn out, smiling at every man and putting it out.

A man was running past Falk. He stopped. He was terribly excited.

'It's John Docherty,' he said to Falk. The man was out of breath. 'They've found him murdered. In his underpants. In maintenance.'

Falk looked concerned. No play-acting about that, he told himself. Still he didn't feel any fear about. Everything was all right.

'And the London Shuttle is boarding in ten minutes,' the man said.

The man rushed off. There were a lot of men rushing about. Falk heard a voice asking: 'Who are you?'

Falk turned. A man in a suit with a necktie was looking at him. The man looked anxious. He was red in the face.

'Security,' Falk said.

'Well,' the man said, 'you're doing a marvellous fucking job today.'

The man went off towards the maintenance shed. Falk went into the luggage shed. There were men in there working.

'What's going on?' one of them asked Falk.

'John Docherty's been killed,' Falk said.

'Good God,' the man said. 'And he traded days off with Danny Long.'

Luggage was being loaded from the conveyor belt on to a flat trolley. Behind Falk's back at the entrance to the shed a man was saying: 'There's Army and police all over the frigging place now. Yes,' the man said, 'now that poor John's gone they're all over the frigging place. But why'd they ever want to kill him? Of course, he was in the Volunteers for a time,' the man said. 'Christ, we'll never get home today. They'll be questioning us till midnight. That's my lot,' the man said. He climbed into the motorised truck attached to the loaded luggage trolley and drove off, leaving Falk alone in the shed.

'We left your beautiful book of poems behind.' Kitty pressed close to MacBride, looking up at him, with one arm round his waist. He could feel her breasts against him. 'It's going to be great for you at Princeton,' she said. 'Don't worry, MacBride. It'll be the best thing that ever happened to you.'

They were walking through the boarding gate on to the tarmac. The runway looked like glass, reflecting the sun against the purple sky. Beyond the runway, the countryside looked like a dark crayon mark, merging with the almost black clouds on the horizon. The line of people going to the London Shuttle had stopped moving. Kitty turned and faced MacBride. She was standing as close to him as if they were doing an old-fashioned slow dance. I'm trapped, he thought, but it feels good. There'd be Princeton. She'd come and stay with him. 'You'll be happy,' Kitty said. 'Before it's all over you'll be happy. I just know it.' The plane they were about to board stood turned towards a lurid sun which shone orange against the purple cloud.

'I'll bring you to New York and show you off to my friends,' Kitty said.

'I thought you said I had my head in the sand?' MacBride said.

'No, no. They're beautiful. Delayed reaction – Something, something –' MacBride felt happy. The line moved forward and they turned to go with it.

'No, no, don't tell me,' she said, 'I know it. "Delayed reaction, remote control, no warning given/As a bomb and also sudden love/ I –" I've forgotten the line – no, don't tell me, I'll remember it. It goes –'

Kitty looked up, smiling at MacBride. He leaned his head down to whisper the lines of verse in her ear and then his head wasn't there anymore.

'Oh, Jesus!' a woman behind Kitty was screaming. Kitty found herself sitting on the floor. There was something grey on the shoulder of her pullover. MacBride was stretched out on the floor at her feet. There was a lot of screaming. People were running back into the airport building. Kitty didn't think she would be able to rise to her feet. While she was sitting with her legs stretched out in front of her, she took the pullover off without touching any of the stuff and, not knowing what to do with the sweater once it was off, got to her feet and put it over MacBride's head.

When he fired the shot, at first no one seemed to notice the limping figure of Falk. He was muttering like a mad man, pushing his way through the screaming passengers. He was furious with himself. If he'd gone for a body shot, the drunken pen-pusher wouldn't have got in the way. But he'd aimed for the head, and at the last minute the fool nodded forward so quickly he'd taken the shot meant for her. Now there was fear all round. Falk was not afraid, but he knew the fear was travelling with him. He'd seen her knocked down when the pen-pusher fell, but he'd lost her.

They had all been milling about bleating like a flock of sheep after the drunken fool was dead in his whore's arms, kissing her whore's mouth. At least she'd never forget that. Wasn't much left to kiss goodbye.

'There he is,' Falk heard another bitch shouting in a high screeching voice. He turned and faced a crowd of them. 'He's got a gun. Mind that gun,' one of them shouted. The bleat of bleating sheep. 'Oh dear God,' a woman cried. Up and down the voices were going in hysteria.

Falk stood with the .38 in his hand. The sheep were bleating and rushing about and he turned and ran into a shed. The sun bright in the doorway, and through the window. The rest all dark. Like inside a church, all cool inside. Falk went behind some packing cases. He got down and assembled the rifle. It snapped together fine. It was a good rifle.

Nothing stirred outside. There was such bright sun at the window that Falk could only just make out the men on the roof.

It'll be today, he thought. He'd never get out of there alive.

There was some movement out in the sunshine by the side of the doors. An RUC man with a loudhailer was asking Falk to come out with his hands up. Falk made no reply.

They'd shoot him down like a dog when the parachute boys came, Falk thought, running in shouting to make themselves feel as brave as the Laundrymen in the snow. No bugles or gongs, though. That'd been real fighting.

The sun was not so bright now. Falk could see through the big window on his right. Up on the roof a man was standing large as life. A long shot like that, shooting up. It wouldn't be so difficult. Then they would all come charging in and he would turn and face them.

I could've been a limping old wreck, full of soldiers' stories at the pub, Falk thought. Better than blathering in a public house, rolling up the trouser leg to show the knee, old men talking in the pub, compared to this, which was a soldier's death that no one could take away.

On the roof, two young soldiers, one a Parachute captain and the other a lieutenant in the Scots Guards, were chatting.

'Who was he?'

'A university professor. And a poet.'

'There were two of them?'

'No, all in the one. A professor who was a poet.'

'Why ever should they want to gun down a poet?'

'Who can tell what they think? Maybe it's not them at all. Maybe he was playing around with the chap's wife. He was a poet.'

'Or a chap's brother,' the Guards officer said. 'The point is – where have we got to now?'

'You won't believe this, Sandy,' the captain said, 'but he got all the way to the fence before he was spotted. Wearing overalls, they thought he was one of them.'

'Where's he now?' the young lieutenant asked. He was a tall soldier, with sandy hair and a freckled face.

'He ducked into the maintenance shed.'

'Which is?'

'That one down there,' the Parachute captain said. The captain was twenty-six and the Guards officer twenty-two.

'Your chaps don't want to rush the building?' Sandy said.

The captain could see he was joking.

'They certainly do,' the captain said. 'But the RUC is down there now, using sweet reason on him through a loudhailer.'

'Do you think he might come out?'

The captain shrugged. 'He may. But the thing is one can just about see him from where we are.'

'Oh? We can?'

'Yes. Through that window there.'

From their position on the roof the young lieutenant looked down and saw through the window.

'He popped up for a moment a while back,' the captain said. 'He's got a rifle. One saw him quite clearly. We only have these automatic weapons. Shoot hell's own amount in nought nought seconds, but no good for a shot like this.'

'Perfectly useless for it, I should think,' the tall lieutenant said.

'Then I thought, what about young Sandy Browne and his ancient

219

but magic Lee Enfield that he's always gassing about? At least you were gassing about it the other night. Do you have it?'

'Boot of the car,' Sandy Browne said.

'Will you have a go?'

'I don't see why not.' Lieutenant Browne turned. 'Macpherson,' he said to a Guardsman squatting on the roof talking to a larger paratrooper.

'Sir?'

Browne tossed his car keys to the Guardsman. 'Go to my car, will you, Macpherson, and bring my Lee Enfield up to me. Mind you don't start leafing through my excellent collection of pornographic magazines or you'll be all day.'

'Very good, sir,' the Guardsman said.

'Very good, Macpherson,' Browne said.

The Parachute captain could see his own men watching and listening to the aristocratic Guards officer and the Guardsman. Toy soldiers, the paratrooper thought. Still, the captain thought, he had that target practice rifle.

When the Guardsman climbed back up on to the roof, the captain could see that the old World War Two Lee Enfield was a beautiful piece of work. When Browne let him hold it, he could smell the linseed oil that had been rubbed into the wood of the stock. It smelled like an old-fashioned cricket bat, the captain thought.

'Don't you have a telescopic sight?' he asked.

'I've got this,' the young lieutenant said, reaching into his breast pocket. He had a spy glass. 'That's all I ever use when stalking,' he said. 'It was my great grandfather's.'

I'll bet it was, the captain thought. He handed the Lee Enfield back.

'You know,' Sandy Browne said, 'it has only this moment occurred to me. Here we are standing about up here in plain view. I mean, if we can see that chap down there when he wiggles about behind those packing cases, he can jolly well see us.'

'I suppose I should have told you, Sandy,' the Parachute captain said, 'but I was hoping he might take a pot at us up here, so my fellows on the ground could get a look at him.'

'Oh,' the lieutenant said.

That's got through the Eton manner, the captain thought. That got to young Browne.

'Well,' Browne said, 'if it wouldn't disturb your grand strategy I think I'd best assume the prone position if I ever want to get off any sort of decent shot at this range and angle.'

The tall Guards officer lay down on the asphalt rooftop and gazed down at the maintenance building through the antique brass spy glass. At one point he rolled over on one elbow and looked up at the paratrooper.

'You just remain standing there, Billy,' the lieutenant said, 'and when he shoots you I'll pot him.'

Kitty was aware of hands all about her. She felt numb. She and three other women, who had been close behind MacBride when the terrible thing happened, sat in a small office drinking cups of tea, watched over by a young policewoman. A doctor had provided sedatives. They were all on edge, though, and their hysteria asserted itself in unnatural but persistent anxiety that they would miss the plane.

'What's it got to do with us?' one of the women kept asking the policewoman, who was the only one very calm.

'Just a few questions,' the policewoman said. 'It won't be long. They're holding the plane for you.'

The nervous woman sat still. She seemed to be gathering breath to ask again how long it would be.

'Your luggage is still on the plane,' the policewoman said.

'Our luggage is still on the plane,' the nervous woman said, turning to Kitty. 'What does that mean?'

'It means they're not taking it off,' Kitty said. She was surprised at the sound of her own voice. 'They're keeping it on the plane for when we go.' The woman seemed placated.

A policeman in plain clothes came in and took one of the women out with him.

Kitty stared out over the expanse of grass towards the airport perimeter fence on the skyline. It stood out in stark detail against the oddly coloured sky, like something painted for a poster. The office did not overlook the apron where they all knew something was happening, but towards the open country to the north. There were a few private executive jets standing on the grass. The sun was losing its fight against the huge purple banks of cloud which now covered all but a narrow sliver of blue sky. Kitty felt completely empty. What was going on around her seemed to be happening through a thick fog.

They called her name three times before she heard them.

'Mrs Lawrence?'

The policewoman took her arm and pushed her gently towards the plain clothes man who was asking her politely to follow him. He seemed bored.

The police were in a small office nearby. The new policeman was older than the other. He had sad brown eyes and a drooping moustache. He made apologetic noises for bothering her, and offered her more tea. 'Just a few questions,' he said.

'Of course,' Kitty said.

'You are Mrs Katherine Lawrence of Holford Park, Massachusetts?' Kitty took out her passport.

'Yes,' she said. 'Katherine Lawrence.'

'Were you acquainted with the deceased?'

There was a silence.

'Mrs Lawrence?'

Kitty looked down. Then she raised her head and looked the policeman in the eye.

'No,' she said. 'I've only been in Ireland a few days. I know no one here.'

'You didn't know him at all? Or why anybody should want to shoot Mr MacBride?'

'MacBride?'

'The deceased, Mrs Lawrence. George Albert MacBride. Did you know him? The woman standing behind you in the queue for the London Shuttle was under the impression you were together.'

'Oh,' Kitty said, 'I'm an American. We talk to strangers at airports, train stations, bus stops. It's a national failing. It gets us into no end of trouble. But there was no connection.'

The policeman smiled.

There was no connection. What good would it do MacBride now to go back through those few hours which was all they had had together? She could, of course, rise and scream and look tragic.

'What was your purpose in being in Ireland?' the policeman asked.

'I'm just a tourist,' she said.

'You don't have friends or family here?'

'I'm an American,' she said. 'I talked to the guy while we were waiting in line. How was I to know?' Oh, MacBride, she thought, the policeman believes this hard-faced American bitch all right now. That's the sort of woman he can understand. I'll feel bad about you later. 'Delayed reaction, remote control, no warning given/ As a bomb and also sudden love,/Killing old dreads and little fears. New sorrows to come/ Unimagined in the unforeseen instant.' See, MacBride, I remembered it.

Later, walking out to the plane with the other shocked passengers across the stretch of tarmac where his body had been, she thought, Poor MacBride, in your bummy suit, you'd have charmed all the girls at Princeton. Three maintenance men in brown overalls were winding up a hose they'd been using to sluice the ground where he had died. There was nothing she could do. She would buy his books, and learn all his poems by heart when she got home, and never tell a soul, not even Sidney. MacBride was the one who never wanted to be involved.

There was a flurry of activity beyond the maintenance shed, close to the perimeter fence. An ambulance, and a tall blond soldier carrying his rifle in a self-conscious manner, like a hunter no longer in the forest.

'Well, Sandy,' another soldier was saying to the tall, languid one with the rifle, 'I owe you a drink.' 'A drink?' Sandy Browne said, 'You owe me an entire dinner, Billy.'

The ambulance men were loading something brown on to a stretcher.

'They got the man that did it, then?' the woman who had been so nervous said. The woman now obviously felt linked to Kitty in the collusion of shared misfortune.

'Thank God for that,' Kitty said. She had to catch her breath at the sudden feeling she had, of joy and of a bitter sense of justice done. They had got him, that loathsome Falk. He was the dead bundle being lifted. She was quite taken aback at her own fierce reaction. The nervous woman, surprised at her vehemence, shook

223

her head and moved away. Inside the plane it was half empty. Kitty sat by a window. There was an empty seat by her. A very presentable-looking woman about her own age but wearing very bright colours and hoop earrings, sat down beside her. The woman's clothes were all too new and shiny.

'Do you live here or London?' the girl asked in a very loud voice, high and nasal. She had a buck-toothed grin, like a waitress in a diner. She was an American. She didn't wait for Kitty to answer. 'I'm from Pittsburgh,' she said, 'but I've got tons of relatives in Ireland, both in north Ireland and south Ireland.'

'Oh, really,' Kitty said. 'Excuse me.' Kitty got up and moved into the back of the plane.

'One of those,' the girl from Pittsburgh said. 'One of those stuck-up Wasps.' The nervous woman came and sat by the Pittsburgh girl. The nervous woman said she had seen a man shot dead. The Pittsburgh girl said that was really terrible. She hadn't seen anything like that. On the contrary, she said, everyone had been really nice.

25

Doyle sat on in the Shelbourne Bar, gazing out of the window waiting for the rain to ease. There had been a cloudburst and Doyle had taken refuge in the Shelbourne, but he was wearing the yellow tie with red dots, so he had been planning a celebration anyway.

The rain meant it started earlier than planned. Outside the rain-spattered window, the heavy early evening traffic was making its way round the St Stephen's Green one-way system. Doyle could see the sudden downpour making the usual maniacs out of otherwise sober citizens hurrying home to the suburbs to harassed wives and kids with homework. But Doyle wasn't a traffic cop anymore. The rain was keeping the less than sober citizens off the streets for a time. But soon they, and the kids with no homework, would be out robbing one another, pulling knives or taking drugs or sniffing glue. Doyle wasn't that kind of a cop anymore either.

He had one of the London tabloids in front of him and was having a lot of fun reading it. There were pictures of G.A. MacBride, Poet of the Petrol Bomb. Doyle almost missed the paragraph which reported that a prominent Ulster businessman had been charged with murder after the mutilated body of a woman was discovered in her Belfast sitting-room.

But the capture of the woman terrorist Kitty O'Shea at Shannon Airport by a special team from Dublin was given a new lease of news life. The paper had been going strong on Lionel Thompson as the murdered British hero, an undercover agent murdered in the name of the IRA harridan. But now it had to tell its readers he was a wacko who thought he was an Irishman.

The London tabloid couldn't quite figure out how anyone could be that crazy. They had hired a psychiatrist to explain it. 'Moving from one racial category to another,' the London tabloid's trained

225

shrink said, 'is well documented.' But, he said, usually it was 'a move up' the social pattern. Many blacks in the States, he said, 'passed into white society every year'. In Nazi Germany, many Jews passed as Aryans. There was a theory that Hitler himself had been 'of Jewish blood'. The tabloid had a second story: 'Was Hitler a Jew?' to underline its point. But, it said, American whites did not become black. No Christian in Nazi Germany turned Jewish. But Britain today is producing a 'new species of wall-bangers, nutters who actually want to be Micks'. Doyle had a good time reading that. He wondered just where the tabloid's man had studied psychiatry.

But Britain, anyway, was shocked. In Croydon someone had pushed something nasty through Lionel Thompson's mother's letter box. There was a photograph of the father of Liam O'Tomas with a chest full of war medals. 'Damn You To Hell, Son – A Father's Curse' the headline said. The newspaper demanded an investigation of Trinity College, Dublin to find out how many other IRA hitmen like Liam O'Tomas were hiding there.

Doyle put the tabloid aside and ordered another drink. He'd save 'Was Hitler a Jew?' for later.

There were a number of middle-aged American tourists in the bar. They were not drinkers. They were waiting for the rain to stop. One of them was standing alongside Doyle.

'Is this the famous Irish mist?' he said, looking at the pools of water on the pavement outside.

'That's Scotch mist,' Doyle said. 'Irish Mist is an alcoholic drink. But in Scotland they have Scotch mist.'

'Scotch?' the man said. He sounded suspicious. Doyle could see the way he was looking at him that he was an American hick and thought Doyle might be a conman out to trick him. 'I always heard "Irish mist",' the American said. His voice was almost angry about it.

'Scotch mist,' Doyle said.

'You a native here?' the man asked. Doyle nodded. Yes, Doyle thought, he's some hick all right. 'You don't sound Irish.' Doyle laughed. That didn't please the man at all. 'My Grandad,' the man said, 'he was a real Irisher, born and bred, a real Irisher, and he didn't sound like you.' The man was wearing a brand new Burberry raincoat and he was completely sober, which was amazing for a man to be when he was as aggressive as that. He was about fifty, heavy

226

round the jowls, and he moved away from Doyle, keeping his eye on him all the time, as though Doyle were up to something. Doyle laughed and he could tell the man didn't like that at all.

A pretty middle-aged American woman, wearing a Scotch plaid skirt and a raincoat with a tartan lining, came into the bar. She didn't look like a hick but Doyle could see she was obviously the hick's wife. She went and stood with him. The hick said something and she looked over to where Doyle was near the window. The pretty woman was holding a Dublin street guide and a copy of *Ulysses*. She was the type, Doyle thought, who didn't read the local papers. They wouldn't know what was going on. They didn't look Irish to Doyle, not even Irish-American, like the Kennedys were supposed to look Irish. But, he thought, they probably gave to Noraid and wore something green on St Patrick's Day.

There was a tall boy with large round spectacles standing next to Doyle. He was gazing down at the front page of the London tabloid.

'I knew him,' the boy suddenly said, smiling at Doyle. 'Liam O'Tomas. He worked at Trinity. He did the lights for the Players' Theatre.'

The boy had one of those cultured Anglo-Irish voices. 'Extraordinary,' the boy said. 'I had a play at the Players' – an adaptation of Dostoyevsky actually – and this Liam O'Tomas in the papers was the electrician. A most peculiar chap came and took him away. I had to do the lights myself. I keep thinking it must have had something to do with all this business.'

'That's amazing,' Doyle said, but his voice didn't sound amazed.

'Yes,' the boy said. 'But the most amazing thing was, that night I came here and who should I meet for the first time but G.A. MacBride, the national poet of Ulster, the one who was assassinated.'

Doyle didn't say anything. He remembered the tall student now. He'd seen him that night, but there had been a crowd of them, boys and girls, Trinity students, and Doyle had remembered more clearly than the boys a pretty girl wearing a shawl.

'MacBride spent the night in my rooms,' the boy said. 'In my bathtub, actually.' He laughed. Then Doyle could see the boy remembering that the death of the poet was a great tragedy for

Irish letters. He stopped laughing and stood there looking serious, staring out of the window at the street in the rain.

Doyle thought he should say something so he said, 'That was a coincidence.'

'I'll tell you what is even more of a coincidence,' the boy said. 'The man who came to collect Liam O'Tomas that night, the man who said Kitty O'Shea had been in an accident, you know, Kitty O'Shea the American terrorist, the newspapers said.'

'Yes,' Doyle said, 'I read that.'

'Well,' the boy said, 'he's standing over there.'

'Where?' Doyle said, turning to look round the room.

'No,' the boy said. 'Outside. In the street. He's standing under that tree. Sheltering from the rain.'

Doyle looked out of the window. Paddy Kiernan was standing in the street. He looked like a wet mongrel dog.

'That's him,' the boy said. 'I'd remember him because he was such an Irish type. And the confused story he told. I was sort of studying him, as a type, an Irish type, a disappearing Irish type.'

'Yes,' Doyle said, 'you would.'

'But, this is extraordinary,' the boy said, 'it means I knew all about it. But unfortunately I didn't know I knew.'

'I suppose,' Doyle said, 'the Gardai are always up against that sort of puzzle.'

'Yes,' the student said. Doyle could see the boy was getting excited.

And outside in the rain Paddy Kiernan was pacing back and forth under the trees overhanging the pavement from St Stephen's Green. He moved with his arms held stiff at his sides. His big red wrists hung out from the end of his sleeves. I ought to have sent him to the sun, Doyle thought as he watched. He was waiting for someone in all that rain. It must be love, Doyle thought. He should definitely have sent him to the sun.

'You see,' the boy was saying, looking intense and agitated, 'there is something that wasn't in any of the papers. I read them all. None of them mentioned that G.A. MacBride was also involved with Kitty O'Shea.'

'Oh?' Doyle said.

'That's right,' the student said. 'MacBride was going on and on about her all night. He was supposed to meet her, in here, in the Shelbourne, in fact. Then the next day I helped him telephone all the hotels. He was very drunk, of course. I told him someone had come to Players' and said Kitty O'Shea had been in an accident the night before – the man out there in the rain, it was in fact. How extraordinary. But he was drunk.'

'Who was drunk?' Doyle said.

'MacBride was drunk.'

'Oh,' Doyle said.

'He didn't seem to connect the two names. I mean to say, the same name, not the two names. He didn't connect them, he was so drunk.'

'Were you drunk?' Doyle said.

'Not very. Not until much later on.'

'I hope you didn't drive,' Doyle said, but the boy didn't take in the sarcasm.

'I wonder if I should go to the police?' the boy said. 'I mean, there's that chap right outside there now.'

'I shouldn't bother,' Doyle said.

'I suppose,' the boy said, 'there were two Kitty O'Sheas.'

'It's a common enough name.'

'Is it?' the boy said.

'What'll you have?' Doyle said. 'My name's Doyle.'

'Oh, same again, thanks,' the boy said. 'I'm Jim Parsons.'

Outside in the rain Doyle could see a thin black-haired girl hurrying along the street. She was smiling at Paddy Kiernan, and Paddy Kiernan was smiling at her. They stood for a moment smiling at each other, then they walked off, not in the least bit in a hurry in all that rain.

The running, fleeing Kitty had panted, gasping for breath – the tight-skirted anxious heroine, all nervous bird movements, with red lips and permed hair in the green jungle twisting a high-heeled slipper and stumbling in the forest, hearing always the persistent shuffling clichéd step behind her in hot pursuit all through a day in London and a long night of flight across a dark Atlantic.

She did not sleep. Her right hand was full of pain again. Her head also throbbed and her eyes itched. The glaring light of the dawn sun at the window of the plane was like a horrible primitive mechanical light that was being tried out and would obviously prove unsuccessful. Her head was full of the fanciful notions of fatigue. Seated, peering down, she felt like an Old Testament prophet raised up by angels in the chair he sat in and whirled about the sky. But the scene below her was bleak and cold, a dark and forbidding moonscape landmass which certainly was no Promised Land.

The cloud cleared as they flew over Maine. Then, of course, she began to see signs of the domestic and the familiar. A road appeared, with a car moving along it, and then the weird ritualistic markings of the baseball diamond; here and there, the aquamarine jewels of swimming pools; then the curious altar and totems of a drive-in movie. She was among her tribesmen. The plane stopped in Boston and she heard the deeper voices of her own North of Boston people as transatlantic travellers got out and modern, local adventurers, who would make the short trip to Connecticut by air, got on.

An elderly woman, clutching a paperback book came down the aisle and sat beside Kitty. And after a little while the sound of the aircraft's engine changed as the plane turned and started to descend. Kitty could see the Connecticut River Valley in sparkling sunshine, and she suddenly felt so emotional that she thought she might weep.

'Are you all right?' the elderly woman seated next to her asked. The woman could see Kitty had tears in her eyes. She had been a silent companion, for such an elderly American woman. She had read the paperback during the flight. Kitty looked at the cover, *The Idle Time of Love*.

'Have you been out of the United States for a long time, honey?' the old lady asked.

Kitty laughed. It was the way the old woman pronounced 'the United States' in the precise manner of the New England matron, like someone making a speech to the Daughters of the Revolution, and then tossed in that sudden unexpected 'honey', like a waitress in a truck-drivers' diner. She was going to be one of them, some day, she thought. A little old lady using the odd and out-of-date salty expression.

As though on cue the woman said, 'That sure does look swell, don't it?' It was the river valley. The plane had swung away from Hartford and was now over farmland. The seat belt sign went on.

The pilot's voice said, 'There seems to be some fog over Hartford.' The passengers laughed and groaned. 'Everywhere else is clear as you can see,' the pilot's voice said. 'But Hartford is fogbound. But it won't last.'

The big plane started a slow, tilting circle. They could look down and see tiny motor boats in the river. The mountains were green again with new maple leaves. There was a large sprawling red-brick former house of a mill-owner. Irish cooks, maids and scullery girls – all of them sending money home – had raced about, black-skirted in white caps and aprons. A large electrified sign in blue letters announced it was now the YMCA. They were flying very low, above the sparkling white stone or shiny black glinting granite of a cemetery, with among them a few large squat mill-owners' family mausoleums, full of nesting pigeons. Kitty could see the pale birds taking to the little patch of sky above the grave. The ugly scars of milltowns appeared, then disappeared, and it was all woods and green with now and then the white-steepled churches and bandstands.

'That's Granby,' the little old lady said. 'I've a college chum lives right about there.'

Kitty knew the towns: Granby, Orange, Wilbraham, Belchertown, Southampton, Easthampton, Longmeadow, Windsor Locks.

'My daughter lives in Boston,' the old woman said. 'She's a grandmother herself now. All my grandchildren are proper little Bostonians. But I couldn't live there. It's not the weather. Boston's weather's something awful. But good heavens, we've got weather here, and they don't get snow in Boston like we do. But –' the old woman stared out of the window. They could see Hartford, buried under a halo of shining white fog.

The plane turned and circled again, with the brown, plain as coffee grounds milltowns offering themselves up for a moment and giving way to green mountains and picture-postcard New England villages. The river had been deeper at one time. English explorers had come up against the current, their tall masted ship had lain at anchor on some bright morning such as this as they rowed ashore full of expectation. Some old ancestors of hers, Kitty thought, had also come up the river in less romantic circumstances and decided that this would be their home. But it was never home to them as it was to Katherine Lawrence. She had no memories of any other home.

'We're going to be terribly late,' the old woman said. 'Do you have anyone meeting you?'

'No,' Kitty said. 'I thought I'd just slip in.'

'Yes,' the old lady said, 'same as me. Soon as we land,' she said, 'I'm going to get out of this plane and into a dry martini.' It was an old joke. Kitty laughed. The salty old woman said, 'Will you join me?'

'I certainly will, Mrs –.'

'Burr.'

'Mrs Burr.'

'Good,' Mrs Burr said. 'That'll be fun. A real American dry martini'll make you feel right at home, Miss –?'

'Mrs Lawrence. Katherine.'

'Katherine. I'm Prudence. Prudence Burr.'

Kitty smiled. The plane kept circling.

'It'll be nice to get home after two weeks in Boston. Home,' Mrs Burr said, 'it's in the genes, and I don't mean the blue jeans.'

They were flying over another dirty milltown. It seemed hacked out of the beautiful mountains, like an act of senseless vandalism, but that was also home. They had circled far round. She could see the bridge across the Connecticut river at Willimansett and then the dam at South Hadley Falls and the roofs of Mount Holyoke College in South Hadley Center. And, circling, she saw the old covered bridge was below them and black and white cows out to pasture going down to the river bank for a drink. On the river, there was a tiny red seaplane, gliding along the water and then lifting off. Only a few cars moved on the old highway, the old road which followed the more ancient trail of the Mohawks. Just barely visible, peeking out of all the new green trees was Holford Park, or, Kitty thought, perhaps not. If you blinked, she thought, you miss it.

The great plane was tilted, circling in the clear morning sky. Beneath them the river was blue under the blue sky and the fields were far more green than a week before, with long stretches of early wild flowers. The big jet rose up and down, giving the passengers their first real sensation of being airborne since they had left the airport. They were whirled about, riders on a carousel with the bright brass ring of home just out of reach. The pilot announced that the fog had cleared, and that they would be landing in ten minutes.